PERDIDO RIVER
BASTARD

D. B. Patterson

PERDIDO RIVER BASTARD

D. B. Patterson

DBP Press 2014

First Printing: 2014 | ISBN: 978-0-692-24629-0

DBP Press c/o Byron Patterson
Post Office Box 399 | Tarpon Springs, FL 34688

Facebook.com/dbpatterson.author

For Dad, who still lives,
and Mom, who still loves him.

FOREWORD

Although inspired by my own family, the book you have in your hands is a product of my imagination and takes place in a world of my own making. Many of the characters share traits and names with real people, living and dead, but they are fictional creations (this ain't no autobiography). The Southern geography is real enough too, but I've poetically tweaked some of it to suit my narrative (this ain't a damn Rand McNally road atlas either).

I spent nine years crafting a story about myths and sins, memory and history, secrets and lies, life and death, magic and mystery, rebirth and redemption, good and evil—all the sublime beauty and insanity I call the Deep South. Inherent themes of race, prejudice, and bigotry come with the territory, but this novel isn't about inciting revolution or calling for imposed societal atonement for past transgressions.

It isn't about blaming others for things they can't possibly help, like the color of skin, the sins of fathers and mothers, or broken pasts.

Simply put, this novel is about finding love through forgiveness.

Whether that's good, bad, or lazy is for you to decide, Dear Reader, but the notion is worthy of discussion, as it seems to be the one people easily dismiss for being too quaint, simple, and idealistic.

I disagree. And so would, I believe, the preacher from Alabama who died for that simple idea.

I'd like to express my gratitude to three important people.

Pamela Sapio, thank you for the years of friendship and support, dear Goddess of Words and Cupcakes.

John Shelby, my cool-as-a-cucumber uncle, thank you for reading (and enjoying) the crappy versions of this story before everyone else.

And Tina Patterson, thank you for encouraging me to finish what I'd started back in 2005—because you cried like a big ol' baby for an hour after you finished reading the final draft, I felt good about letting go and letting God.

—D. Byron Patterson, June 2014

Prince, I know of a wood where store
Of hanged poor folk to the branches cling,
Lapped and shrouded in leafage hoar:
It is the orchard of Louis the King.

— John Payne, from *Theodore de Banville*

He who is devoid of the power to forgive is
devoid of the power to love. There is some
good in the worst of us and some evil in the
best of us. When we discover this, we are
less prone to hate our enemies.

— Martin Luther King Jr.

THE FOOL

Chapter 1

In the Name of the Mother
and Her Prodigal Son

Tampa, Florida—Thursday Night, May 26, 2005

Two years had passed since we dropped his empty casket into the grounds at Magnolia, and Brandon Doogan's body was still missing. Nobody anticipated Dad's miraculous return except for Mom, who simply refused to believe he was dead until she tucked his bones into the earth with her own hands. Who cared if she didn't want to say goodbye to her husband yet? She had a right to believe everybody was wrong until she was ready to change her goddamn mind. I sure as hell wasn't cracking to bits over a fancy burial box with no corpse inside it. A hole filled with something filled with nothing wasn't worth one of my tears.

Still, it was hard to believe two years had passed.

Mom called Thursday night before the Memorial Day weekend began, but she didn't want to talk about the ugly anniversary. She wanted to talk about what happened after the ceremony, when I woke in a Charleston hospital after I tried killing myself the wrong way. Two years gone meant talking about my promise to Mom and my godmother. I could hear Hattie telling me my chickens had come home to roost.

Mom was more direct. "Where's the money, sugar?"

"I only have a third of it," I said, "but if I had another—"

Mom laughed. "Sugar, sugar—two years ago, you did a stupid thing that put your ass in Crazy Town for an expensive month of therapy," she said. "We gave you money because it's what families do—you made our gift into your debt when you swore to repay it one way or another. Since you don't have the money, you promised to do anything we told you to do, no questions asked. You just keep what you've squirreled, sugar, because tomorrow morning, you're gonna take me to Pensacola."

"Mom, what's happened?"

"What part of 'no questions' was hard to understand?"

All I could manage was a feeble, "Yes'm."

Using her sweet-tea voice, Mom said, "Play hooky from work, get your butt up here, and we'll go have a weekend full of *family-fun.*"

We both laughed at that.

Family-fun was a euphemism to describe our special brand of unlucky togetherness, which occurred at the junction of Planned Activity Street and Murphy's Law Lane. A promise of togetherness that often put somebody in a jail cell, or a room at Sacred Heart Hospital, or a grave at the Beulah Baptist Church cemetery. The hysterical misfortunes of beloved relatives, but with clowns and balloons.

"*Family-fun* is NOT an incentive, Mom."

"Neither is a dog shit sundae, sugar, but you're taking me to see my mama and daddy," she said. "Half of Escambia County is waiting to squeeze the pudding out of you. It's time, Duddy. Call in sick and get up here. End of discussion."

Calling in sick wasn't necessary.

I was currently unemployed, not that it mattered.

Mom would've told me to quit any job if my employer didn't like me taking a day off without notice.

In my family, breaking your word was a cardinal sin, which brought the wrath of an entire coven of women upon your head. My grandparents lived north of Pensacola, in Cantonment, a small town spitting distance from the Perdido River where Florida's tip wedges Alabama's underdangle. Shelbys had lived there for generations, which meant visits with relatives I hadn't seen in years. I fumbled my excuse about the end of next week being better.

And so, it came to pass that Brenda Shelby Doogan gave me one her *family-famous* silences.

God knows when it began, but Shelby women used silences that raised conversational tension to an art form. Mom was THE homecoming queen of pregnant pauses. As melodramatic as a Scarlet O'Hara fainting spell, they seemed to precede some revelation or apocalyptic truth. This particular silence was so sweeping it scared the shit out of me.

Silence.

Finally, Mom said, "You've avoided making amends long enough. I don't care how smart you are, you don't know half as much as you THINK you do." Her voice broke. "Sugar, I want you to think about the summer of your accident. I need you to prod the memory again."

Promise or no, this question was within my rights.

"Why?"

"Because we're going to Flomaton first," she said. "Duddy, try to remember something. A tiny detail could be the key."

"Key to what?"

"To what happened to your daddy, sugar."

An hour later, I was standing barefoot in the kitchen drinking wine straight from the bottle.

The summer of 1980 wasn't my happy place.

It was a big year of history—American hostages in Iran, murdered kids in Atlanta, Mount St. Helens, Ronald Reagan, and the death of John Lennon. In my world, a July 4th reunion put me in a coma, replete with a broken arm, a busted collarbone, a skull fracture with concussion to match, and bruises on my near-photographic brain. Memories on or around that afternoon had all but vanished. I'd grown accustomed to the gap in my mind.

Did I really want to start poking that soft spot again?

Schools of fat catfish flip-flopped in my gut. It was too late for a jog around the block to settle my nerves, so I took a sedative and packed for the trip. I paced the floors of my empty rented South Tampa bungalow waiting for the wheels in my head to stop spinning. I never made my house into a home. No painted walls, no artwork, no bookshelves—just a bunch of unopened boxes stacked in corners.

"Story of my life," I said to nobody.

After I climbed into bed, I stared at the ceiling and told myself nothing horrible was about to hunt me down, eat my brain, break my heart, or give me an STD. *Family-fun*, I thought with a sleepy smile.

Waves of waking and dozing gave way to a monster nightmare. An empty beach at sunset. Sand suddenly becoming soil and damp leaves. Me doing a weird flying-hopping thing in a forest where Dad was a tree. Him telling me where to find his body just as a gunshot blast blew his trunk into bloody splinters.

And that was my four o'clock wake up call.

Turning on the lamp, I wiped my eyes and opened my nightstand. Keeping a journal since my hospital stay was an ugly habit, but my therapist said it was important to put my thoughts and dreams to paper for reflection. Staring at the blank page, I suddenly felt ridiculous. Too tired and cranky to give a flying monkey shit about therapy, I chucked the book across the room.

Fuck you, Diary.

It was time for me to grow a set.

I got out of bed and made coffee. I showered and dressed, locked up the house, and stood in the driveway. I gazed at the star-filled sky and prayed for Dad's soul. I climbed into my rusted Jeep Cherokee, affectionately called Jeepers, which had no AC and was as ugly as homemade sin. I loved the piece of shit with all my heart, and I vowed to keep it until it died or someone carjacked it.

Leaving Tampa before dawn wasn't bad, not with the windows down and a pot of strong coffee riding shotgun. With the windows down and white noise roaring in my ears, I ignored the shame telling me to turn around. I focused on my promise. How did my childhood accident explain why Dad went missing 25 years later? I saw no connection, but a penance was a penance.

Jesus Christ, was I naive.

Generations of history and secrets from crisscrossing branches in a family tree dominated by Mom's side were about to crush me. I couldn't see beyond my manic-depressive feelings about Dad. I'd needed him to be a counterweight to Mom, but he couldn't, wouldn't. He refused to be what I needed him to be.

Nothing connected me to Brandon Doogan except vague memories of hope for some dream that might've been. The legacy a father leaves his son can be more sacred than the Ark of the Fucking Covenant, and Dad made me feel like a trick-or-treating Charlie Brown.

For every bit of history told over a pitcher of beer, for every war or love story, and for every showing of scars, the conduit between father and son strengthens and binds.

And me? I always got a fucking rock.

But Brandon Doogan did leave something behind, and he made for damn sure I'd go through hell for it.

Less than two weeks from now, I'd find myself on the Styx River in a boat called *Heart of Darkness*, with a woman named Sharon, a half-black man named Joseph Conrad, and the cousin of a redneck drug lord who happened to have my father's bones hidden in his mobile home deep in an Alabama swamp.

I'll do my best to tell the story as it happened without spinning it too much, but forgive me if I do.

After all, I am my Southern mother's son.

Chapter 2

Miles to Go, Promises to Keep

Ponte Vedra Beach—Friday Morning, May 27, 2005

Mom lived in a seaside town south of Jacksonville and north of St. Augustine. Dad had dreamed of retiring there, so my mother moved into a posh seniors-only community to feel close to the man she'd lost. Being three hours away from her post-suicidal son gave her peace of mind too—a short drive to my side if I ever did something stupid, like slice my arms or eat some pills.

A winding road through well-groomed fairways and bike paths dumped me in a cul-de-sac in the back of the complex. Mom was reading her paper, smoking her cigarette, and drinking her cup of coffee on the patio. Even from a distance, she was striking. Not pretty, mind you— she wasn't an oil painting, all perfectly blended brush strokes of colors to match the sofa. Her beauty was earthy and timeworn. And she always smelled of tea roses. It was easy to see why Dad loved her.

Nodding to the plate of warm biscuits on the glass table, she lit another cigarette and went back to her paper. Until Mom got through her coffee and the personal ads, she talked to nobody and growled if you did. While she read, I settled into my chair and ate breakfast.

Her condominium had a view of the Atlantic. Sunrises here made your heart just ache, and the way those colors broke across the water gave you chills. Wood storks waded in the mangroves and saw grasses nearby.

Breezes from there carried sweet scents of decaying, expired sea things. On warmer days, you could smell the salt marshes and oyster lagoons from the estuary, and those tides brought manatees sometimes.

A footpath cutting through the high dunes there led to a stretch of beach where a quartet of German spies had landed on June 16, 1942. Hidden somewhere nearby was (well, to a few older Ponte Vedra locals) the REAL Fountain of Youth.

"You forgot your guitar," Mom said. "I wish you hadn't."

"Shit, I'm sorry."

And I meant that too.

I enjoyed playing guitar, but my brother Tyler and cousin Mike were much better musicians than I was.

I hated not bringing it.

"I guess I won't reminisce about falling in love with Brandon."

"That's like saying you refuse to remember your favorite bible verse," I told her. "I say bullshit to your Southern sulking and superficial sadness."

Mom flipped the bird as she told her sideways love story.

"On a fall night in 1971, Brandon Doogan climbed to my window on a two-step ladder, hauled me to his Mustang, and drove to the preacher. Your Granny helped with our secret nuptials. Your Grandpa hated Doogans more than he hated Asians and refused to speak to me until the day my water busted in Miss Eva's barn. Sugar, you changed your Grandpa's mind about letting a Doogan love his daughter—he couldn't wait to see his grandson."

I shook my head. "Mom, three months of heavy petting in the backseat of Dad's car wasn't love. Leaving third base to steal home plate wasn't a reason to get married."

She giggled. "None of you damn kids would be here if it weren't for Brandon stealing my home plate, sugar."

"Gross, Mom."

She poked me with her bare foot. "Hurricanes work in less time, sugar, so don't you dare tell me falling in love's any different," she said. "Three months, three days, three minutes, three seconds—doesn't matter. When love flips the poles of your heart, *shift happens*. Hattie will tell you the same thing, Duddy. Shift happens."

"Hattie's love doesn't kill anybody," I said. "Your love's psychotic and alien. It kills people. Mommy Dearest, you are FULL of shift, and I reject your suddenly-in-love crazy talk."

Shift happens, she says.

Not to me, it won't, I say.

"Just 'cause you once were married to a Maybelline-painted Yankee to spite your Southern family doesn't mean you're immune, sugar. It'll hit you hard, boy—I can feel it. And when you have kids, I hope they're all JUST—LIKE—YOU. That's a curse for you."

"Love's a curse," I spat, "unless it can perform miracles."

She didn't need to know about my vasectomy.

No one needed to know about it.

After Mom took one last drag of her cigarette, we left for West Florida. We crossed the Central Zone and went back an hour in time. The ruins of Santa Rosa County, her towns still nursing wounds from Hurricane Ivan's rampage from last year, were staggering.

Pine forests were snapped matchsticks from Beaver Creek to Happy Valley. Everywhere you looked something was in disrepair or worse. I'd seen damage like this when Hugo gutted South Carolina back in 1989.

"Talk about a hurricane," Mom said. "I was seeing this good-looking older man in his mid-20s, but the moment I laid eyes on Brandon, I forgot everyone and everything, including my own name. I knew I'd crumble without him, sugar. I had to marry him, HAD to."

Mom fiddled with her hands. "He claimed me, sugar. He fought for the right to love me even as I was spilling you onto the floor of a horse stall—hey, ease off the pedal there, Dale Earnhardt."

"You lost your head because Dad claimed you?"

"Only a woman understands that feeling."

Against my will, I bit my tongue. Dad's struggle to earn my mother could've bonded him to his firstborn son, could've made our relationship special. If anything, it did the opposite.

I needed a happier memory. "Remember Brenda's Folly?"

Mom giggled. "Son-of-a-bitch wanted to see if my name would sink his homemade raft," she said. "And when it sank to the bottom of the river, I spent the rest of the day spitting fire at him like I'd swallowed a whole volcano. But he kept grinning at me, like he was seeing Jesus. I know he wanted to knock my teeth in most days, but not that day."

Mom's bottom lip quivered. She absently touched the pewter crescent moon dangling from a chain Dad bought for her. Her charm matched the sun he wore on a diving watch he never took off. She let the moon fall to her chest, a weight that haunted her heart and bound her to the ghost living there.

"I know we fought, sugar, but I loved him with all my being. I hated him for making me ache so much—I still do. Every day I die when he doesn't come home. I swear, lovin' Brandon Doogan will turn me to dust before I'm sixty years old."

It was no secret Mom loved Dad's looks, but sometimes just the sound of his voice punted her to either end of love or fury. If she wasn't screaming in ecstasy, then she was screaming in rage. The inevitable volcanic eruption between them happened a week after my brother was born.

Dad had picked up an extra shift one night, so Mom took Tyler and me down to the movie theater near the apartment to see the only one playing. When Dad came home, he found me under my bed terrified my baby brother would kill me in my sleep. Tucking me back into my bed, Dad gave Mom a piece of his mind.

As I lay beside Tyler, screaming for my soul in his bassinet, I listened to dishes smashing and parents shouting in the kitchen.

"THE OMEN? You went to see THAT movie? If you want to destroy that boy of yours, Brenda, just tell him the Shelby curse will kill him. Or make him watch Eskimos club baby seals on PBS for free. Christ in a hula, woman, you oughta see *The Exorcist* next!"

Mom hurled plates piled with hot epithets. "Curse?" *Crash!*

"Eskimos?" *Shatter!*

"You're the Devil!" *Slam!*

"Get out, Brandon Doogan!"

And so, it came to pass that Dad took a leave of absence and left us for three months. He came home, but they never spoke of why he left or where he went. The Satan Baby incident marked clear battle lines between my parents—a Doogan might've seeded Mom's garden, but she'd claimed ME in the name of her maiden Shelby.

"DEAN ADAM DOOGAN," Mom shouted, snapping her fingers. "Sugar, I've been telling you to slow down since we turned onto Highway 29. You're going too—uh-oh, see?"

In my rearview mirror, the screaming sirens and flashing strobe lights of the Florida Highway Patrol cruiser following me. "Shit," I said, pulling over to the shoulder.

Mom giggled. "I tried to warn you, sugar."

"You're not helping."

Florida Highway Patrol Officer Enos Percy took my license. Mouth of white teeth, the trooper horse-smacked his gum and asked where we were going and why I was in a hurry to get there. Mom tried to take the heat by telling him she made me go faster to get to Flomaton sooner. Officer Percy had no sympathy. He handed me my ticket, tipped his hat and drove off.

•

Finding Flomaton, Alabama was like stumbling into Brigadoon—you didn't know you were there until you were there. It was one of those blink-or-you'll-miss-it towns perfectly content to shuffle along at its own pace.

Mom was behind the wheel, so I only realized we'd arrived when she stopped on the shoulder of a dirt road. This two-mile stretch of road ran parallel to farmland that stretched to where Bill's Dollar Store once stood. Shelbys once owned several hundreds of acres in this part of Alabama and more south of Cantonment, Florida.

As far as I knew, our cousin Pidge (and her mother, my crazy-as-a-bed-bug Great Aunt Clara) owned the last of those parcels, which wasn't much. A sloping hill rose from one of their fields like some stubby, bald mountain. "There it is, sugar," Mom said. "On the hill there."

"Yeah, I see it," I said, getting out for a better look.

The house of *family-famous* legend Cotton Wilson sat atop that hill. His given name was Ewell Curtis, but folk only knew him by his nickname and bone white skin, which camouflaged his mixed heritage of dark-skinned Creek Indian, Sapelo Island Gullah, and Perdido River redneck.

By all accounts, he was a horribly unlucky man.

Misfortune followed him all his life, which is why he put my godmother Hattie into the care of my grandparents before he disappeared for ten years. Mom got a black sister when our white Southern family adopted Hattie as one of theirs, in the early 1960s too. Cotton Wilson returned to Flomaton in 1972 and built his house on that hill. He mended his relationship with Hattie and kept to himself mostly.

My accident happened up there.

It happened in HIS cellar under HIS workshop behind HIS house.

And there it was.

Seeing it was always a punch to the gut.

My childhood ended on that hill. I still had the scars from my fall. Here, under my jaw, behind my ear, across the crown, down my spine— hundreds of stitches and months of recovery.

Putting my brain together like Humpty Dumpty pieces made me curious about other things I didn't know.

I remembered asking Dad about my Doogan kin from Alabama and him telling me I'd get the beating of my life if I asked again. Of course, I fucking did—kids ask questions.

My beating was so brutal I couldn't walk for three days.

A teacher saw the bruises on my arms. I spent a week with a school psychologist who didn't believe my excuses. I never forgave Dad—covering for him broke something. It later made it easy to abandon a family who loved a man who hated his son. Seeing Cotton Wilson's house again was proof I hadn't forgiven him.

The car horn honked.

The sky growled with distant thunder.

Vertigo knocked me on my ass. I blacked out and came to as Mom was helping me to my feet, which felt like it happened before. I was accustomed to a déjà vu chaser after a dizzy spell, but it was still unsettling. "You know, I had lots of therapy for this shit," I said. "But I'll try to remember, for Dad's sake, I'll try."

Mom squeezed my arm. "Do it for your own, sugar," she said. "I trusted what Brandon and Cotton Wilson told us, but if they lied, it wouldn't be the first time somebody hid the truth. Maybe they were trying to protect you."

"Protect me from what?"

"That, sugar, is the mystery. Secrets can't be kept forever in this family. Maybe the one in your head'll help you forgive your daddy one day. Maybe if you forgive him, you'll forgive me."

"Forgive you for what, Mom?"

Silence.

Chapter 3

Strange Fruit, Oddly-named Vines

Flomaton, Alabama—Late Friday Afternoon

There was nothing like crawling over a dirt road with the car windows down. There was music in the gravel popping and the clay cracking into powder beneath the rolling tires. And there under a sky of sun-stained clouds did the dried-up chambers of my withered heart pulse with new blood.

Rounding the bend of trees, our cousin's big romantical farmhouse came into view. Three stories of white siding, John Deere green accents on all the shutters and the wide front door—a picture postcard country home with gardens of flowers, creeping muscadine and scuppernong grape vines, and blooming shrubs of every color.

Sunlight from the tin roof spilled over the eaves and into the Billie bees swarming over a woman waving to us on the porch. Dressed in *family-famous* overalls, Pidge straddled the porch rail, pendulum kicking a leg and chugging iced sweet tea straight from the pitcher. Diffused light made the frizz of her silver head into a fuzzy halo, which made me smile so hard I cracked my brain stem. She nearabout flipped ass-over-feet when I eased our car next to her rusty Wrangler.

Pidge was a hard hugger. Her flailing arms brick-smacked into you and wrapped around you like redneck swaddling clothes. Only God kept you upright.

Although Mom warned me about her weight loss, Pidge still bore some breadth and nearly knocked the wind out of me.

"Duddy-darlin', you look so much better," she said, cackling. "HA! I bet your mama drove you crazy all day too."

Her husband's death had aged Pidge hard. It was odd not seeing old Jervis. He was a skin-wrapped skeleton with an Adam's apple the size of a bull's testicle. He was painfully shy, but he loved my cousin, and he spent every waking hour proving it. His violent, accidental death was no more shocking than Pidge being responsible for it.

Death is family, as we say.

Mom and Pidge wept bittersweet tears as they held each other.

I busied myself with our bags and took them into the house. When I returned, they were in the gazebo, a rickety gray beehive with rusty cranks and retractable awnings. A rotted wooden bridge took me to the octagon-shaped dome with its wall-to-wall benches and table bolted to the floor. We drank iced sweet tea from purple plastic tumblers and made small talk for a while.

After a quick supper, we popped a few corks of Pidge's latest batch of muscadine wine and played cards. Poker wasn't just a Shelby family tradition—it was a sacred institution and damn-nearabout a full-blown religion. I was a horrible player, but I did win two out of nine hands.

Pidge opened a bottle of scuppernong brandy and filled Mom's plastic tumbler. "Duddy-darlin', when you bluff, your eyes twitch more than a squirrel on speed," she said. "The day a Doogan man wins at cards on a bluff is the day a Shelby woman joins a convent. HA!"

Mom snorted brandy from her nose. "Shit that burns!"

Behind the distant storm clouds, the sinking sun pulled thunder up from the horizon like weeds. Wind swirled dust into devils that danced around the gazebo as the light faded.

Gusts rustling the trees flipped their leaves into steel-green rain catchers and stirred the sweet summer smells of fresh-cut grass and jasmine. My mind wandered back to Cotton Wilson's house. It gnawed at me, and I couldn't take my eyes off the bend in the road.

"Duddy-darlin', what's on your mind?"

"Were Cotton Wilson and Dad close?"

The question hung in the air until Mom threw up her hands. "My job was getting him here, Piddy-pat—your turn now," she said with a sloppy smile. "Do your duty for my precious Duddy."

Pidge shot her a raspberry. "You're drunk, Bren—lightweight."

Mom flipped her the bird.

Their screaming and vulgar name-calling was good for them. Mom's laughter once was as *family-famous* as Pidge's cackling or Hattie's hooting, but its music left when Dad did. The chain smoking didn't help either. Her joy sounded hollow, like clanking cowbells instead of tinkling chimes.

And that's when Pidge broke wind.

A hand to her mouth with a fake look of surprise, she threw her silver head back and cackled madly. Her sophomore effort rattled like two gators growling under her backside. Her last one was the kicker. It came out caddywumpus and shook the gazebo.

It was some time before we could speak.

Finally, Pidge said, "Duddy-darlin', after I drag ol' Otis into the house and put her drunk ass to bed, we'll talk."

Mom giggled. "It's a big secret, sugar—shh."

Rolling her eyes, Pidge muttered something about needing a bigger boat as she left the gazebo with Mom. Wiping down the table, I cleared away the plates and cards as the sky opened and then abruptly closed.

Hours of rumbling, and all we got was a five-minute shower and wet night heat. To prepare for the squadrons of cockroaches, mosquitoes, and junebugs about to lay siege, I cocooned the gazebo in a blanket of Cutter fog and citronella candle smoke.

Pidge returned with two uncorked bottles, one in each hand. Her wine wasn't exactly fine, but it wasn't Mad Dog either—it was my favorite adult beverage, even more than beer.

Behind her house, Southern grape vines weaved through wooden fences that dotted an area the size of three football fields. She made batches every year—her barn was full of caskets and bottles. After years of doing this on her own for fun, she was slowly turning her hobby into a real business. She figured it would take another five years, as long as she found the right people to help her make it happen.

Pidge poured two glasses filled to the rim.

"I got Bren drunk on purpose to give us some privacy," she said, taking my chin. Staring into my eyes, she said, "Dean Adam, I love you, but I need to say this because I do—you're a grown-ass man, almost thirty-four years old, so stop draggin' crosses and blaming Brandon Doogan for your ignorance and misery. Acting like a surly Blanche Dubois won't bring him back from the dead. Even if it did, I'm FIRST in line to hit him AND Brenda with a baseball bat."

"Why?" I asked, trying not to laugh.

Pidge let go my chin. "All I'll say is your mama made a promise she won't keep. Something important just came to our attention, so your godmother and I put together a plan to get you here. You'll learn the rest this weekend. Brenda won't."

"I don't understand."

"You don't need to understand yet, Duddy-doodle-doo—you're taking baby steps and toe-dippin' the pool," Pidge said, sliding a large manila envelope across the table. "Open that up. Might as well start."

"Jesus Christ, you women are all nuts."

"HA! Ain't THAT the truth. Now open it, shitbird."

I unclasped the fastener and tipped out two newspaper clippings from *The Pensacola Journal*—one article dated three years ago and one dated July 7, 1980. The recent one was about Baldwin County Sheriff Silas Doogan's war on drugs along the Perdido River, especially the swamps north of its Styx tributary. The older article was about Hank Doogan, reported missing on July 5, 1980. The faces of the two men were familiar. My hands trembled as I stared at the same square jaws and wide-set eyes I saw in my own face.

"These men are my cousins? My uncles?"

Pidge slapped a mosquito on her arm. "Brandon's older half-brothers," she replied. "Hank and his identical twin Dale were child molesters. Your daddy put Hank in prison, which got Silas elected Baldwin County Sheriff. Hank was paroled July 2, 1980, and was last seen in a bar down the road on the night before our reunion. It's possible he ended up in Cotton Wilson's cellar to sleep off a hangover."

"A convicted child molester may have seen me up there," I began grimly, not daring to finish. "Shit, Pidge—even if it was true, how would it connect to Dad?"

"That's your mystery to solve, Duddy-darlin'," she said, adding, "but it's important you see the faces of your kin. Ol' Sheriff Silas is still a good man. Hank and Dale, not so much."

Sliding the envelope back, I said, "What about Dale?"

Pidge shrugged. "MIA since Hank dropped through the floor of the world, but I heard rumors he was running meth on the river."

"Do you know Silas?"

"Yeah, I know Silas," Pidge said with a smirk. "Crooked-as-hell when it comes to keeping office, but hardworking, loyal, got a heart of gold. Oh, and Hollywood handsome too—HA! I always liked Silas." She swallowed a lump and took a breath when she said, "If you get a wild hair up your butt, look him up. He'll wanna see you, Duddy-darlin', and so will you."

"What, does he know about my accident?"

Pidge threw up her hands. "A brick fuckin' wall," she said. "I wish you'd take a hint and quit asking questions—it ain't like you're ready to march up the hill to see what you remember. Duddy, I suspect you're too book smart to see the forest for the trees. It makes simple wisdom harder to understand and doubles the work Hattie and I got to do."

The sky thundered, as if on cue.

Pidge took my hand. "Brandon was pigheaded, selfish, and other things I won't say out loud. The best way to understand how to forgive him is to learn the truth about your family tree, Duddy-darlin'. Both sides. You ain't cursed, even though you were born in Miss Eva's barn."

That was actually a true story—well, it was true enough as long as I don't mention the added bit about the cow.

On June 3, 1972, I was born in Miss Eva's barn.

Mom christened me Dean Adam Doogan, as she lay sheet-covered and spread-eagled over two bales, her bird legs akimbo. Granny held one leg, Aunt Belladonna held the other, Pidge held her hands, Hattie cradled her head, and Miss Eva was the accidental midwife after Mom went down in that horse stall.

"I love that I was born in a barn—that ain't my curse."

"HA! Your curse is ignorance, Duddy-doodle-doo, which means you can fix it up and change your stars." Pidge clapped. "Okay, you got two choices: either put on your big-boy britches tomorrow and mosey up to Cotton Wilson's cellar to see what memories come; or drink some brandy with me in my history den tonight while we look at old pictures."

"Brandy's good," I replied. "Tomorrow's another day."

Pidge countered with a look that spoke volumes as much as it said nothing, a facial expression Hattie called *devil-thinking*, and it was often worse than Mom's silences.

•

The hall clock spat out its cuckoo eleven times.

Pidge cackled.

"HA! Aw, here's one of you as a tiny drunk, Duddy-darlin'," she said, lifting a picture of me as a toddler with a cigarette dangling from my mouth and a beer in my hands. "Your rotten Grandpa."

On the stereo, Billie Holiday was singing about her worthless man. We sipped homemade scuppernong brandy and sat on the sofa flipping through photo books and her *family-famous* wall of framed photographs.

Generations of framed arrested moments from ceiling to floor.

Mom, Hattie, Uncle John, and Belladonna drunk as skunks on Granny's porch. Tyler and Amanda playing poker at the kiddie table with our cousin Mike, dressed as Popeye. A faded Olan Mills portrait of the Hell's Belles—Granny, Miss Eva, and Aunt Clara, who wore a movable eye patch even then. The *family-famous* picture of Hattie, Mom, Pidge, and Granny marching behind Martin Luther King Jr. struck me hard—I'd done nothing with my life.

Your curse is ignorance—fix it.

Pidge put away the photo book.

"Your Grandpa was stationed in Taiwan when the itch for hard drink and cards nearly got him thrown in the brig. Your Granny saw the signs and reported him to his commanding officer. She knew what sins slept in the Shelby blood. She had to get him straightened out—she knew Uriah Shelby always did his worst when he was shit-faced."

I sat up. "I didn't know that."

Pidge got up and walked to the fireplace. "Blood has a memory— it stores and tucks things away like secrets," she said. "Heart disease, webbed feet, identical twins, albinism—they run in our family." She took a book without a dust jacket from the mantle and tossed it to me.

The title in gold letters read, *An Incomplete History of Perdido River Families—1798 to 1998.* She opened to the photos.

"Murder, suicide, rape, incest, addiction, the crazies, gambling—those things run in our family too," she continued. "Here's the bastard responsible—we exist because of this man, and we're still paying his debts. I swear when he was born, God forgot to put the soul in."

Uriah Ephraim Wilson Shelby.

My mouth went dry from looking at his craggy sunken face and vacant John Brown eyes gazing at ghosts haunting outside the frame.

I had nightmares about his eyes and the horrors they must've seen over his too-long life. Seeing Uriah's eyes made me wonder whether those visions lingered somewhere deep in my blood, waiting for me to dream them. That we existed because of this man was enough to unhinge the mind and capsize the soul.

"Book needs a new title," I finally told her. "A catchy one that'll market itself to the sins of our family's forgotten past."

Pidge didn't laugh.

Turning to a different photo of Uriah Shelby, she said, "Knowing the evil he did, I made a promise never to run from tragedy, Duddy. Or hide from my pain. Or blame someone else for my sorrows. Did Brenda tell you about what happened to Jervis?"

"Just that it was an accident because of the curse."

"HA! And what's the curse?"

"Who the fuck knows," I said, laughing. "I'd say love, but don't tell Hattie I said that."

Pidge nodded. "Shelby witches have an itch in the blood we gotta scratch, either with a lit stick of dynamite or a heaping pile of bullshit—there's a curse. Loving hard and killing husbands for sport or spite, there's two more. Just ask folk on the other side of the river. Gossips over there STILL talk about your sister killing HER two husbands 'cause of her Shelby blood."

After gleaning the doomsday parts from both testaments and the plots of pulp fiction paperbacks, bad luck somehow came to life like a bumpkin

Frankenstein, loaded for bear and drunk as Cooter Brown.

Our family cliché was a bad penny you couldn't lose.

The sky flashed as thunder rattled the windows.

"How did he die?" I asked, adding, "Jervis."

Pidge sighed. "Jervis and I were doing some spring yard work. I'd decided to trim them oak branches from the damn roof, so I made him hold an old ladder while I sawed 'em off. Can you picture him holding ME up? HA! Damnation station, what was I thinking? Mountain ass me wielding a gas-powered Black & Decker chainsaw on a rickety ladder over my husband six feet below."

Pidge wiped her nose on her sleeve and continued.

"That damn tree was a barky, hateful thing, tickling my bedroom window day and night. I was mule-headed persnickety about cutting it down. Jervis let the ladder go when the dog snuck up and yipped. Down I came. Branch killed my dog. Chainsaw killed my Jervis. Cut a crescent under his neck. He bled to death in my arms. I know it's my fault, but I'll spin my tragedy into a comedy about the dog and goddamn curse until I die. I wouldn't do either if I didn't know my family history."

Silence.

"HA! Death is family, Duddy-darlin'. Remember that. Now, take this book and skim through it before you go to sleep."

Pidge always knew what lurked below the surface, how big the iceberg was. Kissing her cheek, I went upstairs and got ready for bed.

My brain wasn't as fuzzy as it was earlier, but my imagination was on fire now. I paced the floor, too nervous to dive into the pages, so I studied the strange shelves in my room. They interlocked, like jigsaw pieces built into the wall, and framed the window with a bug-snug reading bench. And every shelf had something.

Knick-knacks, books, magazines—National Geographic and LIFE, mainly—a set of 1972 World Book Encyclopedias, cat tchotchkes, several moldy Reader's Digest condensed classics, a few books Pidge had written as a ghostwriter when she was younger, and a small, plain-as-paper music box that played a sweet tinkling melody I'd heard before, although I couldn't recall from where.

Falling into the window seat, I flipped through the history book.

It read like a farmer's almanac with easy-to-read vignettes about who did what to whom. I skimmed records, farming charts, birth and death tables, maps of unknown creeks, tidal grids for the streams and marshes of the entire watershed. In the back were recipes, rustic wisdoms, and a family tree with names missing or erased from it.

My ancestors weren't handsome folk, but they had remarkable faces, weathered with time and life.

I found myself staring at Uriah Shelby again.

Bourbon-drunk since leaving the womb, he'd carved his legacy into the 19th century.

> *He hanged for killing a senator's wife in 1893. Until then, he wandered the South with the devil's luck, an insatiable lust and a night-black soul. Hard liquor led him to rape and incest. Gambling led him to killing and thieving, catching fugitive slaves, and murdering them for fun. God only knows how many girls, his daughters and granddaughters, bore his countless bastards, all of them doomed to suffer for his sins. The powder keg of chaos on the Perdido River exploded when 12-year-old Annie Doogan gave birth to Earle Adam.*

Pidge knocked on the door. "Yoo-hoo may I come in?"

I pointed to the glasses she carried and shook my head. Ignoring me, Pidge handed me a glass. "Drink the ice water first," she said, swapping it for the next glass. "This'll bite the dog's hairy ass before you wake up—drink it fast or you'll puke."

It was a moonshine toddy, which was rubbing alcohol and the sweat of an old woman's cracked feet, with a splash of Tropicana for color. She sat next to me and flipped through dog-eared pages about Shelbys and Wilsons, Doogans and Percys, Ravenhairs and Freedmans, and Lincolns—a lineage proving I was part of something special, something greater than me. "Duddy, remember when I gave you two black eyes?"

I burst out laughing. "You told me if I put my fists together my knuckles would smell like strawberries. When I sniffed them, you smacked my fists and I hit my face. Two black eyes, two knocked out baby teeth."

Pidge cackled. "HA! You looked like a slow Hamburglar, with your little raccoon eyes and missing incisors," she said. "Bless your heart, and when you told Brenda a stranger came up and punched you out of the tree, I near 'bout pissed myself."

"The week before the family reunion," I said, smiling.

"I got bored babysitting you that afternoon," Pidge said. "I WAS a wicked woman, but I was curious about what you'd do. You took it. You didn't cry. You told me to apologize and hugged me after I did. I just started sobbing from the guilt. I fell head over feet in love with you that day. You got a strength nobody else has, Duddy. You can shoulder heavy weight and go on."

A lesson only *slightly* cruel in hindsight. It taught me the consequences to ignorance and proved to Pidge I could take a hit or two and shake it off. The ignorance was more my concern—I could fix that with a through crash course on family history.

Take what happened in Cotton Wilson's cellar.

I never would've gone there had I known the smell of moonshine meant something dangerous—wait, moonshine? Sniffing my empty glass, I closed my eyes.

And then I sniffed again.

No, I was certain I'd smelled this before.

I remembered it clearly, as if I'd lifted the rotten log of my brain to find a pale colorless worm squirming in the sudden light.

"Pidge, I think my block cracked," I said, sniffing the glass. "I remember this smell when I was throwing stones in a pond. This was on someone's breath. I'd swear on a stack of bibles."

There was no need to say whose breath it was.

Pidge threw her arms around me. "I say we go to sleep on a high note, Duddy-darlin'! Give me my book. You can look through it again when you come back to visit next weekend. Hell, maybe I'll mail it to you before then."

"Next week? You and Hattie are plotting already?"

Ignoring my questions, she waltzed across the room with the glasses. "Sweet dreams, Duddy-ducklin'—I'll see you off in the morning when y'all head down to Cantonment."

"You're not coming with us?"

Pidge smiled. "I got errands."

Turning off the light, she paused inside the open doorway for a moment. "You're stronger than you think, Duddy-darlin'."

I wasn't in a mood to argue.

There were plenty of sayings about genies and bottles, Pandoras and boxes, toothpaste and toothpaste tubes, so I was content to shut my mouth and let sleeping dogs lie.

Chapter 4

One Plague, Two Houses

Saturday Morning, May 28, 2005

The sun mule-kicked me in the face. Pidge's magic midnight moonshine nip did its job and kept my hangover at bay. I was achy until I was showered and dressed for breakfast. Orange juice, eggs and bacon, and hot buttermilk biscuits waited for me in the nook. Mom was too busy sipping coffee laced with aspirin to talk to me. I sat quietly in the bay window seat and studied the new lake in the yard.

When I'd stuffed myself, I loaded our bags in the car and walked to the bend in the dirt road to look at Cotton Wilson's house before we left for Cantonment. I debated whether I should go up there.

If a whiff of moonshine could snake charm details from my brain, what would a stroll do?

With the sun already baking, I doubted it'd do a thing. The sky was too bright. Everything was so green I wanted to punch a baby duck. Hearing rustling behind me, I turned as Pidge parted the branches of a pine tree. "I thought I saw your skinny ass," she said, snapping her overalls. "How you feelin', Duddy-doodle-bug?"

"Better than Mom," I said with a laugh.

Pidge cackled. "HA! Oh, the shit party she's throwin' in the kitchen. So, you gonna go up to see Ewell Curtis Wilson's house, or are you gonna stand here and pick your nose?"

"I'll go up there next week," I said with a pathetic sigh. "Shit, what if Dad caught me doing something in that cellar and beat me so hard I fell? Were they hiding what HE did to me, or was it some other Doogan asshole? Do I even want to know the truth?"

Silence.

Pidge smiled. "Flawed as he was, Brandon wasn't a monster. Whatever happened will stay hidden unless you get some skin in the game, Duddy. If you want truth then fight for it. It's in your blood. Spanish moss once covered the entire tree in his front yard," she said, pointing. "The branches went bare after Cotton Wilson's wife Alice hanged herself after he died. This past Thursday, I went up like I do each week, and I swear to God, there were two new drapes high in the tiptop branches where the mistletoe grows. It's a sign."

"A sign you're full of shit, Piglet."

Mom waved as we approached the front stoop. She was about to say something when a horn blasted from behind and scared the hell out of us. A golden-brown 1985 Lincoln Town Car swerved around the bend. Its engine coughed and sputtered when it came to a stop in the drive. I couldn't tell who was in the car, but they weren't welcome.

Pidge gripped my arm. "Go fetch my shotgun from the hall closet," she hissed. "Move your molasses ass—we ain't got much time."

I went to the closet and returned to the porch, handing the gun to Pidge. I joined Mom at the foot of the stairs. Two of the four men got out of the car and tottered to the front bumper.

The one in the black tee didn't move—he looked at his feet and kicked the gravel. The one without a shirt took a few steps toward the fence as Pidge hefted the butt of the gun on her hip. The other two young men were sitting half-in and half-out of the backseat now. They had buzz cuts and looked half-starved. The driver was the only one without a shirt, and he had a swastika tattooed on his right forearm.

Pidge wiped the shotgun barrel with a sleeve.

"Cash Doogan, you're an idiot to come here," she said. "I see you brought your poor brother Darl and two chicken shit Percys in the backseat too. What's your business, Cash?"

Cash Doogan shot a snot ball between the slats of the old fence. The two Percys laughed. Darl didn't, but he looked up long enough to catch my eye. He quickly looked away. Turning his attention to me, Cash nodded to himself, as if he were agreeing with the voices inside his head.

"I got somethin' for you," he spat. "You the one called DOO-dee? Well, How-DEE Doo-DEE!"

Only two in the redneck coterie laughed.

Darl wasn't one of them.

The laughter stopped when Pidge popped her weapon into position, aiming at Cash's smile. Without blinking or flinching, he casually dropped a manila envelope and half-lifted his hands in the air as he returned to the car, never taking his eyes from me.

What in God's name did I do?

"Next time, keep that lead foot in check when you're in these parts, Doo-dee. Wouldn't want the wrong people to access your information, would you? Brandon Doogan's son can't slow his roll, or keep his women in line when he ain't around. Speaking of Alabama porch monkeys, I don't see your nigger sister here, Brenda. Piggy, did you put her ass to work in the cotton fields? Tell her I stopped by."

Before I lunged, Mom grabbed my shoulders and pulled back hard. Pidge fired the shotgun and blew out one of the front tires of the Town Car. For a few moments, all I heard was ringing in my ears. Then came the cries of crickets and mourning doves and Mom's heavy breathing.

When Pidge spoke, her voice was low with measured rage. "Cash Doogan, you don't deserve to draw another breath, but being that I'm a Christian woman, I'll count to three for the Holy Trinity before I shoot your brother—one!"

Cash Doogan laughed as he started the engine. He continued to laugh as he slowly backed up the wobbly car. And still he laughed as the car disappeared around the bend.

We held our tableau. There was no need to move or speak. It felt good to be quiet in our solidarity. In my mind, I heard Hattie's velvet voice and pictured her face. And I felt her love, which kept me grounded. My godmother practiced what she preached, especially when it came to forgiveness. I wondered what she would've thought about what had happened.

The dust cloud from the car began to dissipate.

I wanted to do great harm to Cash Doogan.

Pidge staggered backward inside the house. Mom tried to follow, but her knees gave and she fell to the steps. I fetched the envelope. I told myself my imagination was making things worse. My knees buckled when I saw the blown up copy of my driver's license inside.

My smiling face crossed out with a red marker, the words 'nigger' and 'lover' with a vulgar drawing underneath them. Ripping the envelope, I told Mom to get her things.

As Flomaton fell behind, I tallied the number of times my skull throbbed trying to forget what had just happened.

Then, out of the blue, Mom slapped the shit out of me.

"Don't—you—ever—try—to—kill—yourself—again," she shouted, a hard slap for each word. Put together, they made an impact, especially since I was a kinesthetic learner and a grown-ass man over 30. "If you ever do that to me again, I'll prop your dead fucking body at the end of my fucking driveway and use your ass for a fucking mailbox!"

It was so sudden I burst into laughter and couldn't stop.

Mom continued to slap me upside my head, the blows came faster and harder as she screamed, which made it impossible for me to keep the wheel of our wildly swerving car straight.

A wide pitch sent us careening into a gas station parking lot where a stripped phone pole finally stopped us from doing a Thelma and Louise down an embankment. No real impact, but the bump was an abrupt ending. That we lived was a miracle, but with 15 miles left to go, anything was possible.

Mom kept sobbing.

I couldn't stop laughing.

•

Cantonment, Florida—Saturday Afternoon

Two years had passed since last I saw Granny and Grandpa. Five years had passed since my last visit to their tiny house beyond the railroad tracks. Muscogee Road snaked through Cantonment, taking us past the St. Regis paper mill, A Touch of His Grace Nail Care, St. Luke's Baptist and Junior's Food Store. Turning left at the fork, we continued winding south, and when I saw the house, my face began to hurt from smiling.

Pulling up a steep drive, we parked beneath an oak tree in the yard and then made our way to the back porch. Beside the gate was a splintered post with a tarnished bell that hung below a sign that told us to 'Beware of Dog' in faded red letters. When I rang the bell, the kitchen door opened with a loud groaning thwack.

A slobbering Boxer bounded onto the porch. Granny stood defiant in the door frame, her fists balled on her tiny hips. "Hell's bells, it took y'all long enough to get here," she said, bursting into tears when she saw me. She rocked me in a hug and mumbled about how long it had been and thanked God for bringing us safely to her.

We went inside and settled around the dining room table with glasses of my aunt Belladonna's *family-famous* sweet tea. After a few moments of small talk, Granny asked about my sex life, which was my cue to go. I went down the hall, passing a bookshelf filled with paperback science fiction and fantasy books Grandpa hadn't read since his stroke. I poked my head inside his dark bedroom, the smells of Carter Hall pipe tobacco and Old Spice filling my nose and kicking my head with nostalgia. There was a Maxwell House tin pregnant with coins, a picture of Granny beside a clock with brass mermaids.

And on his nightstand were pictures of his grandkids, the last things he saw before he went to sleep. Kissing his forehead, I went outside to fetch our bags from the car.

Flomaton suddenly felt like ancient history.

Blooming honeysuckle mingled with a stink from the belching paper mill you could taste in the back of your throat. I tripped on a pair of tree roots diving in and out of the sandy ground like barky sea serpents. Luckily, I didn't fall or drop the bags. From where I stood, I could see the railroad tracks curving around the bend of pine trees on Muscogee. When I was a boy, Grandpa would take me here to watch trains carry cargo to the paper mill. I remembered him holding my hand as they rumbled by.

As I got older, watching trains was no longer fun.

My imagination craved make-believe, and the yard was a creative playground for Tyler and me. We used to lay tracks, build forts and secret outposts, and raise all kinds of holy hell with our own version of World War II as the backdrop.

And this beautiful oak tree I'd climbed many times as a child. Spanish moss covered most of the branches now. Hattie once told me the gray draping mosses in these trees were memorials for lost and forgotten souls, as if all the nearby dead in unmarked graves had heaved themselves into the branches for the wind to remember.

Hattie called them Graveyard Trees.

In the kitchen, Granny was tossing bologna on toasted slices of Sunbeam bread slathered with yellow mustard and piled high with beefsteak tomatoes and iceberg lettuce. When she started talking about how the steroids for her eyes made her feel like Superman, I went to the living room. My favorite things were here, perfectly preserved since my childhood. The Magnavox Astro-Sonic console under the window, the laughing Buddha, the ceramic praying hands, the store-bought painting that matched the couch, the grandfather clock, the sets of Time-Life books, the vinyl LPs of the Beatles, Johnny Horton, Yma Sumac, and Elvis.

The summer I stayed here, *Urban Cowboy* was my morning soundtrack. Even now, I get teary-eyed at the steel guitar intro to 'Looking for Love'. Mom joined me when Charlie Daniels started singing about chickens picking dough in the bread pan. Suddenly, Granny trotted out sporting a 10-gallon cowboy hat that swallowed half of her tiny head. Mom giggled. "Mama, whose hat is that?"

"Hell's bells, it might be the dog's for all I know—I found it under Belladonna's Ouija board in her closet," she added. "Lord, this song takes me back. How 'bout you, o' boy?"

Flicking up the brim, I said, "It sure does, pardner."

Until the reunion in July, memories of the month I stayed here were unsullied. Vacation Bible School with Granny, movie outings with Belladonna, my Boba Fett action figure, George the Family Ghost, Miss Eva's fruit orchards and barn, Aunt Clara taking me downriver in an inner tube, Grandpa firing a shotgun at Belladonna's ex-husband.

On the day of the reunion, I recalled the pig in the fire pit, the horseshoes clanking, kids screaming, me throwing rocks in a pond, and smelling moonshine breath.

"DEAN ADAM DOOGAN!" Mom shouted.

The first side of *Urban Cowboy* had ended in spirals of repetitive static. "What?" I asked.

"Sugar, are you having a fit? That's twice since yesterday."

"I'm fine," I said. "It's been a while since I've stepped foot in this house, you know. Let up a bit."

Had Belladonna not opened the kitchen door and called for help so dramatically, Mom might've pressed me. Granny got up, kissed my cheek and left. Mom looked at me without expression, studying my face for cracks. She knew lying wasn't a thing I did well—like bluffing, my tell was easy to spot, and she knew what to look for.

That afternoon, armed with a pitcher of iced sweet tea, the cowboy hat, and a Walkman I dug out of the hall closet, I sat outside in the heat and listened to a mix tape with songs from Guns 'n' Roses, Christopher Cross, Metallica, and Dolly Parton.

The kitchen door thwacked open.

I turned just as Belladonna closed the gate and began her graceful march toward my spot under the Graveyard Tree. Mom often joked her sister wasn't a witch so much as she was a delusional pothead who dressed in black clothes and memorized all the Halloween recipes from every October issue of *Martha Stewart Living*.

Of course, Belladonna often joked Mom was as smooth as a Jezebel aspirin and sped 100 miles over the bitch limit. "Hey, babe," my aunt said, sitting next to me on my root seat.

And that was all the catching up we needed. Belladonna and I always had an easy-going, I'll-see-you-next-time-I-see-you relationship that made it easy to be close without any stress. Life had a funny way of making people feel guilty when time passed without updates. For a while, we talked small as we passed the pitcher.

"Mom tell you I got a speeding ticket yesterday?"

Belladonna laughed. "I told her to make sure you were careful driving here." She reached into her ink-black dress and took out a palm-sized box of cards. "Don't tell your Granny I have this Tarot deck in her house— she'd shit a brick." The charms on her bracelets clicked as she handed me five cards and lit a clove cigarette.

"I used to make decisions from readings up until my sixth divorce," Belladonna said. "At least I got stories. I might've stayed with my third husband if he wasn't such an abusive asshole and I wasn't a lesbian. Keep quiet about that or I'll hex your pecker with a pox. I think your Granny knows—if I hear about how nice the two les-bun nurses in her doctor's office are, I'm gonna slap her with my big gay hand. Jesus Barking Christ, it's hot. Anyway, it's a curious reading, and you're a curious person, Duddy, so..."

"A fat fucking lot of good that's done me," I said. "Sorry. Heat makes me cranky. Tell me what the cards mean. I am curious, really."

It wasn't a lie. I liked that Belladonna made crazy seem normal. The cards, in order, were The Fool, The Lovers, The Hanged Man, The Tower, and The World.

Belladonna exhaled a long stream of spicy smoke. "This reading basically says the circle of life is gonna bitch slap you over the next week or so. I'll be happy to talk to you more about it tomorrow," she said, getting up. "You're in my old bedroom, if you didn't know that—supper's at six. I'll put your plate in the fridge if Rick doesn't get you back in time."

"Rick Shelby?" I asked. "Am I going somewhere with a cousin I haven't seen since a hundred years ago?"

"Oh, shit, babe—I forgot," Belladonna said, putting the cowboy hat on her head. "How do I look?"

"Like Stevie Nicks at a barn dance—what about Rick?"

"He called me since I'm the only one who talks to him," she said. "He heard you were in town and wanted to take you out for a beer. Anyway, babe, he'll be here soon." Her bangles and dangling baubles and rings and bracelets clinked as she flicked the brim of the hat. "I don't know why everybody's so mean to him. People make mistakes. That's why black sheep should stick together. I'll see you tomorrow, in case I don't see you tonight. I got a date with a belly dancer, and I'm wearing this hat."

I laughed as Belladonna went back to the house.

Rick Shelby was a distant cousin of ours who worked for the Escambia County Sheriff's Office. Sometimes Dad was sent here to help Rick's undercover investigations with the Coast Guard, DEA, and the Baldwin County Sheriff's Office. Dad and Rick trained new deputies and other local law enforcement officers recruited for the dangerous work. They remained close until a few months before Dad disappeared.

That Belladonna was the only one who spoke to Rick anymore didn't bother me as much as it intrigued me. I mean, who was I to judge any man by his sins, rumored or otherwise?

A forest green Land Rover rumbled up the steep drive. Rick Shelby got out and barreled into me. Jesus H. Christ. Rick was so tall he would've been halfway home if he ever fell over. "D-D-Dean Adam D-D-Doogan, it's g-g-good to see you," he said, flashing his dimpled grin. He bear hugged me a second time, bouncing me over to his SUV before throwing me in. "Soon as I saw your t-t-ticket in the s-s-system, I had to see you," he said. "Let's t-talk over a pitcher."

I'd forgotten how thick his accent was. Rick's drawl and stammer belied his intelligence. His being in law enforcement (and often undercover), you could see how a stammer might be an advantage in certain situations—it didn't seem to faze him, which I admired.

"Hang on," he said, banking a hard right. "Here we are."

Light from the late afternoon sun passed through the trees on the shoulders and dappled the road with mottled beams. We headed for a gravel parking lot filled with pick-up trucks and motorcycles. A pod of diving topiary dolphins and other mystery topiary animals filled the lawn surrounding a squat cement building with a sign that said, 'BAR.'

The fenced picnic area behind it had a charred grill that looked like a blackened steam engine belching thick smoke. A sweaty bald cook tended sauce-covered rib racks and meat slabs from one end to the other. Beneath tents along the fence were sad, greasy men smoking Marlboro reds and passing bottles of bourbon.

Only a handful of those men were eating barbecue. And others were doing something worse—I saw pipes and needles.

We passed a topiary sentry bear and a god-awful green dragon slithering alongside the walkway to the front door. Hanging from the branches of a sapling pine was a lumpy snake that hovered above a row of dollar signs and shark fins. At closer range, you noticed the manicured shrubs were shapes molded from chicken wire, wrapped in green Christmas garland, and secured with white garbage ties.

"What the hell?" I muttered.

Rick laughed. "The owner of the b-b-bar has a son who's a bit t-t-touched in the h-head—nice as hell, d-d-dumb as a post. If his brains were d-d-dynamite, he still couldn't blow his nose. All right, D-D-Duddy, this is a rough place. Don't expect Ruby Tuesday's, okay?"

A bell above the door jingled as we went inside and waited for our eyes to adjust. The night-dark room was cold and smelled of stale smoke, mildew, and sour sweat. Several stools sat around a square bar in the center. Empty beer bottles lined a shelf that wrapped around the walls a foot below the ceiling. And there were obligatory neon beer signs, whiskey and cigarette posters, and photos of scantily clad, bare chested women on Harley-Davidsons.

The jukebox next to the cigarette machine was playing, 'I Found Jesus on the Jailhouse Floor.' Surrounding patrons were smoking, drinking, watching television, or staring blankly ahead. Others were shooting pool, playing video poker, or throwing darts. We went to a corner booth under a confederate flag stretched across the back wall. The flag didn't bother me as much as its size did—it was a fucking circus tent.

The barkeeper brought us a pitcher of Bud Light.

A penance is a penance is a penance.

"Listen, D-Duddy, so you know I'm not d-d-dicking you around," Rick said. "I got myself into s-s-something shady a few years b-b-back, something I'll d-d-do time for when I d-d-decide to turn myself in. Brandon knew I skimmed off the top, that I used extricated contraband for my own extracurricular activities. He never held it against me. T-t-t-tried to help me, but it was too late by then. I was over my head before he disappeared—it's gotten worse. I know y'all didn't get on, D-D-Duddy, but he was a good man. He tried. I mean, I'm flailin' and floppin' like a fuckin' fish trying to figure things."

"Join the club," I said, draining my mug. "I'm surrounded by women pulling at me like I'm a goddamn puppet." With a nod, Rick let me stew in my irritation, which ended when Garth Brooks stopped singing about the thunder rolling. "Didn't mean to bark at you. I'm sorry you're in trouble and have nobody but Belladonna to talk to, but my emotional plate is full at the moment—I mean, unless you know where Dad's body is."

Silence.

Rick refilled my mug. "D-D-D-rink up, D-D-Duddy," he said. "I'll need more of this if I'm g-g-gonna talk anymore."

By the second pitcher, the number of customers had doubled. A small group began playing darts not far from us. Between sounds of swearing and laughter, I heard HIS voice.

"I'd give my left nut to see a nigger lynched," he said. "Stringin' 'em up was a family affair back in the good ol' days when Earle Adam Doogan kept the peace in these parts. A great man makes for a great Grand Wizard, and Earle Ad—Darl, you clumsy fuck, pick up that dart 'fore I stab your face with it. What the hell are you lookin' at, Daniel Pussy Percy?"

"Shit," Rick hissed under his breath.

"If you brought me here to meet him," I said, "I already did."

Cash Doogan made a few more jokes about stringing up faggots and kikes with dead Indian guts before he threw his first dart. Rick grabbed my arm and pulled me back down into my chair. "D-d-don't start a fight," he said through gritted teeth. "Cash Doogan doesn't know we're here—goddammit, I thought he was up the Styx River tonight. Somebody must've t-t-told him."

"Told him what, that I was here?"

"Thought you'd be safe," he said, irritably. "Hidin' in plain sight usually works well enough around these hicks—s'what I get for tryin' to d-d-do the right thing." When Hank Williams Jr. started singing about family tradition, Rick got up to hit the head.

A scuffle erupted close to our booth. From the corner of my eye, I saw Darl Doogan writhing on the floor holding his face—his lip and nose were bleeding. The singing was so loud I couldn't hear Cash Doogan breaking a beer bottle on the cigarette machine. And because I was staring at the bathroom door waiting for Rick, I didn't see Cash Doogan come up behind me until he cut my ear and spat in my face.

"Hey, cousin Doo-dee," Cash Doogan hissed, his breath sour from too much beer and too many cigarettes. "If Darl hadn't fallen on the floor, I never woulda known Traitor Ricky actually brung you here. Christ, I wanna cut the rest of your pretty-pretty face now's I see you. It'd be like fuckin' an underage virgin. You'd look fine as shit in a dress and makeup though. You like boys, DOO-DEE. Runs in our family, you know. Did your daddy not tell you? What about that black whore of a godmother, did she—?"

That did it—*forgive me, Hattie.* It was all a blur, what happened next. Even now, I only vaguely recall the events.

I was walking on a slant by then and filled with renewed anger. Somehow, my knee found his groin and my fist found his ear, an unfortunate miss that gave Cash the chance to return the favor by cutting me up. He didn't get to use his bottle hand because Darl held it back.

"LET GO'ME, DARL—I'LL KILL HIM," he shouted, as someone grabbed his other arm. Cash flailed as they pulled him back, but it only made the rage and fury twist his face into something unrecognizable. "RICK SHELBY, I knew you wasn't gonna play our game too much longer—thank GOD I got better men on my side. I'LL KILL YOU AFTER I KILL THIS DOOGAN FUCKER. DO YOU HEAR ME, RICKY?"

With some help from the barkeeper and a brutally muscular young man who must've been a bouncer, Rick Shelby ushered me outside and threw me into his Land Rover. He climbed in and took several breaths—his hands were shaking so badly he dropped his keys twice. He started the engine and blasted the air conditioning.

When he was calm enough, he flipped the passenger-side visor up and directed its light over my face. "If nothing else, maybe a shiner'll remind you to steer clear of Cash D-D-Doogan next time you're itchin' to fight—things could've been worse," he said, swallowing hard. "Jesus H. Christ, that was close—God Almighty, what an idiot I am."

It was a short trip back to the house. We didn't speak much, not that there was enough time to talk about what happened (or wasn't said). Maybe the cheap beer made me paranoid, but Rick seemed to know something about Dad and yet telling me would get him into trouble somehow. It was just a hunch—or beer-fueled suspicion—so I left the confession entirely up to him. When we pulled into the drive, I said, "Please tell me the rest of my kin aren't like Cash Doogan."

Rick lit a cigarette. "Not even close, D-D-Duddy, but the watershed's a breeding ground for criminals, and he's the bad apple they follow," he said. "Cash has a real t-t-talent for bringing out the best worsts in weak people, so they'll stick with him until he gets killed, or they do. I haven't been able to keep him in line since Brandon went missing."

Rick wore a strange look that might've been *devil-thinking* had it not been so incredibly sad. "The officer who wrote your speeding ticket—his name's Enos Percy, and he brought it to Cash Doogan's attention because they work together and share information. The only reason Cash went to Flomaton was to size you up and to spite Pidge."

"Darl is nothing like his brother," I said. "Just an observation—I wouldn't be able to back that up with facts. It's just a hunch."

"D-D-Darl is innocent—he's just trapped," Rick said, adding with a sigh, "like I am. You just d-d-don't know the hell this mess has become. I thought I'd be able to tell you what it was I wanted to tell you, but I think I need some more time to put my shit in order, D-D-Duddy. I promise, next time you're in town. Here's my number—"

"Just tell me—I'll remember it until I die," I said, wincing as I touched my eye. "Haven't had one of these in years."

With a laugh, Rick told me the number. He was either playing me or helping me—for what reason and to what end I didn't know. I could see the cogs in his mind turning as he struggled with the burden he carried. "Thanks for seein' me, D-D-Duddy," he said, shaking my hand. "Call me if you need me for anything—God knows what might happen the next time you're headin' this way and you don't have a friend."

Stumbling out of the Land Rover, I waved to Rick as he drove off.

It was eight o'clock when I opened the kitchen door. I shoveled down the plate of food Belladonna left me. With a wave to Mom and Granny, I said goodnight and went to my room. I was beginning to hate secrets. Keeping them was a deception, regardless the intention.

For protection, for concealment, for a rainy fucking day, for the good of the family, for saving your own skin—keeping a secret was nothing more than an excuse to lie.

I knew that better than most.

Chapter 5

Music and Lyrics by Secrets and Lies

Sunday Morning, May 29, 2005

I woke to see Granny leaning in her cowboy hat grinning at me like a buck-toothed beaver. "G'morning, Grandson," she said. "Get up, brush your teeth, get dressed. I want to visit my mother and you're driving. I made you an ice pack. Been a while since I've seen a shiner like that."

"Well, it's been a while since I got one."

We hopped in her gold T-Bird and drove south to Beulah Baptist Church. Muscogee Road went under Interstate-10 and forked. I took the narrow gravel road that dead-ended at the church parking lot. It wasn't the first time I'd heard the church mentioned, but always a surprise since we weren't Baptist. "I thought Shelbys were Lutheran," I said.

"Shelbys in these parts are Southern Baptist, but Wilsons come from strict Missouri Synod Lutheran stock," Granny said, securing her cowboy hat. "Your rotten old Grandpa never cared where we parked our butts on Sundays 'cause he refused to go to any church. We used to attend St. Timothy's up in Farm Hill every Sunday with Clara and Eva until we found out our Lutheran church had too many damn Methodists."

The Shelby cemetery had been on the grounds of Beulah Baptist Church since the mid-1880s. Most residents had been dyed-in-the-wool Southern Baptist save for a smattering of Wilsons and Percys who'd married into the family.

"The plot I bought for your Grandpa and me is under them Grave-yard Trees," she said, pointing to the corner. "See that pretty white bench across the way? Get some daisies and meet me over there."

The yellow and white flowers were blooming along the length of the chain link fence. I gathered an armful and joined Granny. She put the posies in a stone vase and sat beside me on the bench. "Like most Perdido River folk, my daddy's people came from Uriah Shelby's loins," she said, "but my mother's people were Kentucky Shelbys, direct descendants of Isaac Shelby. Pity more of HIS blood didn't get passed down—most of his land and money's gone."

I laughed. "Now you're spinning history, Granny."

"Oh, hell's bells, I am not," she said. "Isaac fought with the Swamp Fox during the Revolution and Andrew Jackson during the War of 1812. He was the first governor, Grandson—no need to spin him bigger. Uri-ah Shelby doesn't need it either. I didn't bring you here to spin anything anyway. I wanted you to promise me something at my mother's grave."

"She won't haunt me if I break my word, will she?"

Granny laughed. "She was a hard woman and meaner 'n a snake, but she weren't cruel," she said. "Only the past haunts us, o'boy. Besides, you wouldn't break a promise—I'm a simple woman, but I know that much about you. I want you to promise me at my mother's grave that you'll be kind to your smiling soul and never try to take your life again." Wiping a tear, she pointed to the scars on my forearms. "Promise me, right now—promise me you will NEVER do that again."

Swallowing a lump, I nodded furiously. "I promise."

We sat in comfortable silence watching the traffic of sparrows and honeybees. A large tombstone, the one obelisk in the cemetery, caught my eye. "Who's buried there?" I asked.

"Lilly Middleton's husband," Granny replied, getting to her feet and adjusting her cowboy hat. "Mama, we're done visiting, but I'll be back soon. All right, pardner, follow me."

A marble spire ten feet tall stood at the center of a small fenced plot. Engraved in capitals around its base was, 'Jonathan Wakefield Shelby—1888–1939.'

"Why wasn't he buried in Charleston?" I asked.

Using a finger, Granny cleaned dirt from the letters. "He didn't know he was one of Uriah Shelby's bastards. He only knew his mother died in childbirth and his Wakefield grandparents died in the Johnstown Flood. He went to school and used his fortune to court Lilly after moving to Charleston. Some years later, they came here to trace his roots and moved into a cracker house down the road from Uncle Justice and Aunt Ruth. Jonathan learned what Uriah did to his mama and drank himself to death—God rest him. I was twelve when I stood here with Cotton Wilson and his grandmother Confederate Jasmine. Lilly went back to Charleston, but we stayed in touch. Did you know she was my schoolteacher?"

"I didn't know Jonathan was another Perdido River bastard," I replied. "We're stars in a night sky—longer you look, more you see."

Granny took my arm and nodded to the gate.

"Grandson, do something that makes you give a damn about others," she said. "And I want you to do something that makes others give a damn about you. Would you make me a promise to try?"

Of course, I would.

We took the hour-long scenic drive back to Cantonment.

Pidge's Jeep Wrangler sat behind Belladonna's car in the yard, but I didn't think anything of it until we got to the porch gate. The unmistakable smells of my godmother's Southern cooking greeted us before I climbed the steps to the kitchen. My hand on the doorknob, I turned around and said, "You deceitful old woman, you tricked me. Hattie's here."

Blinking innocently, Granny said, "Did I not tell you?"

Grandpa mumbled an incoherent greeting and waved with his good arm as Mom rolled him into the living room to play one-handed Legend of Zelda and watch television. Belladonna patted my cheek and brushed past me to help Granny in the kitchen.

I followed the sounds of laughter and clapping, and the scents of cocoa butter and Hot Six Oil (two of my three favorite fragrances since the day I was born). Turning left into the hallway, I poked my head into my bedroom. Hattie and Pidge were waiting for me there.

Unable to stop smiling, I cleared my throat, looked at my cousin, and said, "So, you had an errand to run."

"HA! Surprise! Now, c'mon in and shut the door, darlin'."

Hattie opened her arms and squeezed the pudding out of me. "Duddy-baby," she said, turning my face to look at my eye. "Tsk-tsk-tsk-tsk, Lord ha' mercy, what have I told you about not keeping your temper, Dean Adam Doogan? You are a grown-ass man, and you know how I feel about fighting."

"It's what I get for defending a woman's honor."

"I'll make you a paste to speed up healing."

"No, Hattie," Pidge said. "Devil-may-care is sexy."

Hattie put a hand on her hip. "Piglet, I'll whoop you with my spoon." Turning back to me, she said, "Other than the obvious, you look good. Still too skinny, but good."

"I'm not the one's too skinny in this room," I told her. "That African muumuu ain't fooling nobody—you've lost weight, Hattie."

"Hush your face and hug me again, Duddy-baby."

Hattie Louise Wilson, the Great Mother Yin to Brenda Shelby Doogan's Great Mother Yang—or, if I added Pidge to make it a trio, Hattie was the second of my Three Southern Fates. My godmother was a turbinado hurricane, a caramel crème-colored blanket of love, and the only woman ever to break my defenses and arrest my heart.

Hattie nodded to Pidge, who reached for something directly behind her on the bed. It was another plain-as-paper music box. With its unfinished wood, matte shine, tiny square size and shape, and tinkling melody, it was identical to the one I saw in Flomaton.

But this time, as the song played the same familiar melody I couldn't place, Hattie began to sing.

> *I'm just a poor wayfaring stranger*
> *A travel'n through this world of woe*
> *But there's no sickness, no toil nor danger*
> *In that bright world to which I go*
> *I'm goin' there to see my Father*
> *I'm goin' there no more to roam*
> *I'm just a-goin' over Jordan*
> *I'm just a-goin' over home*

"I'm goin' home," Hattie finished, face beaming as her voice faded.

"Remember when I used to sing that to you?"

"Yes'm," I said, grinning. "Is this your music box Pidge?"

"Mine's back in Flomaton," she said. "Not that it matters."

What the hell did that mean?

"This one's mine—I brought it as an example," Hattie said. "Duddy-baby, when I got cancer all those years ago, Cotton Wilson, my daddy, gave me a music box every time I went to have chemo. It's why I got a cabinet full of 'em in my basement. Twenty boxes, one song. My mother used to sing it to comfort me, so Daddy made sure I could hear it when a needle put poison in me. I love Melba and William Hubert for taking me in, but I've missed my mama since the night I saw her killed."

Silence.

"You ain't the only one to have something taken from you, Duddy-baby," Hattie said. "I wish I didn't know what happened—I wish I could forget it. That doesn't mean you don't deserve to know what happened to you. I know what happened to you in that cellar."

"We both do," Pidge added, taking Hattie's hand.

"But how—" I began. "I don't understand."

"I know you don't, which is why you gotta trust us until you do, Duddy-baby," Hattie said. "We won't tell you outright, but we will help you put the pieces of your broken memory back together and set you on a path to finding the other half of your family you don't know."

Pidge smiled. "We ain't guiding you, Duddy-darlin'— we're pushing your ass off a high cliff so you don't have time to think too much about what you'll be doing as you tumble headfirst to the ground."

"We wanted to do something two years ago, but you went and did the dumbest thing in this entire damn world," Hattie said, tsk-tsk-tsking me. "I guess you weren't ready for truth anymore than you were ready for death."

Defeated, I said, "What will I be doing then?"

With a quick look at the door, Hattie smoothed her gown and took a deep breath. "You'll be learning 'bout your family tree, root to stem—that's all you need to know right now," she said. "It'll seem like a wild goose chase at first, but only if you forget your promise to do whatever I needed you to do, NO QUESTIONS ASKED."

"So, again, what is it I'll be doing?"

"I'm missing three music boxes that look just like this one," Hattie said. "They're special to me and to this family. Next week, I want you to get the boxes and bring 'em to me. I don't want 'em mailed, and I won't be able to travel after my next chemo treatment."

"TREATMENT," I said, too loudly. "The cancer's back?"

Pidge patted my shoulder. "Ease the thunder, darlin'."

Hattie took my hand. "The music boxes are the last ones my daddy made, and I'd like them as soon as possible. Lilly Middleton has the first box I need you to bring me."

Strange coincidence, I thought. "I'm visiting Mom for my birthday, so I'll just head up to Charleston Friday morning and bring the box to Montgomery by supper time."

Pidge harrumphed. "Leave your mama in Ponte Vedra," she said. "Lord, deliver me from chicken shit Shelby women—I swear I'd wring her neck if I could get away with it."

Hattie rolled her eyes. "Lord, deliver me from vulgar women in overalls," she said. "As your godmother, I promised to do right by you if your mama doesn't. What you're doing for Piglet and me is your business, not hers. This cancer comin' back is MY business—you hear me? Nobody outside this room needs to know my business."

"Yes'm," I said.

Kissing my forehead, Pidge left me alone with my godmother.

Hattie took my hand. "Brace yourself, baby," she said. "I won't promise you your memory'll come back, but I promise you'll know the truth about things you've asked and wondered about. Whether you'll be better off for knowing isn't up to me, but you'll get what you've always wanted. You'll get a few other surprises too, but we'll talk about those after they happen. Lord knows I've got to clear my schedule for that talk—you might need to stay with me in Old Alabama Town for a week or two."

"Great, Hattie—just effing great."

"Today, we're gonna eat good food and love each other hard, and pretend like I'm not sick and you ain't got nothing to do."

"Sounds like I plan," I said. "How sick are you, Hattie?"

"Enough to say this might be the last time I see my Shelby mama and daddy," she said. "Doesn't mean I won't, but somethin's not right with the stars, and I'm not talking about mine. I wish I had my grandmother's Gift. Or Auntie Claudia's, Lord ha' mercy—this one time I went to Charleston, I spent the day at the market with Claudia watching her weave baskets and tell Gullah stories. That woman changed me before I left South Carolina."

Changed was a feeling I knew well.

Later, as I was setting the table, Granny shouted at the women giggling like teenage girls in the dining room. "If y'all don't stop with this silliness, I'll douse you with holy water—I'm talkin' to my Grandson," she said. "Maybe if y'all knew I'd be dead and gone tomorrow."

Belladonna shouted, "Don't say that, Mother!"

Granny stormed out with a cleaver. "I'll say what I damn well please in my own home," she said. "Hell's bells, 'dead and gone, dead and gone!' Leave an old woman alone."

"Old woman, I came here to make sure you didn't have a foot in the ground already," Mom retorted. "Maybe next time I won't bother leaving Flomaton. I'll just keep heading south to Pensacola and stay at a Sheraton on the beach."

"Good riddance," Granny said. "I'll die with a smile on my face."

Pidge cackled, Mom and Hattie whooped and hooted, and Belladonna screamed. Red as a lobster, Granny was too distracted to finish her earlier thought, but it didn't matter—she was too happy to care.

Hattie's *family-famous* cuisine was its own food group.

Buttermilk cornbread and homemade honey butter, spicy brown sugar-glazed ham, skillet fried okra, fresh creamed corn, flat beans, and collard greens. She shucked, scraped, sliced, pared, traced, and creamed it by hand and then added heaps of *nothin'-but* (Hattie's shorthand for L-O-V-E) to finish her masterpieces of comfort. You savored every bite, which is why eating was an all-day affair.

It was time for Grandpa to retire for the night. Before Granny wheeled him to his bedroom, he looked at the woman he'd taken in all those years ago. His own daddy had taught him to hate her for having brown skin. My once-bigoted Grandpa found humanity and redemption through his love for Hattie. He slurred his gratitude for her visit and called her daughter, and he wept as he struggled to touch her face.

•

After a long hot shower, I went outside with a pack of cigarettes and half a bottle of Pidge's brandy. I'd had plenty to eat, so my buzz was warm and smooth, and it put me in a relaxed mood. As I sat on the old root, I stared up at the sky drifting in and out of *devil-thinking* and twilight-dreaming. I didn't know how long I'd been there before an unfamiliar car turned up the drive and stopped in front of me.

"Dean Adam Doogan, I need to talk to you," the driver, a female, said. "Get in."

Although I couldn't see her face, I was lubricated just enough to be lured by her voice. She didn't give her name, but I didn't ask for it either. There was an air of mystery about the woman, so I tossed my brandy bottle and hopped in the car. Who was I to deny the request of a strange female I didn't know?

Not me, bub.

I didn't give a shit about not talking to strangers. Besides, I needed a break from the heavy fucking things in the house behind me.

To hell with the consequences, I thought.

The bar was a badly sanded plywood plank glued to a rickety old counter in a storage room behind Junior's Foods. Concrete walls, shelves of sundries, bottles of spirits and myriad tobacco products, adult magazines, dirty movies, and performance pills.

In the corners were lava lamps teetering on stacked boxes. Overhead were strings of blinking Christmas lights. Sam was the short bald owner who looked twice his age. He poured tequila shots—one for me and three for the lady, who tossed them back with a smile.

"I'm Sharon, by the way," she said, shaking my hand.

"That your real name?" I asked.

"You tell me," she said. "Is Duddy real, or is it Burmese?"

That made me laugh.

"What do you do for a living, Sharon?"

That made her laugh. "I'm holding out for a hero in a middle management position over in Bumble Fuck, Florida," was her reply. "In the meantime, I've been dividing my time between here and, uh, *north* of here for the past few months. And what do YOU do for a living?"

I took a shot of tequila. "Absolutely nothin', ma'am."

A retro jukebox played Merle Haggard when I was introduced to the only other patron there, an older woman named Eunice Percy. She only had eight teeth in her head, but she smiled as she shook my hand anyway. Eunice had been coming to Sam's for her nightly glass of Johnny Walker since her husband died.

When we'd settled back on our stools, Sharon looked at me for a long, awkward moment. "You know, that black eye's a knee-bender, Duddy—I wasn't thinking about getting laid tonight 'til just now," she said with a slow smile. "Get over it—I'm not a whore. I'm just no talker unless I've had some tequila, which is also my sexy elixir. Relax and listen to what I have to say before my libido takes over. Sam, an ashtray, please?"

Sharon lit her cigarette.

She didn't look like the lonely, crazy type. If anything, she looked the exact opposite—but then so do most people with borderline personality disorder when you first meet them. She was determined to connect with me, as if she'd been putting it off and had mustered the strength to do it.

She wasn't beautiful in any conventional sense—the package store lighting wasn't the best, so don't hold me to that.

Still, I couldn't take my eyes off her.

Getting laid suddenly sounded like a good idea.

"I'm married—hope that doesn't bother you," she said.

I took a drink. "I married the wrong person once," I said. "Cheated on her too, but that could've been the drugs."

"I didn't say I married the wrong person," Sharon said with a smirk. "I didn't say I married the right one either. And you ain't the only cheater, Duddy Doogan."

"How the hell do you know who I am?"

Sharon smiled. "I know all about you, Mr. Doogan—did that come out sexy or really creepy?" She laughed a sparkly fruity laugh as tendrils of smoke seeped slowly from her smile. "You're just gonna have to take me at my word for now."

The jukebox changed songs, and I half expected Olivia Newton John to start begging that barfly mister of hers to *not* play B-17, but Tammy Wynette started telling us how hard it was to be a woman who stood by her man. The song inspired Eunice to croon along.

It was atmosphere, if nothing else.

"We're in the ass-end of Cantonment," I said. "Why?"

Sharon laughed. "This ain't the ass-end of Cantonment, I promise you," she replied. "I heard about your tussle with Cash Doogan yesterday. The bar owner's a family friend and he saw Rick Shelby bring you in there. Don't get me wrong—no Doogan's a saint, but Cash is a monster. I'd swear he's Uriah Shelby reborn."

"So what?"

"I told you to relax and listen," Sharon said, blowing a ring. "No, you don't know me from Eve's left tit, and I don't personally know you from Adam's left nut. But I've known you from a distance for a couple of years now, so put those hackles down. You'll know why soon, so enjoy a pretty girl's attention until then. I didn't expect you to get in my car, you know. Either you got a thing for strawberry blonde strangers or you want to follow me down the rabbit hole."

"What if it's both?" I asked.

Sharon smiled again. Now I was certain she was more than pretty.

I finished my beer. "All right, what are you playing at?"

"Well, after I heard about your bar fight, I wanted to tell your stupid handsome face to be careful about trusting Rick Shelby," Sharon said, looking at her hands. "I know he's kin, but he's been a lost soul these past three years. Be careful."

What in the hell did Rick get himself into?

Sharon kissed me before I could ask the question.

"Look, you're gorgeous, but my night was heavy before—"

With another fizzy bubbly laugh, she kissed me again, harder this time. I was surprised at how quickly my confusion evaporated. The moment I felt her lips, my questions vanished—poof, all gone. I suddenly realized how lost I'd felt, how alone and isolated I'd been—Rick and I had those things in common.

Another kiss finally did me in. I always thought kisses were small things. I'd kissed plenty of strangers in plenty of bars—I wasn't exactly a monk. But this kiss was different. It rendered me powerless.

Sharon ordered one last shot for each of us, paid the tab, and led me outside. Then she continued to lead me past her car and across the dark street. I had no idea where we were going, and I didn't know what time it was. I just let her take me.

There was an empty public park a few hundred yards from the bar. We walked beneath an old rusted swing set and headed for the merry-go-round on the other side of it. The wobbly wheel creaked under our weight as it spun us in lazy circles, carrying us nowhere as we passed a cigarette in our dizzying round-n-round silence.

Other needs took over by the end of our spin.

And when the moon had gone from the sky and the night had coated everything with dew, Sharon put on my T-shirt, slipped her bare feet into her sandals, and went to sit on the swing.

As I fumbled naked in the wet grass trying to dress myself, she clapped and whistled, cat-calling *sotto voce* for more. My jeans were inside out. I left my socks and boxers where they fell and didn't bother tying my shoes. After I gave her the rumpled wad of her clothes, she tossed her blouse onto the broken slide and rolled the pants under an arm. Rising from the swing, she led shirtless me back to her car and took me home.

As the car idled, Sharon took my hand.

"Next time you're in town, I'll do more talking and less tequila," she said, kissing my knuckles—an intimate gesture as alluring as it was terrifying. "Duddy, tonight didn't go the way I'd planned it—to tell you the truth, I had more to say than just a warning about Rick Shelby."

"So, until next time," I said. "How will I find you?"

"Oh, I have your Tampa address—'night."

What the hell?

As I watched her leave, all I could do was stand there and marvel at my luck. Wonder quickly evaporated as I trudged my drunk ass into the house—too good to be true usually was.

For a brief moment, I thought of Belladonna's Tarot reading.

The Fool and The Lovers were obviously in play.

The Hanged Man was up next, and then The Tower, and neither card promised candy and roses. Not that any of that mattered.

I couldn't have cared less if Cash Doogan himself was about to put the noose over my head and chuck me off the roof of an oceanfront highrise.

Someone else occupied my thoughts now.

Although she didn't tell me the whole truth about who she was, Sharon didn't lie about the tequila.

Chapter 6

Death is Family and
Other Just-so Homilies

Memorial Day Morning, May 30, 2005

After a long night of my secret sexy she-devil doing a Texas two-step on my loins, heart, and head, I opened my eyes to see Hattie's smile under the brim of the cowboy hat. "Must you women be in my face every morning?" I groaned.

From the dining room, Mom told me to eat shit and die.

"What the hell did I do," I said, adding, "pardner?"

Hattie hooted. "Came home at three o'clock without so much as a phone call," she said. "She'll take you off the kill list if you go apologize—it'll be a long drive, otherwise."

Mom ignored me until breakfast was over, the car was loaded, and it was time to leave. I kissed Grandpa on the forehead. I barely escaped a Pidge and Belladonna snuggle sandwich (and tried not to laugh when Mom shot me the bird behind them). Granny hugged me hard. "I should hop in my T-Bird and drive to Tampa."

"Why's that?" I asked.

Hands on tiny hips, Granny said, "To work on my damn suntan— hell's bells, can't an old woman visit her grandson and take him to a fancy dinner at the Village Inn?"

Hattie pinched my backside when we hugged. "Remember what I told you—keep your mama out of this."

Mom cleared her throat. "Let's go, thoughtless son."

Leaving the house in Cantonment filled me with a pain that only deepened with the passing time. Like a faint bone ache, a post-visit malaise settled into my joints, swallowed my joy, and blew out the candles in my heart.

Dulled from departure (and lack of sleep), thoughts of Sharon left my mind when I began to miss Dad more and hate him less.

Today, it felt good to miss him.

"Death is family," I whispered.

Mom sighed. "Amen, sugar."

At least we didn't suffer alone—two years had taught us that much. Two years had passed since I stood at his empty grave at Magnolia Cemetery. It rained that morning. As everybody else passed the gates, I sat in the arbor under two weeping sweet gums. Hattie joined me on the bench. We held hands as she talked about the times to every heavenly purpose, but I found no comfort in her words. Dad was gone, and I felt as if the one to go, to disappear, should've been me.

And so, it came to pass that I decided to make Brandon Doogan's memorial about me in order to spite Dad and God at the same time.

A penance is a penance is a penance.

It was a quiet return trip to Ponte Vedra Beach, otherwise. Sometimes we listened to talk radio or the white noise of traveling. Neither quelled the emptiness I felt, like an echoing, hollow cry in the dark I couldn't answer. Hours after we reached the safety of Mom's screened lanai, the twilight sky had begun to change into its darker evening clothes. We ate supper and listened to the surf.

I loved the beach at night, especially when the first stars were coming out. Our trip to Pensacola felt like a dream now, a green mile leading you toward an undiscovered country.

And Christ, I couldn't get Sharon out of my head.

What she did to my body was one thing—what she did to my heart was hardcore Whack-a-Mole. I nearly told Mom—you know, to exorcise the succubus from my mind—but I talked about how strange I felt instead. "Me too, sugar," she said. "If today weren't the ugly anniversary it was, I'd swear there was trouble coming."

"What kind of trouble?"

Mom shrugged. She was right—something in the family cosmos was cow-tipped askew, a tilted feeling that stayed with me long after I said goodbye and left for Tampa. The upside was the two cases of Pidge's muscadine wine and brandy waiting for me on my front porch.

In one of the boxes was a note that read, "I wanted you to have this when you got home. I enjoyed our visit, Duddy-kins—Hattie and I got plans for you, so drink into a happy dream 'til we call you up for active duty. P.S. See you Saturday."

•

Tuesday morning, Tropical Storm Arlene formed in the Gulf of Mexico. Hurricanes and tropical storms were harbingers of doom (according to all the witches in my family). While I couldn't accept that as gospel, I was determined to keep an open mind about all the things I couldn't rationalize. Still, a storm named Arlene made it hard not to wonder if other unstoppable Southern things were heading my way.

Wednesday afternoon, a letter arrived.

I opened the envelope too quickly and got a paper cut for my trouble. Inside was a page with a phone number and time to call scribbled on it. At ten o'clock, I called two wrong numbers before the correct one. Our conversation didn't begin so much as it exploded into being like, a tiny Big Bang. We didn't stop talking until five in the morning.

10:32 PM

Sharon sighed.

"Had Uriah Shelby kept his dick in his pants, we wouldn't be here. When he wasn't fucking his own daughters or granddaughters, he was burying his hatchet in some other poor woman. All the bastard did was drink, rape, and kill. He fathered most of the Perdido River, but folk 'round here don't know the whole history, only a last name they've been taught to hate for generations 'cause they don't know any other way. At least there's hope that'll change soon. At least there's that."

11:04 PM

Sharon shouted.

"Since Brandon disappeared, the watershed's gone to hell because he was the only one who kept Cash Doogan in line. When he was around, weed and shine were dangerous—not much crime there. When he wasn't around, the meth came overnight, like an operation was in place. Say what you want about him, things got worse after he disappeared."

12:32 AM

Sharon giggled.

"Self-esteem? I don't know what that even means—I live day by day, I love my family and my God. I don't bother thinking too much. I know my yesterdays inside out. I know what I'm doing each time I draw breath. I don't waste time worrying about tomorrow because it'll come with or without me. I know who I am and where I come from. Call it what you want, but I couldn't give two shits about some hoity-toity phrase created by a Yankee psychologist."

01:57 AM

I cleared my throat.

"I was living in an efficiency south of Boston. I hadn't told anybody I was divorced. I don't know why I took Dad's call Thanksgiving night, but I did. He wanted to bring me home. I was sitting on a milk crate when I told him no. Two weeks later, he went missing. Six months later, we buried his empty coffin. Had I let him help me, he would've been alive, so I thought I deserved to die. I was an idiot and lost too."

03:21 AM

I continued my thought. "My sister Amanda took the curse to a new level when her two husbands died on their honeymoons. Hubby #1 went head first through a car windshield after falling 30 stories off the bridal suite balcony. Hubby #2 died after Amanda backed over him in a fully packed SUV before a romantic drive on the Blue Ridge Parkway. She's vowed not to love again and has since become a vodka-bottle-a-day gal. The curse is people having a shit time. All the superstitious story spinning and jinx talking are ways to cope. But what do I know? I'm still earning my way into the fold."

04:42 AM

I chuckled.

"My brother didn't talk to anyone BUT me his first three years. People said the curse scrambled his brains. I remember a buck-toothed cousin said something about it to Mom. 'The goddamn family curse's made yer boy a RE-tard, Bren'a—better take him to church and git him bap-IT-ized.' Tyler just looked at me and screamed, "DUDDEE! DUDDEE!" His Frankentoddler skewering of 'Dean Adam' stuck. So, yeah, my little brother named me."

05:09 AM

As I lay on my bed staring at the ceiling with a stupid grin on my face, listening to the radio and thinking about Sharon, I wondered what fresh hell I'd gotten myself into. I slept until the afternoon and was heading west on I-4 by three o'clock.

•

Ponte Vedra Beach—Thursday Evening, June 2, 2005

Sea breezes hushed through the bamboo lining the back fence.

With the tropical storm out in the Gulf sucking all the humidity from the atmosphere, the night was comfortable and breezy. Sadly, Arlene was speeding for Pensacola, which was unsettling considering the damage still left from the last one—harbingers of doom indeed.

Mom and I listened to Blossom Dearie and drank wine, and we spoke of other things. I bummed a few cigarettes.

I'd loosened up and was feeling happy.

"Sugar, tell me a story, something juicy."

"We were leaving California for Charleston, stopping in Cantonment for a few days first. Even in February, driving through deserts in a hatchback with black vinyl seats and no AC was sweltering. Talk about *family-fun*—you made batch after batch of Kool-Aid in a knee-high Vlassic pickle jar to keep us hydrated. You took a picture of us pissing in the Arizona desert with your Kodak Instamatic.

"After three days, we were only halfway across Texas because Dad misjudged the weight of five people plus suitcases in our tiny four-cylinder car. We were a day behind schedule. To make up time, Dad decided the glass Kool-Aid container would be more useful as a slop jar between fill-ups. At a Stuckey's gas station bathroom, I got pink eye. Both eyes were swollen shut by the time we got to Florida. Our Vlassic pickle chamber pot wasn't accepting deposits either, but with Granny and Grandpa's house only ten minutes away, we waited until we pulled into the yard. You took Amanda into the house while us boys peed outside. Then we trudged dog-tired to the porch, each of us with an item from the car. Dad had the slop jar and put it on the kitchen counter. After washing my face in the sink, I remembered seeing a jar of juice next to the cookie jar. I went to the counter, slid the jar over, unscrewed the lid, and took a gulp. It was warm and tasted like flat club soda with the rank tang of unwashed pig. I forgot it was there—I was so sick and I couldn't see. But Dad put that up there just for me."

Raising my wine glass, I laughed and took a swig.

"Sugar, I'd be more interested in you telling me why you don't have a job—you're a grown man. I want to be friends. I won't judge."

"I got into an argument with a supervisor when we all went out for drinks after work one night," I said. "He was getting belligerent with a woman at the bar and when I tried to take him to the parking lot, he had me fired. That was a week or so ago. I'll find another job."

Mom smiled.

When the phone rang, she answered it and then handed it to me with a yawn and a grin. "I don't know why she's calling so late—those steroids I bet." She smashed her butt into the ashtray and jumped to her feet. "Shit, your birthday card," she said, running to the kitchen. Returning, she said, "Here—sorry I opened it. I'm off to bed. I'll clean up tomorrow. Just lock the door when you come inside. 'Night, sugar."

When I mentioned the late hour to Granny, I got an earful. "Hell's bells, with the steroids for my eye, I can't sleep," she explained in the same sweet-tea voice Mom used. Granny talked a blue streak for an hour about her new strength, her pain-in-her-ass sisters, and how young she felt. "Steroids make you hungry," she said. "Did I tell you I was blind in my right eye before I got my prescription? I bet I could lift my T-Bird. Hey, o'boy, you get your birthday card?"

"Yes, Granny—what's that noise?"

"Dinner's done," she sang as I heard the microwave door close. "I went to the Taco Bell today and ordered me twenty burritos. I like to freeze them and cook 'em when I want one."

"That's a good plan, Granny."

She laughed. "I know I'm making no sense tonight," she said. "Thank you for humoring an old woman, Dean Adam. You did get my card, didn't you?" I looked at the Hallmark card's cheesy watercolor cover and cheesier greeting in calligraphic script that read, 'For my Grandson.' Inside was a birthday check for ten dollars.

"Thanks, Granny."

"Anyway, I'd better go through the supplies I got for this storm. I'm beside myself with worry. We JUST got the damn roof fixed from Ivan. I love you, Grandson—I'm so glad you're still in this world."

It was the last thing she ever said to me.

•

Early Friday Morning, June 3, 2005

The clock grinned the time with bright red teeth. I shuffled into Mom's tiny office to check the National Hurricane Center website. Its recent bulletin warned coastal residents of Florida, Alabama, and Mississippi, from Pensacola to Mobile to Biloxi, that Arlene would become a hurricane before landfall. Satellite images streamed an animation of the tropical storm's growth and movement over the past thirty-six hours.

Arlene had slowed to a northwestern crawl, churning in the Gulf and eying the end of the panhandle. When I phoned Granny to check in on her preparations, I didn't get an answer. It was odd, especially since the woman slept as light as breath. She always had, even without steroids.

I called the house again, but no one answered.

There was still no answer when I called a third time.

I woke Mom, who immediately phoned Belladonna, who called ten minutes later. All I could do was hold Mom after she collapsed to the kitchen floor in a fit of weeping.

Before it passed, she spoke in the strange tongue of grief as she spouted information to me through fish tank sobs. After taking a deep breath, she was able to relay what my aunt had told her. "Granny was sitting in her bed," Mom said through tears. "Her hands were folded in her lap, and her Bible was opened beside her."

No, Mom—you're wrong, I thought.

But I just spoke to her last night.

Granny can't be gone from us.

As the seams of the heart begin to unravel, you succumb to the piston-pump motions of other kinds of going and moving. Turning off the feeling faucet was easy for me when there was planning to do and people to call. And Mom would need me to help her with both, plus driving her to Pensacola when she was ready.

That was the plan until she spoke to Hattie. "But I NEED him to drive me there—I know the funeral will take time to arrange, but that doesn't mean he—dammit, I know that's Miss Eva and Clara's job, but I can't drive without him. WHAT COULD BE MORE IMPORTANT THAN MY MOTHER'S FUNERAL?"

Mom burst into a new fit of weeping.

"Not if that's the reason you and Pidge are telling my son—don't you turn this back around on me, Hattie Louise. Life just shat in my family punch bowl. Yeah, I know Death is family, but you don't know my son the way I know him! No, HE'S NOT READY!"

After a long pause, she shook her head and wiped her eyes.

"Yes, I understand. Okay, goodbye."

Silence.

Mom got to her feet. "Apparently, you're going to Charleston to get something from Lilly first," she said, wiping her eyes. "Hattie says for you to pick up your sister in Atlanta on your way to her place in Montgomery."

"What about Tyler?"

Mom didn't answer—she stared blankly ahead. "I can't believe they took you away from me," she finally said, fresh tears pouring from her red eyes. "I can't believe God took you instead of Daddy. I'll kill him when I see him. He was the one—not you, Mama. God picked the wrong one."

She lit a cigarette, something she rarely did in the house, and poured her a glass of wine, something she never did before noon.

"Tyler's been in Virginia trying to patch things with Laine, so I'll have to fly him to Pensacola," she said, blowing smoke rings. "Are you going to tell me why Hattie has you going to Charleston? No? Well, if you're done eating, then you should leave before I put you on my kill list. GOD-DAMMIT, GET OUT, DUDDY!"

And that's how my birthday began.

With numb resolve, I made my way north on I-95.

The highway up to South Carolina was a diorama of wetlands and forests. Stubby palms, old oak and cypress trees, mangroves, and bone-thin pines grew beneath the network of freeway and throughout the flood plains fanning toward the barrier islands. With Mother Nature's help, my roller coaster morning evaporated in the sweltering heat of afternoon.

Death is family, three simple words that acknowledged shared morality and our proximity to it, was like a sacred tenet from the Tao of Redneck Perdido River Folk. There was wisdom in those words, and it made me realize I'd looked at my family the wrong way all my life. There was honor in keeping a promise. There was pathos in loving hard and feeling punished for it. There was something magical about the women conspiring in secret to bring me closer to the truths about my home, my kin, and my past. As much as I loved my mother, I was willing to jeopardize our relationship to learn them.

Death is family.

History and connections, generations of stories and superstitions, secrets and lies—there was so much life in the spaces between those words. I'd felt incomplete for so long that I had to take care not to drown in the knowledge coating the inside of my skull like thick honey—my mind was dripping with the stuff. My ancestors had lived and died because *their* ancestors had earned for them the same grace now given to me. Did I deserve this chance to bear witness to any of their history? What did I know of struggle or sacrifice when all I've ever been was a fucking tourist in the short time I've lived.

Granny would've disagreed. She always saw your better self, not that she didn't notice your imperfect self. My grandmother had a way to see the miracles waiting for you to discover, and had faith that you would. Now she was gone.

Death is family.

I had to trust Pidge and Hattie. I felt their unseen strings pulling me. Despite the cello music playing in my heart for Granny's passing, I smiled. And I felt blessed to be so cursed by those women.

Chapter 7

Our Lady of Tradd Street

Charleston, South Carolina—Friday Afternoon

It was sizzling, crotch-rotting, monkey-ass hot, and it took me two hours to get across the Ashley River Bridge. Summer driving in the South without air conditioning was like naked ice fishing with your dick in the dead of a Minnesota winter. Both windows down, no cooling breeze, and the harbor's churning waters wafted its festering aromas in the stagnant air—imagine plough mud at low tide and fetid she-crab soup left to rot for a week in a garbage bag.

My mood changed when I started moving faster toward the Holy City's skyline of steeples and antebellum houses sinking into the tops of palmetto trees. After merging onto Cannon Street, I went south on King, its palms like upright bottle-brushes lining the narrow one-way avenue to the Battery. I made a last-minute decision to stop at the market—I was beyond late, so it didn't matter when I got to Lilly's.

Beaufain Street took me into a sea of people. Where did all the tourists come from? And the street performers and sidewalk artists? And the insane number of clopping horse-drawn carriages? And the Dixieland band playing under the awning of that old bank—

—Spoleto!

Damnation station.

Charleston's annual international arts festival ran from the end of

May through the third week of June. People from around the world flocked here. Spolidiots, Spoletians, Yankees from-off, and even locals, all packed the streets and avenues of shops, hotels, and trendy restaurants. I couldn't change my mind, but I needed a parking spot. A frazzled mother of five backed her minivan from the space in front of me—right next to the Dixieland band.

I claimed the spot and honked Jeepers most triumphantly.

Using my last bottled water, I wiped my face and neck before I took a dive into in the ocean of strangers in the Charleston City Market. The 200-year-old open-air bazaar stretched four blocks from Meeting Street to East Bay Street. A hodgepodge of culture, kitsch, and commerce, the market housed merchants in booths and shops selling prints of Rainbow Row, the Battery, Fort Sumter, and seedier offerings, including T-shirts and shell-covered trinkets.

The entrance at Market Hall was a pink-hued Athenian temple ornamented with rams and elevated stoop that looked as if blind masons built it. The exit spat you on the corner of East Bay Street, where you could see the harbor docks and Treasury building where Dad used to work.

I was somewhere in the middle, where vendors were selling flowers, toys, and bald p'nuts. Disparate aromas filled the air with rapturous scents of baking waffle cones, cooling cookies and fudge, and roasting coffees, chocolates, and nuts. I squeezed between tables lined with bags of Charleston rice and recipe booklets for shrimp 'n' grits. I nearly knocked over a menagerie of shot glasses and Gone With The Wind postcards when a pack of swarthy men in wife-beaters pin-balled me into a small group of Spolidiots with thick Boston accents.

They were asking where the slaves had been sold.

I just rolled my eyes—the site for the slave auction house was few blocks to the south on Chalmers Street, a less romantic area than the one where The United Daughters of the Confederacy ran a museum about the War of Northern Aggression or, as it was often referred to here, The Recent Unpleasantness.

Scanning the pavilion, I ignored the Spolidiots behind me asking where they sold slaves and headed toward the end of the second pavilion. A heavy-set woman with nutmeg-brown skin in a bright polka-dot dress was sitting in a lawn chair. Auntie Claudia was one of the famous Sweet-grass Basket Weavers of the Charleston Market. They were descendants of the first slaves brought to the Lowcountry. She and three other women spent all day threading stalks of marsh grasses into baskets, fanners, bowls, boxes, mats, and hampers. Finished pieces sat in honey-colored rows on old linen sheets—a bowl could fetch upward of $500 dollars.

They were shrewd businesswomen who capitalized on what Auntie Claudia called, 'the guilt of certain white folk.' She once told me, "The guiltier they feel, the more baskets they buy."

All the women added a vital sense of history, but Auntie Claudia was a legend in the Holy City. As a boy, I used to sit with her on Sunday afternoons with Lilly to hear her stories and songs. Her booming voice rose above the din of any crowd—and she always had a crowd—but she loved children to gather at her feet. You can imagine what happened when a short pale man in khaki shorts barged through to argue about the prices of her baskets.

Without getting up, Auntie Claudia shouted at the rude man in Gullah by not shouting at him directly: "Tie yuh mout'! Heah? 'E bad mout' me ie een crack muh teet.'" I didn't notice the licorice-dark man the size of a carriage horse standing next to me.

After the Spolidiot stormed off, the tall man poked me on the shoulder. "Excuse me, are you Duddy?" he asked with a smile like a stained glass window.

He smelled like cinnamon pipe tobacco too.

"Yes, I am," I said, shaking his hand—his name was Ned. "Jesus, you're huge. What's your accent? I can't place it?"

"I'm Claudia's cousin from Philly—she sent me to bring you over," he said. "She figured you'd be stopping by."

"Thanks, Ned."

Ned waved as he disappeared into the crowd.

I hadn't seen Auntie Claudia in two years. She had a way of reading you. I mean that, literally—she looked at your palm until a kinesthetic psychic magic thing happened and she told you something that shook you to the core. I didn't put stock into the tool or method she used, but her insight was spooky true.

"Auntie Claudia, you haven't aged a day," I said.

"Hush that white devil tongue and hug me," she said, embracing me warmly. "Here, sit on my upside down bucket seat. Lord, baby, I haven't seen you since Brandon's memorial. And I haven't aged much 'cause I smoke, drink, and eat what I want—the secret's makin' vices from scratch. Sorry to hear 'bout your grandmother. It's the unhappy beautiful way of things—I hope you made your peace with her."

"I actually did, thank you," I said, swallowing. "I honestly wasn't going to stop by for a visit today, but as soon as I hit King Street I had an urge to see you. If I'm imposing then—"

"Tie yuh mout'—yuh heah? Lord, baby, we don't gotta know every damn why all the time," Auntie Claudia said. Clenching the smoking pipe in her teeth, she took my hand and traced the lines of my palm with her finger. "A doctor cut your private bits? Keep from having babies?"

My mouth went dry. "I told NOBODY I did that."

Auntie Claudia laughed. "God's Gift told me," she said, smoothing my skin. "Didn't work like you thought—woo, life's bursting in your man parts. Boy, you can't hide no more than Brandon tried to hide. Who's this woman that's bit into your heart like an apple?"

"Sharon," I answered, nervously.

"Hmm—she might be the One for you, but not all she says is perfect truth," Auntie Claudia said, squeezing my fingers. "Not exactly lyin', but not exactly showing you the real her. She's knocking courage back inside that rattled soul cage of yours though. She's preparing you for troubled waters, dark and cold—I'm talkin' out of the old world kind, like secrets hiding in plain sight all around you, Duddy. Best go on down to Miss Lilly's before the sun catches you in his down. Gimme sugar, and you tell her I'll see her for tea tomorrow."

"You still have tea with her?"

Auntie Claudia laughed. "Baby, I wouldn't miss ONE tea with Lilly Middleton for all the blue blood money in Charleston—without her papa's daddy, I wouldn't be sitting here with you," she added. "Next time, we'll visit properly."

Saying goodbye to Auntie Claudia, I went back into the crowd. Finding my way to the parking lot was easy with Dixieland music guiding my steps. Seeing the bank sign ahead, I did a sideways crab crawl through a pack of giggling girls to the spot I'd left Jeepers—a Mazda sat in the space now.

My heart was rattling like a steel can in my chest. I asked a few strangers sitting on the wall nearby if they'd seen my old Jeep, but they hadn't. Instinctively, I felt for my keys, but my pockets were all empty.

Oh, God, not today—please, not today.

When the band stopped to take a break, I approached the leader, a man named Timey Weathers, who shook my hand with a sad look on his face. He led me to the edge of a knee-high cobblestone wall and sat down. "Sorry, young man, but with so many Spolidiots walkin' 'round, a few o' them gangs from Up-Chuck come do they stealin' bidness," he said. "If you was bumped in the market, then you was marked. You got someone nearby?"

"Yes, sir," I replied, taking a deep breath.

Timey gripped my shoulder. "I been where you standin' now more than a few times—listen, if you're hungry, I can get you a hot plate from Henry's. If you're thirsty, my percussion section has some whiskey. You need to borry a cell phone?"

Shaking my head with a grateful, resigned half-grin, I thanked the old band leader, wished him well, and sprinted toward East Bay Street. Thoughts of Auntie Claudia and Sharon mingled with thoughts of Granny and Mom and Hattie—and of course, it was impossible not to think of Dad now that I was here. As fast and as hard as I ran, I somehow started laughing without losing momentum—the theft of poor Jeepers seemed a fitting end.

At least it didn't die on me.

For the life of me, I couldn't stop laughing, and it was a sign telling me I was heading straight into trouble.

•

The late afternoon sun dressed the multi-tiered Federal-style home in Old South Dreamy. It was built in 1818 with a Charleston piazza, wraparound railing, a courtyard and carriage house, slave quarters, and several gardens spread over a wide lawn. For years, the Historical Society had begged her to make the property a museum, but Lilly was damn stubborn about letting superficial people polish her beautiful home into another prized turd. Standing at the gate dripping in sweat, I rang the doorbell a second time and peered over the wall.

Where is Helga?

I was about to ring a third time when a German voice from the second floor piazza shouted my name. Hair in a permanent long braid, Helga was coming down the outside staircase laughing as she made her way to the gate. Throwing open the metal-lattice door, she reached for a hug and then drew back with a frown.

"Ick, you filthy boy—*ekelhaft*," she said, her accent thick Hollywood German. Pointing to the back of the yard, she said, "She's pruning roses in her favorite spot. Go use the outside washroom for your toilet. Ick, you messy thing—*ekelhaft*—you dirty thing."

With a chuckle, Helga went tsk-tsk-tsking around a corner.

Trees and vines choked off the harbor air, cooling it with shade and fragrances of cut grass, wisteria, and lavender. In a corner beneath a coppice of mimosas and a busty magnolia, a sturdy, elderly woman with bright platinum hair was elbows deep in a rose bush, pruning with her bare hands, which is all you needed to know about Delilah Middleton Shelby. At 103 years old, she only ever answered to her nickname and always wore gray sweatpants, a white Oxford dress shirt, and a double-wide-brimmed straw hat adorned with fake Gerbera daisies.

Lilly had more gumption than the Carolina militia and brooked no excuses—being late because of traffic and a mugging weren't on her list of exceptions. Knowing death was the only excuse she'd accept, I kept my mouth shut and waited.

"Dean Adam Doogan, you're late and yet, still alive—we don't have much time now that the sun's going to bed," she said, still pruning. "I'll give you a pass this once. Come over here, sweetbaby. Let's us have a look at those pretty green eyes."

The way she hummed syllables elevated a genteel Old Charleston Blue Blood accent into something indescribably MORE—hers was sexy and curled, elegantly deep and rich, and went down like Tennessee whiskey on a cold day. She threw a handful of thorns and extended a hand—

not a scratch or drop of blood on the skin.

After I helped her to her feet, she looked at me and smiled. "My, you've filled out," she said, patting my chest. "Good, the world's better off without you being so damned shallow, sweetbaby. Every day isn't a Tradd Street cotillion."

"Hence the sweat suits and sneakers?"

"Poo, sweetbaby—Lord knows I'm a tomboy at heart," Lilly said, slipping an arm into mine. "I wear sweatpants because they're comfy, and I wear tennis shoes to piss off the Ravenels, who'd think I was rich white trash regardless. I'd go starkers to spite them if my breasts didn't look like a pair of used prophylactics. Take me 'round back of the carriage house. Anyway, Father walled off most of the yard so I'd have a nook hidden from nosy eyes and strolling folk *from-off*. Take me down to the sloping walkway through the trees. See?"

There, at the bottom of the hill, was a squat brick building. I'd never noticed it before now. It was so tucked back and hidden you'd think it was a utility shed by the look of it. Vines of dark ivy covered it in leafy green scallops from bottom to top.

As Lilly and I made our way, she squeezed my arm. "Sorry to hear 'bout Melba's passing," she said. "I didn't know her as well I know your godmother, but Melba was all heart. Her older sisters, Eva and Clara— decidedly NOT from the same cloth."

"It was a shock," I said.

Lilly laughed. "Death isn't a shock—life's the shock. Live a hundred candles and then you'll understand. Now, stick your hand in that bush and slap the metal plate with an open palm hard." As a gate opened to a winding path, she tapped her cane on the crumbling cobblestones. "Poo, this'll wreck my hips—hold me steady, Dean Adam. I don't want to fall. One more bionic implant and I'll have a TV show."

The path took us under a Graveyard Tree next to the small building. Moss hung between cracks, forks, joints and fingers, and dripped over the door. Lilly tapped it with her cane and smiled, only slightly out of breath—old age didn't touch her.

"Lilly, how do you stay in such good shape?"

"Poo, sweetbaby—I'd trade a healthy lung for less wrinkles. I look like one of them Shar-Peis," she said, taking a key from the band inside her hat. "Lord Almighty, this door looks like it hasn't seen paint since the Reconstruction."

With careful back-and-forth motions, she took out a clunky old key and, with careful back-and-forth motions, jiggled it inside the lock until it clicked. She pushed open the door and flicked a light switch. "This is more than a cellar," she said. "Laws, that's a big lady long legs. Shoo, girl. Shoo. Better than a family of palmetto bugs, I suppose. Watch your step, sweetbaby."

For a moment, I didn't know if I could step into the unknown—an irrational fear tried to throttle me up through my ass—but we quickly floated down the stairs like a pair of old Charleston haunts.

Lilly turned on the AC unit at the bottom and told me to look around. The cellar was bigger than I'd imagined. It was cleaner too, clean and brown with musty odors of earth and dusty soil, and memories—the smells of history.

The mottled clay floor was hard and dry enough to support counters and metal racks with empty jars and cans. Rusty pots and forgotten utensils dangled on hooks. Ornate rugs hung on pegs in each of the exposed brick walls, save one wall.

A case of shelves filled with dusty tomes from floor to ceiling.

"Not all secrets are shameful," Lilly said. "Take me to the books there, and I'll show you what it means to hide a secret in plain sight. I wish we didn't have to rush this, sweetbaby."

Rush what, I wondered.

Hidden behind a book with a crushed spine and no title was a handle that made a clacking pop when Lilly pulled it.

The entire wall of books and shelves glided inward and left on metal tracks, locking in place out of sight. We stood before a small room roughly 12-foot by 12-foot. The urge to take off my shoes was strong—it felt like standing on holy ground. Lilly lit a kerosene lamp on the bureau and sat on a chair against the wall.

"I was five when Father brought me here and told me my great-grandfather had the cellar built after Thomas Jefferson was the president," she said. "He had this secret room built in 1818 and hid runaway slaves in it. And his son, my grandfather, would take them to New York in one of his cargo ships. He continued the work HIS father began with *my* father, who said they purchased whole families to keep them together when they secured their freedom. It was a miracle no one discovered our very dangerous stop on the Underground Railroad, but we weren't interested in parading about like royalty either.

"Our branch of the Middleton tree was pruned before my father was born—we aren't mentioned in any known history of Charleston, not any like the Grimke sisters. Still, I am proud to say we freed 163 souls from bondage, Claudia's and Hattie's people included."

"Hattie's people hid in this room?" I asked.

Lilly smiled. "After supper, we'll talk more."

We ate in the solarium. And after two helpings of Helga's unbelievably decadent Black Forest chocolate cake and three glasses of port, my tongue loosened. I sheepishly told my story about the theft of Jeepers at the market earlier. "I don't care about the money or clothes—or my cell phone, I just—"

"Hush now, sweetbaby—Helga-dear, a pad and pen, my address book and the cordless phone, please and thank you," Lilly said with a look telling me to keep quiet. "It's time to call in some favors I'd never thought I'd get to cash in."

"Really, Lilly," I protested.

"I told you to hush," Lilly said. "I've done a great deal for a great many people over the years, so let an old woman have fun. Go upstairs and take a shower, you ingrate. Helga will put out some sleeping clothes and wash what you're wearing now. Shoo, Dean Adam."

As promised, a T-shirt and pair of shorts were waiting on the bed beside the music box, lid opened, the same song playing. There was a square of folded pages covered in words written with an old typewriter.

At the top of the first page was a place and date.

Still in my towel, I sat down to read.

•

Cantonment, Florida — June 10, 1919

Margaret Shelby should have reached the Wilson place by now. She trudged north along the river with a howling newborn in her arms. His wrist badly broken, the baby screamed himself hoarse between fits of shock and silence.

The early hurricane had begun to assault the watershed, but it did not frighten Margaret as much as Earle Adam Doogan and his men hunting her down.

Margaret lost her footing and fell hard on her backside, rattling her teeth and bones. Wobbling to her feet, she searched for landmarks — nothing was familiar. Swirling in the ravine below were the remnants of a bridge and a mangled carcass of a panther. A wayward branch knocked her down again.

"Hell's bells, Lord — I can't do Your work if I breakin' the damn baby," she said, spitting a tooth. "Hep a sinner, Lord!"

As Margaret waited for the vertigo to pass, the ground beneath her collapsed. She tumbled toward the troubled water and rolled into a boulder. Ignoring the pain, she did her best to calm the infant clutched in the crook of her arm.

He's going to die soon, she thought.

The hairs on her arms tingled. A flash of light cracked the air and split the trunk of an oak tree perched on the edge of the wall. The flaming tree fell into the ravine and pinned her, the mud beneath her now like quicksand. Debris collected into dams of dead animals, leaves, wooden posts, toys, and refuse. She needed to free herself.

Spying a row of sapling pines directly above her, Margaret used a sticky trunk to pull herself from the muck. She climbed the charred trunk of the burning tree and passed its curtain of exposed roots at the top of the steep bank. The house she sought was in the clearing ahead — she nearly danced a jig when she saw the windows aglow with light.

Hiking her sopping dress, she went to the house, a beacon shining atop its dark hill, and fell on the steps to the front porch. "Justice Wilson, git out here," Margaret shouted. "You, Justice Wilson!"

A black-haired man with a shotgun and a lantern opened the door. "Margaret Shelby? Woman, I didn't expect you 'til tomorrow."

"Damnation — gimme the gun an' take this child 'fore he drowns," she said.

"Dear Heavenly Father," Justice said. "Who did this to him? Answer me, woman."

"God did it to'm," Margaret spat and went inside the house. "God did it to us when He let Uriah Shelby fill the watershed full of bastards. Tend to the baby while's I tend to my sister — how's Ruth?"

"Baby was stillborn," Justice said without emotion. "Ruth doesn't know. Becca took care of her mama when Confederate Jasmine didn't come. She did what you both taught her — and I thought she was too young for midwifing."

"Like all men, you're ignorant," Margaret said, tossing her bonnet to the family table as she went to the back room. "See to that baby. Save his life an' you'll have the son Ruth couldn't give you."

"What aren't you telling me, woman?"

There was a long silence. Outside, the wind and rain railed against the house. Inside, Margaret smiled and said, "Behind the bible on the mantle is my flask. Have some whiskey and pack my pipe."

Another squall shook the roof. Justice took the quilt from the rocking chair and placed it on the table. Laying the baby on it, he removed the soiled wrappings and sucked his teeth. A small voice behind him spoke. "Papa, the storm's loud again."

Justice looked over his shoulder. Tucking raven-colored hair behind her ears, the girl moved beneath his arm and gasped. The baby's white hair, the filth covering his body, the broken bone, and his ripped flesh filled her with pity.

"I thought the baby died, Papa."

Justice calmly set her to task. Becca returned with a basin of soapy water and a wooden spoon from the cupboard. She fetched a quilt and the baby

clothes she helped Mama sew, and she watched her
father work. He explained what he was doing as he
washed the angry flesh, reset the bone, and stitched
the skin. The arm was dislocated at the shoulder,
but with Papa's help, Becca popped it back in place.

The baby stopped screaming. And when Becca
dressed him and cradled him in her arms, the baby
stopped shaking. "Such blue eyes," she cooed. "Will
Mama feed him? I can make a pap if I need to."

Justice had not thought about feeding the child
until now. He said a silent prayer to God asking His
forgiveness for not grieving for his dead son. There
was new life in need of saving still. Becca was as
bright as a polished silver pot and knew not tell
her mother about the child she held.

"Hello, little brother," she said.

Justice looked up when Margaret touched his arm.
"She's weak as a kitten, but strong enough to feed
him. Becca-girl, take him in. Say nothing 'bout him,
that's a lamb." Margaret took the bloody sheets she
had been hiding behind her to the sink. "I told Ruth
his arm got twisted up in the cord and broken when
she pushed him out. No, you sit while I do my business in here. I'll tell you everything when Confederate Jasmine comes. Just know he's yours."

With the body of his stillborn son cleaned and
wrapped for burial, Justice went to see his wife.
The copper-metal scent of blood greeted them before the light of the candles did. Ruth smiled, her
cheeks pale pink as the infant suckled hungrily at
her breast.

Justice sat beside her. "Does it hurt?"

Ruth winced. "More'n the labor — I had a dream he
was dead, but he can't be. Look at the white hair on
his head. Is the storm here yet?"

Justice shook his head. "The worst of it is hours
off, so don't worry yourself." He helped Ruth button
her gown and took the baby. "What's he called?"

"Ewell Curtis Wilson," she said with a smile. "A
strong baby needs a name to help him survive this
God-forsaken watershed." She yawned and said, "Ewell
Curtis, his head looks like a cotton bud."

Later, as the hurricane crept up the river, Becca read from the Book of Matthew in her room. Justice held his living son at the table, as Margaret smoked her corncob pipe and sipped corn whiskey from her flask. The scratches on her face and neck looked as if the devil had whipped her.

"Ruth's right," Margaret said. "God has a plan for him, which goes double for us sinners takin' care of him. He's a cursed blessin', if you ask me."

"Margaret Shelby, I won't have curse talk in my house," he said, his eyes narrowed. "I don't care what you or your sisters say about the taint of Uriah Shelby's blood. I'll put you out like a cat."

"You'll taste my knuckles if you try," she said, trying not to smile. "These folk will see this albino baby as cursed whether you will or won't, so git right with the talk. Pray for strength to hep the boy weather the storm his life will be. After God's done with him, he'll suffer more than the Devil's own. It's always God's children who suffer most."

"Woman, what are you not telling me?"

Margaret took a drink. "He's the bastard son of JJ Doogan," she said. "Confederate Jasmine's youngest daughter Echo gave birth last night – she died. My sisters would drown Doogan spawn for sport, but he's the grandson of Confederate Jasmine too, so... I set out this morning to get here before the storm hit, but I had to hide in Cantonment."

"Who's after this boy, Margaret?"

The sound of Becca's shuffling ended the conversation. "Papa, do you know those men in the backyard," she asked. "They woke me up with their swearing."

Margaret gripped her arms. "They see you?"

"No'm, my candle was out," she said. "They talked about a nigger baby the Shelby witch brought here. Aunt Margaret, you didn't bring a nigger baby here. That's baby's white as Christmas snow."

Justice gently patted her. "Don't say nigger, Becca," he said, grabbing the shotgun. "Margaret, who are they?"

"Earle Adam Doogan and some of his kin," she re-

plied. "I hoped this storm would stop 'em in Cantonment, but I knew it was a small chance. I'll pay for
it. My life ain't worth that much."

Justice swallowed. "Becca take the baby in to
Mama, lock the door and say nothing."

"Yes, Papa."

Justice turned to Margaret. "Get the gun on the
shelf over the cupboard — protect my family, and
that includes you, you old harpy. Earle Doogan isn't
so powerful without his entire posse. He'll leave
soon, one way or another."

"But you got HIS property," Margaret countered,
pointing to the bedroom. "The property that'll be
suckling at Ruth's teat while you're squaring off
with his evil grandpa."

Justice glanced at the neatly folded lump of
clean sheets at the end of the table. He was surprised at how quickly the thought came, that his
dead son might be their salvation. "Margaret, you're
mistaken," he said. "There's nothing in this house,
alive or dead, belonging to Earle Adam Doogan."

Outside, the wind brought in the rain sideways.
His eyes adjusted to the darkness as he searched for
trespassers. Justice heard no one, saw no one, but
he felt eyes watching him. He knew the river and its
tributaries intimately. He had a sixth sense about
life here. A strange quiet from the west told him
eyes were on him.

A gust from the back of the house carried the
stench of sour sweat, chewing tobacco, moonshine,
and blood. It was the perfect place for hiding
— Justice could see the spot from the end of the
porch. He aimed his shotgun high at the trees there
and squeezed the trigger, the blast bringing down a
loose branch from a tall elm.

"That's your warning," he shouted, lowering the
barrel. "Earle Doogan, go and live, or stay and
die." Wind was his answer. Aiming, he squeezed the
trigger and fired.

"JUSTICE WILSON, I GOT THE NIGGER JASMINE WOMAN,"
shouted a voice.

Justice lowered his gun. "Jasmine?"

No reply came, only the dim light of a newly lit kerosene lamp peeking through the trees. Two men, the one holding the lamp and the other dragging a large sack, headed across the lawn for the porch. The one with the light was limping badly — the one with the sack struggled against gusts of wind and the prisoner inside his bag.

Justice aimed. "Earle Adam Doogan, I'm a God-fearing man, but you're trespassing, and I pro-tect what's mine."

"I protect what's mine - all's I want is justice, Justice," Earle spat, thumbing behind him. "I got an ace shot in them trees and his pistol's pointed at yer face. Them Shelby bitches kilt my JJ. I know Margaret stole my bastard grandson. I'll trade what I got in my sack for my property you got in your house. Be still, you nigger piece-of-shit!" Earle kicked the soiled canvas bag.

Justice winced. Earle's nephew Lucas lurched, nearly dropping the lantern. "I need to sit," he said, dry heaving. "I'm dizzy, c-c-cold, Uncle Ear-le. Please."

"Quit whinin'," Earle snapped. "We'll git the hell gone soon's I got what's mine. Boy, don't you bleed out. Justice Wilson, give me my half-nigger grandson. Dead, alive, don't matter. I ain't pro-tecting life. I'm protecting my family honor and my own goddamn legacy. My name will be remembered with fear and awe for generations."

The front door opened.

Margaret Shelby walked onto the porch with her shotgun aimed at the man.

"Earle Doogan, you ain't fit to lick the devil's feet," she said. "I'm a better shot than anybody you got hidin' in them trees. Leave the bag an' get the hell gone, or I'll kill two Doogans just to give a pair of angels upstairs some wings."

"Goddammit, y'all killed my boy!"

"He wasn't no boy -- he was a monster named JJ Doogan. It didn't matter to him that he had two

little ones at home. He had to plant his evil seed
inside an innocent girl. So, we cut him to bloody
bits for a secret backyard burial. You won't find no
grave. Earle Adam, since I ha'n't slept in two days,
my trigger finger's itchy as a chigger bug bite."

Earle pulled his prisoner out by the nape of her
neck. Confederate Jasmine was an older woman, but
her eyes were wide and defiant, and they blazed with
fire. A knife suddenly in his hand, Earle pressed the
blade to her face. "I wonder if I got me a bleeder,"
he said, caressing her skin. He removed the gag but
then drove the tip of his blade into her shoulder.

"Don't cut her!" Margaret shouted.

Earle Adam whistled a strange bird call to the
trees – there was no response. "I told my boy there
to hold off — I'll kill this nigger and die a glorious death, if Margaret shoots proper. Either way, I
protect what's mine," he said. "Justice, better control that Shelby bitch, or get another dog."

Margaret spat. "A Doogan couldn't bluff hisself
out of a fist fight with a dumb crippled blind girl."

Justice raised a hand. "Margaret, JJ's dead bastard isn't worth more than Confederate Jasmine's
life." He turned to give Margaret a hard stare until
she lowered her gun. "Get the bundle for Earle."

Margaret understood what needed doing and went
inside the house. Justice Wilson knew this was their
chance. He fought back tears when that evil man took
his stillborn son. After Margaret helped Confederate
Jasmine from the sack, Earle threw in the lifeless
lump given to him.

Suddenly, Lucas Doogan dropped his lantern, keel-
ing over face-first in the mud, dead as a stump. The
wick burned brightly, revealing a dark red pool
around the steps, and went out.

Earle kicked the body. "Now I gotta haul yer ass
home," he said, glaring at Justice as he stuffed his
dead nephew in the canvas sack. Tying it shut, he
hoisted his dead upon his shoulder and smiled.

As the wind blustered, and the clouds emptied
their water, Earle Adam Doogan stood in the middle
of it as he slowly looked at each face before him.

As if he'd been a neighbor stopping by, he said, "Y'all have a pleasant evenin' now," and headed back to the line of trees, vanishing into the night.

"That man murdered your son and husband, Jasmine," Justice said. "His son murdered your son-in-law, raped your daughter, and kidnapped you just to get his hands on his dead son's bastard. You saw his eyes – this isn't over." He sighed. "Echo, God rest your soul. May He bless and keep you. Amen."

"Things ain't exactly as they seem, Justice," Confederate Jasmine said, wincing.

"Jazzy, you're bruised and bleedin' like a stuck pig," Margaret said, helping her up the steps. "Shoulder needs cleanin' an' sewin' — I doubt Earle Adam washes his knife."

"I don't doubt it, but I'm fine – I just drank too much hurricane's all," Confederate Jasmine said. "We ought to tell Justice what we've done tonight — you can be seamstress while I drink me some corn and spin a few stories for this saint of ours."

"If Justice Wilson's a saint then I'm the Virgin Mary," Margaret said as they passed. "He's saint enough, I reckon. Even backwoods saints from Cantonment deserve truth."

Reaching the top step, Confederate Jasmine touched the man's cheek and said, "The hard part's yet to come - steel yourself. We had to cover tracks to do what we did tonight. They won't stay hidden forever."

Margaret spat. "Well, we had to do something," she said. "At least my sisters got a barn out of it. Biggest tombstone in the South, I'd bet."

Confederate Jasmine laughed. "I'll take that bet and raise you a set of twins separated at birth by the Perdido River."

"What have you two done?"

Neither woman answered. They went into the house and left Justice Wilson alone on the porch.

*

THE HANGED MAN

Chapter 8

Road to Old Alabama Town

Early Saturday Morning, June 4, 2005

At sunrise, I turned on my bedside lamp. A suitcase sat on the floor with an envelope taped to its side. Inside was a stack of $100 bills, a new Florida driver's license, and a note ordering me to open my suitcase. My dirty clothes were clean and folded neatly beside some new clothes and the music box. The typewritten pages of story I'd found inside it were still on the nightstand—I put them in the box and got dressed for breakfast on the piazza.

When she saw me coming downstairs, Lilly waved me to the empty chair on her side of the small table.

Helga excused herself and went to the kitchen.

Lilly sipped the last of her coffee and gave me a good, long stare. Before I could utter a word, she raised her hand and growled at me, "Tie yuh mout', Dean Adam. You've a plane to catch. My car is waiting to take you to the airport when you're finished. Brenda and Hattie know what's happened and when to expect you too. No arguing, or I'll lift my shirt and show you my deflated prophylactics."

"I don't need all the money. Really, Lilly."

Helga tsked-tsked-tsked from the hallway. "Sie gerade danke der frau, dummer junge," she said, or something that sounded like it.

"A simple thank you will suffice," Lilly said, glancing back at her housekeeper with a smile. "Forgiveness, gratitude, humility—three things we all must try to master before we die. When in doubt, just listen to your elders, sweetbaby. You need a suit for the funeral, new clothes in your pre-ferred style, plus money for gas, food, fun, accidents, gifts, bail, or bribes. I won't be around forever, sweetbaby, and I can't abide not being useful when I so obviously can be."

"Fine, but I'll say prayers to you all the way to Atlanta."

"Don't you dare make me into a Catholic Saint, Dean Adam Doo-gan," Lilly replied. "I may have more money than the Vatican, but I'm a Southern Baptist, you devil. Helga tells me she found you sleeping on those pages from the music box—I take it you read the story?"

"Several times," I replied, mouth full. "Who wrote it?"

Lilly smiled. "Melba Shelby did—I typed it up," she said. "We'd been writing letters since I left Cantonment in 1939, but she sent me a large en-velope with that story handwritten on lined paper after they took in Hat-tie. I wept when I first read it. She so captured the spirit of those people, sweetbaby."

"And you knew them," I said. "I saw Jonathan's obelisk at Beulah's cemetery. Granny said to ask you about it."

Lilly sighed. "Ten years after Margaret Shelby carried a baby through a hurricane, my husband and I left Charleston for a house not far from Ruth and Justice Wilson's place. I was schoolteacher for the orphans in their care, and three of their nieces, and their ten-year-old albino son, who only ever answered to Cotton, the brat. Jonathan was busy tracing his roots, which was the reason we were there, so I kept myself busy teach-ing. Melba was my favorite student."

Helga returned with a fresh pot of coffee.

"Confederate Jasmine and I weren't close friends until my Jonathan passed," Lilly said. "I invited her to Charleston, and when I made my re-turn, she came with me. Did you not listen to the recording in the music box, sweetbaby?"

"Do you mean the song?"

Lilly shook her head. "No, the audio recording."

"I didn't know there was one."

"Well, now you do, sweetbaby," she said, patting my arm. "Sounds like Hattie wants you to figure out the secret to playing it. At least you'll have something to do on the plane."

And then it was time to go, just like that.

I had all these unanswered questions, and it was time for me to get into a limo, head to the airport and board her private jet to Atlanta. For the life of me, I couldn't look at Lilly now. I didn't know why, but I couldn't lift my chin. Not a matter of concern for Lilly, who wasn't so high and mighty that she couldn't do it for me. We stared into each other's eyes. She gave me a warm hug at the gate. I got in the limo.

Leaning inside the open window, Lilly said, "Everyone's a bastard in the Perdido River watershed. You don't need to act the part, sweetbaby, but knowing who you are and where you come from keeps you grounded. Give my love to everyone—when you can stay longer, come back and visit me."

An hour later, I arrived at Peachtree-DeKalb Airport.

Amanda was sitting on the hood of our rental car. When she saw me, she nearly fell backwards. She hugged me, bursting into tears reeking of vodka. She wobbled around the car to the passenger side like a bobble-head, tossing me the keys and sobbing again.

It was already a long fucking drive to Montgomery.

We stopped at a one-size-fits-all travel station off I-85 in La Grange, Georgia. Every conceivable brand of redneck packed the center, an oasis for road-weary folk heading west. People milled about the mall of pumps, restrooms, and picnic areas. Amanda went to throw up while I filled the tank and bought crap to eat.

As I waited for my sister, I people-watched. A host of overweight families with armloads of greasy foods and sugary sodas, fleshy mothers, fathers, and kids stuffing their faces with fat sausage hands.

Truck horns blasted.

Her face the shade of Doublemint green, Amanda returned with a seasick grin, pointing to the fracas erupting behind the diesel pumps. I ordered her to fill up on water and pretzels.

Amanda grimaced after her rancid burp. "That smells like it came from Aunt Clara's dog," she said. "Miss Hattie's the only reason people should visit Montgomery—I hate that place."

"You hate Hattie's roommate," I said.

Amanda sighed. "I don't hate Sara Nell. She makes me sad."

When we arrived in Old Alabama Town, I kept to the outer streets to avoid the tourists. Clouds streaked in ribbons above us, brushing the buildings and houses with strange sunset colors. Most of the houses were gaudy boxes with too much fretwork and painted in the ugliest shades of Wetumpka marmot—that is, baby shit brown-beige-yellow. North Hull Street had the houses with brighter colors, lovely homes etched with balustrades and cornice porch brackets, columned porticoes, and terraces. We turned into the driveway of Hattie's Italianate-style 1840s manor home and parked in back.

We knocked on the kitchen door. Wind chimes clapped in the eaves when Hattie opened it and greeted us with warm hugs. Her eyes were swollen from crying. Her skin was gray and dry—not a wonder considering the chemo hits and Granny's death.

Hattie ushered me inside and rounded on Amanda. "Babygirl, you smell like Cinco de Mayo—don't even deny it, Missy," she said, easing back and trying not to smile. "Did I tell you 'bout the time Brenda, Pidge, and I drove to Dothan to buy Aunt Clara's cigarettes and whiskey? How we never bothered to come home that night?"

Amanda nodded. "It's my favorite story."

Hattie smiled. "Maybe I'll spin it for you later if I feel better," she said, ushering my sister and me inside. "Dean Adam, put Lilly's music box in my sun room, and both you children need to wash up—dinner's 'bout ready. Babygirl, I'll fetch you some Tylenol."

"Thanks, Miss Hattie," Amanda said.

The house was its usual bone-chill cold. Its familiar smells were the clean lemony odor of wood polish and the thick buttery aromas of baking. We shuffled heavy and hungry down the hallway and dragged ourselves into the candlelit dining room. Three places had been set around a dark cherry wood table whose center leaf leaned behind a matching china cabinet.

Cotton Wilson's furniture was ornate. The table and chairs were the marvels from a Swiss clockmaker's dream. The leaf textures, the Gothic grooves, the curved bevels of nooks seen and unseen. "Oh, my daddy was such an artist," Hattie said, watching me from the kitchen door. "He made this whole set for Miss Eva, but the old bat didn't like the color of the wood—I swear the woman would make Jesus mad enough to slap a cripple lamb. And I feel like I swallowed a porcupine." She blotted her forehead with a towel.

"Hattie, you didn't need to cook for us," I said.

My godmother, of course, ignored my comment. "I gave Sara Nell a sedative, but it hasn't kicked in yet," she said, fanning herself with her hand. "If she says 'colored girl' one more time—YOU KNOW WHO I AM, OLD WOMAN!"

A *thump-thump-thump* from upstairs was the reply.

Hattie shook her head. "She's had a bad day all week," she said. "Banging that broken broom handle on the rug in her bedroom—I'M 'BOUT TO KILL HER WITH IT! She had a fit, spat out her medications, and now we're in the middle of a broom handle drum show."

Thump!

THUMP!

"SHE NEEDS AN EXORCIST," Hattie shouted at the ceiling. "It's like making a bear drink from a Dixie cup. Caterwauling like a banshee, of all days—DEVIL TAKE HER!"

THUMP!

"Miss Hattie, does Mom know the dementia is this bad?"

"No, babygirl," Hattie replied. "Hospice care's what she needs—I'll get around to it after—" She paused to look at me. "After I take care of some estate things and get the carriage house fitted for her needs," she said. "I never should've said y'all were coming tonight."

Thump, thump, thump!

Hattie pulled two small pots from under her chair and banged them in reply, the clamor echoed throughout the house to counter any further broom thumping from upstairs. When she went back to the kitchen, Amanda rolled her eyes and went to see Sara Nell. I went to the water closet under the staircase to wash my hands.

Muffled sounds of arguing preceded my sister's heavy steps coming back down the stairs. Amanda opened the door. "So, I apparently look like a painted whore," she said. "We hugged before she blanked out and didn't know me from her hairbrush, but she complimented me on my makeup as I left the room. You should go up—it's fun."

"No thanks," I said, easing by her. "Excuse me, whore."

Amanda hit my arm. "You're such an ass."

In the dining room, I poured iced sweet tea and piled the plates with food. My sister poked her finger into the sweet potato pie, licked it, and wiped it on the lace tablecloth just as Hattie came through the kitchen door flap.

"AMANDA DEANNA, you KNOW better," she shouted, plopping in her chair. "Nearabout too tired to eat."

"I wonder why," I said low in her ear, my voice thick with sarcasm. "It's not like you don't have cancer to manage."

Hattie gave me a sideways smile. "Hush."

"This creamed corn's off the chain, Miss Hattie," Amanda said. "You shouldn't have gone through this trouble, but you SO should've gone through this trouble."

"Nobody else 'cept the brown folk can cook these days, so what do you expect? Hoo—Amanda-baby, I got business with your brother after supper. I need you to clear and clean for me. Put something other than vodka in your water bottle when you go upstairs to scare your grand-mother again."

"Miss Hattie, I'd be happy to scare her again."

Hattie clapped.

"That's my babygirl," she said, passing me the basket of hot buttered rolls. "Sara Nell's fine when she doesn't spit out her meds. Last week, I whopped her ass with my spoon 'til she stopped her craziness. You'd a thought I stabbed her."

A grin bloomed on her face.

The freckle spots on her nose stretched into crescents.

Hattie was *devil-thinking*.

With a sigh, she said, "I never planned to stay in this house for so long. Brenda and Brandon were going to take her to a nursing home in Ponte Vedra, so I could sell this old museum and move into Pidge's farmhouse. Then Brandon went missing and my godson went cuckoo-birdin', and Brenda stopped living or caring. Somebody had to take care of Sara Nell when old age shook her like a bad junkyard dog. Ain't like I never suffered her before—"

Thump, thump, thump!

The second floor rattled with a loud crash.

THUMP!

THUMP!

THUMP!

"I swear to my Resurrected Jesus, I'll put her in a home—I'LL PUT YOUR WRINKLED ASS IN A HOME!"

As wind gusts threw yard debris against the bay window, Amanda licked butter from her pinkie. "This roll should be a controlled substance, Miss Hattie."

Hattie popped her hand. "Wait 'til I say 'Grace' or I'll put that bun up your exit-only—take hands, bow heads," she said. "We thank you for this food, Heavenly Father, and humbly ask You to welcome Melba Shelby, a beautiful sinner who's been a light down here—may she forever find rest in Your bosom. And Lord, please watch over my babies as they journey south in the middle of this storm. Please carry them safely to Flomaton—Amen. All right, dig in."

Amanda closed her eyes as she chewed in ecstasy.

"Miss Hattie, you're a miracle worker."

"Babygirl, that deep freezer AJ Cobb gave me for Christmas is the miracle," she said. "Your drunk ass would've told me a plate of rice and pickles was ambrosia."

"Your boyfriend gave you a freezer?" Amanda asked, grinning. "How romantic."

Hattie put her fork down. "Young lady, that ain't polite."

"Miss Hattie, I'm not a lady, so spill it."

My godmother cackled as she threw her arms around Amanda and whispered something in her ear. I bit into my second roll and piled my plate with more food. After a round of pound cake and coffee, Amanda got up to clear. I ran to fetch Lilly's music box and joined Hattie in the sunroom, an addition salvaged from the original wraparound porch. As we sat on the cream-colored wicker sofa that creaked like a barn door, she put the music box on the coffee table and opened the lid.

"My sweet Lord," Hattie said, opening the folded story inside the lid. "I haven't seen this story in a long time. Oh, it does paint a picture." Smiling as she shuffled through the pages, she wiped her eyes and said, "My, my, my—they're here, thanks to you, Mama Melba. God rest your soul. Praise you, and praise Jesus. Oh, my heart."

Hattie's dam burst. Her wailing sobs broke through her walls and brought her crashing down in a flood of grief. We embraced until she felt purged. "Now you know how I've been doing," she said. "It just comes, and I collapse under its weight until I let go and give it to God. You should've heard the thumping yesterday when I couldn't stop. Anyway, Duddy-baby, I know Brenda's mad as hell at me, but you belong to Piglet and me now."

Silence.

"Lilly told me there was a recording," I said. "I didn't know."

Hattie picked up the music box. "Each one of these has a secret history or truth. I asked Lilly to take you down her cellar, so I was hoping you'd figure out the puzzle box."

"Will you PLEASE just tell me?"

"You gotta earn it, baby—best way to keep something safe is to hide it in plain sight, like an Underground Railroad Station in the heart of Charleston. My daddy Cotton Wilson learned that from Lilly, who learned it from her father, who learned it from his. Daddy made seven boxes before he died. I got four of 'em upstairs. You'll figure how to work something so obvious."

Something so obvious.

A secret hiding in plain sight.

THUMP! THUMP! THUMP!

"Hattie, is there a key to the music box?" I asked. "There's a keyhole, but without a key to unlock it—ah, nevermind. The whole flight from Charleston to Atlanta I tried to figure how this thing worked—it's got me stumped. Plain sight secrets will be the death of me."

With a chuckle, Hattie fiddled with the box.

"I hope you'll have an easier time making at least one of the others work," she said. "Or it'll be the death of something."

Static, and then silence. After another burst of static, Lilly spoke:

The truth was hiding in plain sight since I met Confederate Jasmine, but I didn't see it for years. We lost Margaret, Justice, and Ruth in 1938. And I laid Jonathan to rest in the cemetery at Beulah Baptist Church in 1939. I had his stone engraved with his birth name and had Shelby added. 'Jonathan Wakefield Shelby,' which spoke to his being a bastard without saying he was. He died filled with a shame not belonging to him, so I took his new surname to South Carolina when I left for Charleston in my private rail car. Jim Crow couldn't touch Confederate Jasmine in my own damn rail car. She and I returned to the Holy City side by side, and there she stayed. Of course, I took her to my cellar and I told her the history. Then Confederate Jasmine told me she was born Harriet Freedman in 1864 to Prisse and Reuben Freedman, that Tobias Middleton of Charleston had purchased them and paid them secret wages, that his son, the man who would be my father, took them to Sapelo Island at the end of the Civil War.

Silence, followed by static, and then:

...at work were greater things than the lives of an old black woman and a young white woman. We put our faith in God...promised to inspire love and...

Static.

...stop the cycle...keeping the truth about Echo Freedman secret was necessary—the only way to save her was to keep the family split...

Silence.
More static, and then,

...finish what Margaret Shelby began the night she delivered them from the reach of Earle Adam Doogan.

Static.
The recording ended.
A twig popped against one of the glass doors to the sunroom.

A wind gust shook the windows and rattled the storm shutters. Strange pressures fluctuated in the room, making heavy and then abruptly light the spaces between objects.

Hattie took my hand. "Things put in motion long before we were born need to play out, Duddy-baby," she said, nodding to the music box. "Lilly recorded that for my daddy when he got up the nerve to go see that cellar and sit in its history. I told you the weekend I went with him."

"Where was I?"

"Doin' some new play in Baltimore," she replied with a frown. "Well, at least that's what you told me."

I remembered the lie I told. I remembered wanting to fly down to see her and Mom, and Lilly. How badly I wanted to ask Cotton Wilson about my accident. I easily could've made the trip. The truth why I didn't go was even more insidious and shameful. Hattie didn't bat an eye after I told her. She just laughed and clapped her hands, as if she'd been waiting at a surprise party and the guest of honor finally arrived.

"Duddy-baby, you can't lie, never have or will" she said, wiping a tear. "My Lord Jesus, everybody knew you and that woman were doin' enough drugs to start a small cartel. I knew you'd stop when you'd had enough. I'm glad you confessed. Always the right thing to do."

"Well, I think it's time you showed me how to work the damn music box," I said. "And I think it's time you told me the truth."

Hattie started laughing again. "Oh, HELL no, you didn't say that—where's my spoon," she said, patting and fanning her neck. "Hoo, I needed that laugh, Lord, I did—hoo-hoo-hoo. You'll figure it out once you stop looking for the answer with your thick head—can't see the forest for the trees."

"What was Lilly talking about, at the end?"

Silence.

Hattie smiled. "Folk with my boxes will find you," she explained, "so try to keep in mind what Dr. King said. Love is your sword and light your shield. I don't want you getting' black eyes on my account—no more fightin', do you hear me?"

"But Hattie, the things Cash Doogan called you," I said. "The way he said the words—he's insane. I had to do something."

Hattie slapped my face. "Then do THIS bit of something the next time you hear that boy say anything about me, my family, my past, my skin color, my people, my history—you will do what my Jesus taught us to do and turn the other cheek," she said. "Nigger's an ugly word, Duddy-baby, but it's a hate word. You don't fight for something hateful. You don't defend hateful. Next time, check yourself."

"Yes'm," I said. "Who told you I got into a fight?"

"Rick Shelby," Hattie said. "All right—lemme squeeze you goodbye. Y'all gotta get on the road."

Why did Rick Shelby call my godmother?

Hattie rocked me in a pendulum hug and swatted me when I brushed her face with my five o'clock stubble. I helped her to her feet. She slipped an arm in mine as we left the solarium. "I suppose Piglet and I are killing lots of birds with the same stone," she said. "Yes, you're the stone, Duddy-baby. You ought to know your history, but it's time to fix the mess Brandon and your mama made."

Amanda waited in the car for me. Hattie and I stood on the back porch trying to get a sense of the weather. Where Arlene was heading was a mystery. The tropical storm still hadn't made up her mind. A gust twisty-turned the hammock between the trees supporting it.

The whitewashed planks of fence moaned beneath the swaying Graveyard Trees. Clouds streamed across the sky in wispy ribbons, hardly harbingers of doom, but the air was cooler. As Hattie watched the sky, I kissed her cheek and turned to go.

She took my arm. "When he shows up tomorrow in that science fiction RV of his, you tell John Shelby he's getting a hex for not returning my calls yesterday. Your uncle's a smart man, but sometimes he's as thick as a gay trucker haulin' Jews to a Nazi pride parade." She shooed me off the porch and waved until I was in the car and buckled behind the wheel. It was hard to leave her now.

Something inside me click-clacked, accenting my broken lifelines and heartaches with a flammable highlighter—memory, fear, love, family, death, truth, history, secrets.

"Please, not her too," I whispered.

Please, God, don't take her too.

We left the tree-lined sidewalks of Old Alabama Town for the Interstate. It took over an hour to get through Montgomery proper. The clouds were dumping rain in buckets and barrels, and the wind gusts were shoving our car from side to side. A sudden wall of water hit us head-on, but I managed to avoid the wreck unfolding in the lanes to our left. Vehicles swerving away from the crash only made things worse. Fear began gnawing at my spinal cord.

My skin erupted into bumps of electric chills as two of those swerving cars smashed into each other directly behind us.

Then, our car hydroplaned.

Turning the wheels into the skid, I guided us safely to the shoulder and rolled down my window to see where I was going—the driver's side windshield wiper blade and its arm were gone.

Amanda screamed.

And that's when all hell broke loose.

Chapter 9

Clarabelle Wilson, Pirate

Flomaton, Alabama—Saturday Night, June 4, 2005

Amanda and I were lucky to be alive. We huddled on the rug in Pidge's den with beach towels draped across our shoulders. Our toddies were hot and strong enough to wake Custer and the horse he rode in on. For half an hour, we didn't speak—not about what happened, not about the weather, not about the funeral—we just sat there waiting for the buzz to kick in. My sister's hair had exploded into a frizzled Einstein nest. Her eyes were fixed in a freakish gaze. She was like the insane conductor of some secret orchestra, her right leg bouncing in six-eight time.

Cupping my palm over her kneecap, I said, "Babysis, you're safe now—we're okay, honey."

"Duddy Doogan, shut the fuck up," Aunt Clara said from her chair. "Slow your roll, Amanda-darlin'—that ain't a Coca-Cola you're chuggin'. Gimme your cup and just ignore your brother whiles I make you another toddy. Duddy, refill?"

"Less booze and no piss and vinegar, you old bat."

Aunt Clara flipped the bird as she whistled down the hall.

Oh, but let me tell you about Great Aunt Clarabelle Wilson. She was 85 years old, the oldest of three (Granny Melba the youngest, Miss Eva in the middle). Clara was a wicked woman, but you worshiped her for it. Her hair was spotted and patchy like mange. She loved Sunday hats. She never wore them, but she loved them. She was never without a homemade pirate eye patch though—she had several of them, which she'd swap out like mood rings, switching them from eye to eye, depending on how she felt. Aunt Clara was also a sadist who made us fetch our own switches, turning us into masochists because we loved her for that.

"I'm gonna rip all y'all's arms out and beat you with the stumps if'n you don't stop acting like a bunch of backyard shit-monkeys," she'd scream. In the next breath, she'd pour another Big Gulp-sized glass of wine and remind us that Death indeed was family.

The kitchen microwave beeped.

Amanda laughed. "She burned the popcorn on purpose."

With the corner of my towel, I wiped my sister's forehead just as Aunt Clara returned to the den with a smoking bowl of Orville Redenbacher on a tray of toddies. After serving us, she fell into the La-Z-Boy and dug into her burned corn.

The corner wall behind her held several framed prints of Elvis Presley, a shrine Pidge had made just for her headstrong mother, whose unyielding adoration for the King kept her sane and somewhat pleasant. As did her love for Goddamn Tater, her ancient flatulent Bassett Hound. Even now, the old dog lumbered into the room and dropped beside her dangling hand, licked it twice and passed a cloud of noxious canine gas.

"There-there, stinky puppers," Aunt Clara said, moving her patch to the other eye.

After another long silence, she slapped her armrests.

"I'm done with quiet time, chirren—what in the blue fuck happened out there? Y'all worried me into smoking two packs of Luckys and some of Eva's weed by the time Rick Shelby pulled up the drive with you shit-monkeys in his backseat. Spill it, and don't tickle me with teasing, or you'll hear what a fat diabetic foot sounds like when I shove it in your asses. Don't forget, I bit off a bitch's ear in a bar fight when I was 57 years old, so don't think I won't hurt you."

Amanda smiled.

"There's my girl," Aunt Clara said, her voice suddenly gentle. "Sit next to me, darlin', so I can pet your head. Move, Goddamn Tater." When my sister settled Indian style next to our insane great aunt, I took a deep breath and calmly recapped the events of our night.

•

Our trip should've been a two-hour drive. We made good time until Arlene stationed her big ass between Alabama and Georgia instead of moving off to the northwest. The highway was teeming with cars headed south—it was a parking lot. For hours, we crawled under buckets, bricks, and animals dropping from the sky.

Of course, a wiper blade would fly off.

Moving to the shoulder, I flipped the hazard lights, took the flashlight from the glove box and got out for a look—in the middle of the storm that put us there. Wind and rain peppered my face as I inspected the windshield. The arms waved, but one had bent in half, its shredded rubber flopping in impotence.

Hitting the hood two times was the signal for Amanda to turn them off. I swapped the missing blade with the gimpy one, which also broke. And then the horn blasted. A blur of panicked hands motioned me back inside the car.

Amanda turned up the radio volume.

A man's voice—then static, and then a voice again.

"High winds...two funnels...crossing paths...shelter—take shelter now." After crackling white noise, three loud bursts, and a long beep, an EBS bulletin warned all motorists traveling between Greenville and Georgiana about the two funnels playing tag around the interstate.

"Christ on a bike," I hissed, starting the car.

I popped my head out of my window and drove on the shoulder. Passing cars refused my attempts to reenter the traffic flow, such as it was, so I kept to the shoulder, swerving around stalled vehicles and moving faster than anyone else. With a chorus of tornado bulletins spurring my illegal action, I continued my act of defiance.

Another hundred or so yards later, a reflecting green exit sign for the ramp to Georgiana came into view—the edge of the danger zone. An updated bulletin extended the warning farther south. Another car honked as I continued my quest to reach safety.

Moving under the overpass, I parked next to a drain straddling the base of the ramp leading up to the bridge joint.

My plan was to sit there and wait out the storm.

Something felt wrong. Another radio bulletin warned of an F-2 tornado spinning for—place undecipherable.

Cracked sounds followed another series of long beeps, and Amanda's puffy red face looked punched. I turned off the car and opened the door. Horns blasted as more cars bullied their way to the overpass. The wind kicked dervishes of debris, carrying dust and rain in spiral drafts. A distant roar displaced all ordinary stormy weather sounds. Cars stopped on the highway.

Drivers and passengers ran to the overpass and up the ramp to where the bridge met level ground. The steel there made a canopy of girded shelter and space was limited.

Amanda grabbed her purse and followed me up the incline. We tucked ourselves under a girder and held hands. A young man and his dog huddled next to us. Others crammed themselves into the spaces beside them, and so on until there was no more room.

The wind hammered us.

A jackknifed tractor-trailer fell from the bridge and crashed into the cars below—ours included.

Two cars in two days—what the hell?

Mothers soothed crying children. Husbands calmed sobbing wives. The dog howled and whined. In a space packed with so many bodies, fear was an unforgettable smell. And then came the roaring freight train of chaos, the winds and the terror and a chorus of *holy-fucking-shit-we're-gonna-die.*

I thought about all the crazy weather in my life. I'd flirted with snow, tap-danced with drought, embraced downpours, kissed my fair share of cold starry nights, held hands with a hurricane or two, made goo-goo eyes at lightning storms—having carnal knowledge of a tornado was something I never wanted to experience again—ever. There I was huddled with my sister and fifty other people as two of these spinning violent bitches tag-teamed raping us.

It was over in minutes.

A collective movement to the cars followed, but Amanda and I stayed under the girders and waited for the wind and the rain to ease. We waited for the fear to leave and courage to return. We waited for the sirens to tell us we weren't alone, that we were safe. And we waited for the bodies scattered around the highway to get up. They didn't.

When we stopped shaking long enough to stand up without our knees buckling, we inched down the ramp. Things were still falling from the sky—rain mingled with sand and splinters, paint chips and twigs, paper and metal pieces and torn cloth, and soft red things I refused to identify.

Our car was gone.

Our things were gone.

"At least it was a rental," Amanda said before she fainted.

An hour later, as helicopters zoomed above and generator lights buzzed nearby, my sister opened her eyes and smiled. The way I cradled her head in my lap spared her the gruesome scene of broken bodies and vehicles. Amanda hugged her purse and swallowed the lump in her throat when I told her Rick Shelby was on his way. Rick was the only one who could make the trip without breaking a sweat. Twenty-seven people died—half of them were in pieces.

"Which is why it was after ten o'clock when Rick finally dropped us off," I said. "We're lucky to be alive. Death is family."

Aunt Clara nodded "Death is family."

"Death is family," Amanda whispered, staring blankly ahead. "I saw them running and heard them screaming when it took them in the sky. I saw them dropping, heard them hitting the ground. I saw."

Silence.

Looking into my empty cup, I wondered how I'd forget what happened. The images in my head weren't as important as how they made me feel. I was good at forgetting horrible things, detaching myself from how I felt about them. I was good at throttling feelings into quiet, perverted submission—so quiet, in fact, that I never heard them screaming to be set free. They haunted me, those feelings I imprisoned, and sometimes, without warning, they escaped.

Not tonight, they wouldn't.

Goddamn Tater farted again. Aunt Clara fed him handfuls of burned popcorn, which the dog ate in sloppy, air-filled bites. Every other minute, he burped or farted, but his silly noises didn't lift our moods.

Amanda stretched and yawned. "It's late. No, Aunt Clara, don't get up. I know where I'm sleeping." My sister shuffled over to me and fell into my lap. "Thanks for keeping me safe, big brother," she said. Kissing me on the cheek, she got to her feet and went to her room.

Goddamn Tater panted and moaned.

Aunt Clara pulled back her eye patch to rest on top of her widow's peak. "She'll be asleep in two minutes in her wet clothes."

Amanda's talent was falling asleep. My baby sister never appreciated her gift until her high school graduation dinner. Dad was about to make some generic toast when Amanda threw her fork.

"Don't toast me—I'm not good at anything, Daddy."

Dad raised his glass and said, "You're the prettiest girl in the world, a fire-breather just like your mama, and my favorite person ever made. But you can do something nobody else can do: you are the BEST sleeper in the world." Amanda tried not to smile as Dad continued. "You fall asleep faster than anyone. You always wake refreshed and happy. My darling girl, you possess the Fountain of Youth, which means—well, at least to my mind—you'll never age, never fade and never die."

It was a great toast.

And it was a great memory of Dad too.

Since I had no suitcase of clothes, I had to squeeze into a pair of Pidge's overalls and one of Jervis' old sweat-stained T-shirts. Amanda was sleeping soundly in her wet clothes, her drooling mouth face down in her pillow, her ass high in the air. A tumbler of scuppernong wine waited for me on a vintage postcard coaster on the coffee table.

There were more coasters, each with a different image. All of them were signed on the backs in the same scrawling hand. Mine was a sepia photograph of two hunters hoisting either end of a pole on their shoulders, a grasshopper the size of a bear dangling between them as they waved to the camera. I used it as a fan after Goddamn Tater bounced through the room, a magically flatulent canine fairy.

Aunt Clara followed the poor dog, spritzing the air with a dime-store perfume atomizer. "Damnation station, dog, sometimes I wish you'd die so's I can get me a new puppy," she said, falling in her chair. "It's Melba's turn now. Eva's next. I'll be the last of the Hell's Belles to go. Death is family." She raised her tumbler with a shaking hand and said, "Melba had the prettiest, sweetest face with the most beam-crooked smile ever. Light shined from inside her, Duddy, like she'd swallowed an angel whole, wings and all—oh, this wine's too sweet. Fuck a duck, Pidge, it tastes like grape juice an' Jesus piss."

I laughed. "Had it last weekend—where were you?"

Aunt Clara cackled. "I live in Cantonment now—I'm only up here to be with you two brats," she said, grinning. "Movin' in with Eva made me nervous at first, but now it dills my pickle—don't tell the bitch I said she's a blessin'. We hide our feelings 'cause it's more fun to insult loved ones than it is to make them feel good. This morning, for instance—after I called her a piss-soaked prostitute passed out in a Perkins pancake plate, she said I was dumber than a blind quadriplegic aspiring to be a waitress at the Howard Johnson's. That's love, Duddy-darlin'. Gimme your cup so I can read your leaves."

Goddamn Tater growled at the wind gusting against the house. The cuckoo clock ticked and tocked. For several minutes, my great aunt stared in my cup, scribbling a cryptic syntax on a notepad perched on her thigh. Sudden psychic explosions were the norm for Mom's side of the family. Aunt Clara's clairvoyance usually ignited after a night binge drinking Pidge's wine.

Clutching the cup, she screamed, "You're gonna die!"

Goddamn Tater started barking. After I jumped, all I could think about was Belladonna's Tarot reading. The card after The Hanged Man was The Tower—a lightning strike to upend the world. Aunt Clara cackled. "Duddy-darlin', your face looks like you done ate a monkey shit taco," she said, clapping. "Yer leaves tell me you're going to be a new daddy soon, but for all I know, that could mean you're about to fill a commode with a healthy brown baby. See? Praise my pine-scented Jesus—I'm fuckin' psychic!"

"I hope you're alive when they bury you."

Aunt Clara finished her wine. "You've been through hell tonight, so you might as well laugh at it—Christ, is that wind? It's two in the A and goddamn M, and the storm is still here. Sometimes, life makes no sense, Duddy-darlin', none at all."

She stared at a far off place for a moment.

The wine had softened her, and she struggled against tears. "Love's the real family curse, Duddy-darlin'. Blinds you, makes you mean, hateful. Mama would start an argument in an empty house she was so mean. Love twisted her heart like an old root after her daddy threw the boy she loved off the porch and broke his neck. She was nineteen by the time she'd pushed Eva, Melba, and me into the world. Mama was an old woman our whole lives."

Aunt Clara threw up her hands. "I don't know what I'm sayin'—I'm feelin' low, Duddy-darlin'. I miss my Melba and I'm feelin' low. Love does too much damage to us hard-lovin' folk. The reason we talk trash and tragedy is 'cause spinnin' keeps us from despair. You're all Doogan, darlin', and I've known it since Eva pulled you out of Brenda—what kind's up to you. They live, die, love, fuck, and hate like everyone else 'round the Perdido—and there's been more than a few good ones. Shelbys aren't saints. Hell, my own damn husband was a Shelby, and he molested Pidge when she was a bitty thing. He died by my hand when I found out. God bless her, she's right as a Sunday rain on most days and stronger than her bedbug-crazy mama every day. I'd kill her before I'd ever tell her that. Love's the curse. Gotta keep love a secret. Always."

"Do you keep any other secrets?" I asked.

Aunt Clara got up from her chair. "Open books have no secrets," she said, shifting her eye patch as she headed down the hall, Goddamn Tater huffing behind her. "Get some sleep."

"'Night, Clarabelle Wilson, you saggy old pirate."

"Fuck you, Dean Adam Doogan."

Chapter 10

Two if by Gulf of Mexico

Sunday Morning, June 5, 2005

The last thing I expected to see was Aunt Clara's face when I opened my eyes, but there it was, eye patch and all, leaning over me. "Get up, darlin', we gotta go now."

"'Mornin'," I said. "Christ, who's dead now?"

"Your Grandpa," she said, sadly. "Wake your sister."

Grandpa's death wasn't the shock Granny's had been, although Amanda wept when I told her the news. Maybe it was a blessing he died— Mom blamed him for killing Granny and planned to murder him anyway. Cantonment wasn't so far a drive with Aunt Clara giving us an earful about Shelbys, Doogans, Wilsons, and Percys that worked the rail line to the paper mill.

"Black families were sharecroppers mostly," she explained. "The younger colored men worked the Muscogee lumberyards with men from the Creek reservation. One Indian fella got killed because some Shelby girl saw him working, fell in love, and got knocked up," she said, switching her eye patch as we passed Farm Hill.

Amanda yawned. "When's Grandpa's funeral?"

Aunt Clara snorted. "Eva's got the local funeral director wrapped 'round her pinkie, so he's expediting a double service for Tuesday."

"Sounds disrespectful—is that even proper?"

"Who gives a rat's ass about what's proper," Aunt Clara spat. "Buddy Lee's been sweet on Eva half his life, so he'll take care of Melba and William Hubert personally."

We entered Cantonment's city limits. The St. Regis paper mill belched thick white plumes of stink into the sky. Amanda's snores from the backseat were coupled with moans about the rotten smell until we turned on Muscogee Road.

My grandparents' place seemed sunken and gray now.

Vehicles I didn't recognize were in the front yard. Pidge greeted us at the kitchen door. She took Aunt Clara by the arm and together they went to see Mom and Belladonna.

Amanda and I looked at the food in the kitchen. Unwrapped casseroles filled the counters like the buffet at Sizzler. A large pitcher of sweet iced tea sat untouched beside a mostly empty bottle of vodka.

"Babysis, you haven't had anything to eat since Hattie's," I said, loading a paper plate with starchy food—I saw her staring at that liquor. "Look, green bean casserole, mac and cheese—I bet Pidge made that. Miss Eva's deviled eggs. Wanna sweet pickle?"

Amanda's glare was my answer. She plucked a dirty glass tumbler from the sink and poured herself a tea and vodka mixer. Through sudden tears, she downed the drink and refilled her glass, this time adding a splash of orange juice.

"Everyone has a breaking point," she said, pointing to the scars on my wrists. "You did, Duddy, and you came out of it—I'm stuck."

"These scars aren't me breaking—just me being selfish," I told her, putting my arms around her. Amanda pulled from me and stared out the small window looking trapped in a gloom of her own making.

"I'm gonna tell Mom what happened to us last night, Duddy," she said, drinking. "I can't shut off my head and heart like you—I can't." With a sudden scream, she threw her empty glass into the corner.

I winced before it hit the wall, but the tumbler didn't break. It bounced around the counters until it dropped perfectly vertical into the squash with a fwoom-plop. The tumbler was faux glass from Bill's Dollar Store (the price tag was on the bottom). As it sank into the yellow mush, with its topcoat of breadcrumbs like quicksand, the tumbler tilted as it finally rested. I didn't need to say anything, but I might've mumbled something about Pisa having a big one just like it.

"I hate you," Amanda said, trying not to smile. "I'm going to go see Mom." A door opened around the corner. I heard laughter and smelled marijuana smoke before it closed again. As to who brought the weed in the first place—who knew.

As Prodigal Son, I'd only recently resumed my study of the mystics, bitches and some-time goddesses gathered in that room—I had much to observe and learn before I presumed to know their psychology.

Bearing witness to their collective rituals was as close as I'd get to knowing most of them personally. In that bedroom was enough magic from the witches of several Southern covens to put my isolated and often impotent worldview into harsh perspective.

"Duddy," a voice from the living room said.

"Git cher ass back here," a second voice added.

"God blessed his handsome face."

"Hush your pie hole, sister dear."

Aunt Clara had three daughters.

Pidge's two older sisters were fraternal twins.

Doris never married, but it was no secret she often had a new boy-friend every week. She drank Doogan moonshine, rolled her own smokes, and out-swore everyone except her mother. Dorothy was the antithesis to her sister. Having never uttered a four-letter word in her life, she was a one-woman moral police force, with two shithouse crazy kids and a hus-band who tried to kill himself after seeing demons.

Pidge was the psychological glue that had kept Doris from sinking to hell and Dorothy from spontaneously riding a chariot to heaven.

"It was best Melba and William Hubert went together," Dorothy said, taking my hand when I sat beside her. "They're both in heaven with Our Savior now."

Doris chuckled, "If'n you think William Hubert's in line for a halo then my ass is a baby rattle. He might be sitting outside the Gates though—down south outside the Gates."

"Doris, don't blaspheme."

"Dorothy, don't preach."

"We shouldn't talk about him on the day of his death."

"I don't have a problem with it," Doris said, tugging me. "C'mon, Duddy, let's go drink, smoke, and gossip."

We went to the backyard. Drinking and smoking on a Sunday morning felt like church to me.

The sunshine sky was as bright as Heaven's picket fence. And the sounds of crickets, frogs, and grasshoppers echoed around us like a choir of angels. We sat side-by-side in lawn chairs under the clothesline beside the chain link fence and sipped the libations Doris made.

"I'll miss Melba," she said with a sigh. "She helped me manage my crazy when my mother wasn't around. Melba was a strong woman. She had to be to put up with your Grandpa, who was more dangerous than a Doogan Klansmen 'til she turned his heart 'round—ask Eva."

"Hell, no—she'll bite off my head if I ask her that today."

Doris laughed. "Then ask her to tell you what happened to JJ Doogan," she said. "He's one of YOUR son-of-a-bitch ancestors, and he's still under her barn. The barn you were born in is the barn built over JJ Doogan's hacked-to-bits body after Margaret Shelby and her sisters got hold of him. Ask Eva. Whoo! My ass crack is a greasy slit, it's so hot," Doris said, getting to her feet. "My glass can't be empty if I plan to be walkin' on a slant all day."

Mom and the other women were in a semicircle on the floor of Granny's room drinking brandy and passing a joint. Miss Eva, Aunt Clara, Belladonna, Amanda, Mom, Pidge and Miss Eva's daughter and granddaughter, Mickey and Kate. Doris sat with them. Dorothy hollered from the living room:

"I'm praying for y'all as hard as I can."

"Don't pray for me," Aunt Clara shouted. "Belladonna, hex my goody-two-shoes daughter while I toke." She moved her eye patch to the other eye. "It's for my glaucoma."

Miss Eva shook her head. "Dean Adam, help me up," she said, extending her hand. "Take me home, so I can bake my casserole for these sinners and take a nap." My other great aunt had shrunk since I last saw her. Her hair had thinned, her voice shook when she spoke, and she had a tiny hump like Yoda's. But that sparkle in her eyes still shined. "I'm tired of these sluts smoking my weed—for MY glaucoma, Clara," she said. "Nephew, let's go before they enlist you too."

"Enlist me for what?" I asked, closing the door.

Miss Eva groaned. "These idiot girls are gonna go help Kate steal a dog. Nephew, now!"

My last visit to Miss Eva's place was years ago.

As if a map lay buried in my brain, I knew the way without needing to ask for directions. On either side of a red clay road were tall peppergrasses and onion weeds, and golden-lashed brown-eyed sunflowers. At the end of a long drive was a double-wide mobile home. Standing guard beside it was the *family-famous* barn—my barn, JJ Doogan's barn—and it looked like a prop from a studio back lot.

"We're here, Miss Eva—wake up."

Her double-wide was much bigger inside than it had seemed from the outside. We sat on low bar stools at the kitchen counter. An ancient tabby named Pyewacket purred under my feet as I sipped some lemonade. He blinked his good eye as the other pale blue one lazed under a half-closed lid. "My cat's twenty-one," Miss Eva said. "We got a year left, I reckon. The pixie girl at the vet's office sent pictures of him to Cat Fancy. Pye was the centerfold, the slut." She opened a drawer and pulled out a small red book. "Here, open that."

"What is it?" I asked, leafing through it.

"Melba's favorite hymn's in there—no, the next page, Nephew—that's the one you're singing at the funeral this Tuesday," Miss Eva said. "Your Grandpa would've wanted something bouncy with beer and breasts—the bastard. Shelby men. Tough shit, I say. Know the hymn?"

"I've heard Granny sing it before."

"If we could haul my old piano out to the cemetery, I'd play for you—I used to play it for Melba when we were girls," Miss Eva said. "Lilly bought Uncle Justice and Aunt Ruth this lovely piano for their house when Becca died—she taught me to play the damn thing, Lilly did. I didn't want to, but I loved Melba's singing, so I learned."

"Anyway," she said, sipping her lemonade, "Lilly married the one Shelby who didn't gamble more than he drank. Being a Perdido River bastard drove him mad with shame. Spent a fortune trying to hide from it and drowned in a liquor bottle. Poor Lilly. At least she had her own money after he died. I'm without a dime to my name 'cause of my husband—you know, all of you kids watch too much damn TV."

Miss Eva's face fell into her hands. She made no sound. Her hunched shoulders bounced as she wept. This woman had farmed and midwifed; she was tough as a tanned teat; she was at home in a chapel pew or a stool in a roadside bar; she swore like a sailor when you pissed her off. Seeing her like this was a shock. I half-expected her to hurl an insult, but she didn't, and it broke my heart.

"Melba was my best friend, the only lady I ever knew," she said, wiping her wet nose on her sleeve. "Damn William Hubert for dying the same weekend—couldn't give her a moment's rest. Now I've messed my mascara. Nephew, tell a soul about me bawling like this, and I'll shove my hand up your ass and pull out your tongue." She blew her nose on a tissue and looked at her face in a compact mirror with a grimace. "A pork butt with eye slits. This face is the curse."

"Grandpa said the curse was horse snot."

Miss Eva laughed. "When he was younger and drunk enough to talk, he'd tell you how the curse made his mama a half-Indian nigger and how it made his daddy hate him. I hate that word—your Grandpa never said it again after he kept his promise to Cotton Wilson."

"What promise?" I asked.

"To do what Cotton Wilson needed him to do when the time came, no questions asked," Miss Eva replied. "Your Grandpa made it after he came back from the Pacific."

"Why?"

"Because Cotton Wilson saved your Granny's life," she said matter-of-factly. "When the time came, Hattie Louise saved your Grandpa's life and redeemed his soul," Miss Eva added, digging in her purse. Pyewacket's steady purring broke in starts and stops, his engine sputtering as he slept.

"Melba was fifteen and ninety pounds soaking wet when she married your Grandpa. She liked how his uniform fit. Ah, found it—look at this photo." Miss Eva showed me a picture of Grandpa looking at the camera with a pipe in his mouth and an infant in his arms.

"Is that Amanda?" I asked.

"All y'all were shit-ugly kids—could be any of you brats," she said. "Cone-headed, snake-skinned, colicky. Pidge looked like a greasy sausage in a pink turtleneck. Mickey looked like an old man the color of a rotten carrot. Kate smelled like piss and blood for weeks. Amanda and Tyler were lemon yellow and sickly. You were a pretty baby, Nephew—I would know. Anyway, look at your Grandpa's face in this photo and picture a feathered headdress on his head."

"So, he's Native American blood," I said. "So, what?"

"His mama was the bastard daughter of a half-Creek Indian named William Ravenhair," Miss Eva continued. "He was the only son of John Ravenhair and Harriet Freedman, a woman you know by a different name."

"Jesus, Confederate Jasmine," I whispered. "Holy shit, are you serious? Her son was Grandpa's grandfather."

"Your Grandpa's mama was Confederate Jasmine's granddaughter. Her great-great-great granddaughter is your mama. If she's Cotton Wilson's grandmother and Hattie's great-grandmother, that makes y'all blood cousins, Nephew. Distant, but blood. Mixed as hell too."

"Grandpa never knew the truth, did he?"

Miss Eva shook her head. "He had a hard enough time with the Indian blood," she said. "But your Granny knew, and it was the one secret she kept from him. He would've killed himself had he known. Anyway, let's get supper started—here's the recipe. You make the food, and I'll take the credit."

"Of course," I said, shaking my head. "Anything else?"

Miss Eva yawned. "There's a music box for Hattie in my china cabinet. Put it in the car with the casserole and my old guitar when you're done. Wake me in two hours."

It was enough food to feed an obese family of seven with tapeworms. An inch-thick layer of buttered broccoli, Parmesan cheese and beer-battered cornbread crumbled over mountains of pulled chicken and homemade doughnut dumplings swimming in a cheesy sea of carrots, onions, potatoes, butter beans, sweet corn, and sugar peas.

After it had cooled enough, I wrapped a quilt around it and put it next to the guitar in the trunk. Tucking the music box under my arm, I headed for the barn. Pyewacket followed, keeping to my moving shadow as I stopped by the fruit trees next to the vegetable garden.

Grabbing a canvas bag from a supply barrel, I picked several sun-ripened Georgia Belle peaches. Each juicy orb was bursting with vermilion and gold, the skin barely containing its sweet white flesh. As I picked, Pyewacket chased bees nuzzling the honeysuckles along the back fence. My bag filled (and face sticky), I splashed myself with water from the rain barrel and went inside the barn.

When the cat joined me, I led him to the far corner of the three-story space. The barn was pristine and beautiful, but it didn't feel the same without the smells of horse and hay, and other farm things. The floor was now charcoal gray concrete, and recently swept clean.

My life began in this stall.

Bags of gypsum, phosphate, and cottonseed meal were its current occupants. I sat down on one next to the cat, who swatted lazily at a curious moth. I put the music box on the floor and wondered about the secret recording.

What was the story? Whose voice would I hear?

For some reason, I wanted it to be Dad's voice. Thoughts of him, like strange electricity, zapped the corners of my mouth, pulling them down and making my eyes burn. I wasn't ready to weep, not for my father, my grandparents, or me—I wasn't ready to unleash years of caged emotions.

Doing as Hattie had suggested, I let it wash over me. Doing as Pidge had suggested, I stopped overthinking. Doing as fools often do, I fumbled trying to make the music box work. Turning it over in my hands, I inspected every nook and cranny of the small cube—there wasn't much to it, believe me. A slide lever, a crank, a mirror, a keyhole with no key—unless it was behind the mirror or...

No, it wasn't behind the mirror. "Fuck-a-duck, Pyewacket," I said, putting aside the box and playing the song instead. "Someone's buried under this barn, kitty."

As I sat there humming, I wondered if my history lesson wasn't locked away in a tiny box, but living and breathing all around me, lurking in the corners and soaring in the rafters. Pining for some hidden way to play this music box only kept me from the real history soaking into my bones and blood right now. To summon all the ghosts of my past, I sang the lyrics to the melody.

I'm goin' there to see my Father
I'm goin' there no more to roam
I'm just a-goin' over Jordan
I'm just a-goin' over home

To commune with the spirits of the dead gathered here, I spoke the words of the only spell I knew.

"On June 3, 1972, I was born in Miss Eva's barn. Mom christened me Dean Adam Doogan while she lay sheet-covered and spread-eagled over a bale, her tiny bird legs akimbo. Granny held one leg, Belladonna held the other, Hattie cradled her head, Pidge held her hands, and Miss Eva played the accidental midwife. Mom was more interested in watching a newborn colt take his first steps than paying any mind to the contractions of her own topsy-turvy stomach." To finish it, I did my best Brenda Shelby Doogan: "Sugar, the instant that foal dropped from Miss Eva's arms and wobbled over to HIS mama, MY water clean busted and down I went in the next stall."

I looked around and waited.

Pyewacket yawned and stretched.

With a heavy heart, I got up and left the barn.

It was hard to leave the place of my birth. To leave the stall where Mom spilled me out and gave me life. It was hard to leave the unmarked grave of my evil ancestor—but what a fucking tombstone for chopped up JJ Doogan! Secret or not, who WOULDN'T want a barn erected atop his dead body until Judgment Day?

•

Miss Eva dragged the small bag of peaches through the gate. "Christ, we'll be packed like sardines in that dick hole of a house," she said, breathing hard. "I'm gonna sit out here with the damn dog—did you put ALL my fruit in this bag?"

The kitchen door thwacked open and Tyler leaped out.

"Wait," I shouted. "Hot food! Old guitar!"

Slowly and carefully on the ground went the dish and the instrument. And then up into the air I went. My brother was more ape than man (that is, if you replaced the dark course hair with tattoos and muscles). His right arm was a sleeve of ocean images, bright blue and filled with colorful fish. He also was sporting a soul patch, which he rubbed on my face as he bounced me and spun me around. He dropped me flatfooted on the ground, rattling my teeth.

Tucking his blond hair behind each ear, he spat tobacco juice through the fence and said with a drawl, "Is that my sexy Aunt Eva?"

"I'm a Southern lady, not an insect—don't you dare squeeze." Winking at me, Miss Eva smacked Tyler's arm and gave him the sacks. "I forgive the retarded their rude behavior, but you ain't slow—you're lazy. You know how I feel about that 'A' word, you little shit. Next time, I'll cut you with my switchblade. Christ, it's hot—I'm going in before I'm an add-on funeral."

We put the food and other items safely in the house. Tyler put his arm around me and led me back into the yard. "I didn't know about Grandpa 'til I got here, boss," he said, lighting a cigarette. "They're all high and talking about a dog they stole. Is there a bar close?"

"I know a place—pretty rough though."

"Since when do you know rough, Duddy?"

"It's about a mile or so down Muscogee."

"We're walking then—fucking sweet, boss."

As we walked to the bar, we made small talk and caught up with each other. He and his wife Laine were talking about a separation, which he refused to talk about with me. He kept changing the subject to his band, going back to school, and how much better I looked—this from the man who didn't speak the first three years of his life. Remembering him as Baby Damien sent me into hysterics. It did the same to him too when I regaled him with the story.

"We were close," Tyler said. "What the fuck happened?"

"The family reunion happened," I replied, showing him my forearms. "And this happened. It's my fault."

Silence.

I wanted to tell him I was sorry for leaving.

And that I'd missed him.

Stoking the secret fires of regret, I kept my cards close for now. Imbibing libations was best for loosening tongues. A half hour and two pitchers of Bud, the prescription for opening hearts and freeing minds. It also dulled the cosmic influence of too many female planets messing with its manly orbit. We reached the narrow drive to the clearing and made our way to the parking lot.

Rounding the bend, Tyler stopped to gawk at the green garland topiary. "Am I seeing dolphins and a giant baby head," he asked, pointing. "I smoked a joint with Aunt Clara, so…"

Clapping him on the back, I directed him toward the gravel sidewalk dappled with sunlight. We made our way to the entrance of the bar past the topiary figures that made the property smaller than it was. Moving past them was like teetering on the event horizon of a redneck black hole, where they dwelled in your mind for all time.

At the entrance, the door opened and nearly knocked us down, as a thin woman with long strawberry blonde hair exploded past my brother and into my open arms. She kissed me under the big bristling green baby head in the lawn. When I came up for air, Tyler waved as he went into the bar. I didn't have a chance to warn him about what he'd might see inside.

"Hoping you'd show up," Sharon said, pulling me toward the line of trees away from the gravel parking lot. She said there was a creek at the bottom of the embankment, and the trees made a perfect wall against anyone or anything that might threaten privacy.

A narrow footpath took us over a small hill down to the stream, which wended east-to-west in a long lazy spiral. Its babbling made plenty of white noise—no one would be able to hear anything but water from the ridge above us.

"Is that the Perdido?" I asked, pointing.

Sharon laughed. "Just another unnamed stream feeding the river," she said. She led me to a larger boulder buried in the muck like some unhatched dinosaur egg. Leaning against the rock, she drew me closer and kissed my neck. "I was hoping you'd come—not expecting, just hoping—

and here you are!"

Sharon studied my face for a moment, and then, surprise of surprises, she slipped her arms around my waist and gently pressed her head to my chest. "I'm sorry about your grandparents, Duddy. I really am."

Admittedly, her affection choked me up more than it should have. I changed the subject. "How did you know I was coming here? Did someone see me and then call you?"

"Yeah, now guess who."

"Man or woman?"

Sharon giggled. "Man."

"Older than fifty?"

"Not yet."

"Close kin or distant?"

Sharon see-sawed her hand.

"Accidental spying or intentional?"

Again, the hand see-saw.

"Criminal or law enforcement?" I asked, drawing out the last syllable. "Wait—Rick Shelby!"

Sharon tapped her nose and pointed to me. Not bothering to explain why, she smoothed my open palm and said, "Sorry if I smell like a hobo—I've been helping the bar owner this week as a favor for my uncle. I'm probably not as pretty as you remember, huh? I hate being a ginger until I straighten out these curls and wear it long."

"Like the night we met," I said, grinning. "When you told me to be careful about Rick."

Sharon shrugged. "I know, but things have changed since then," she said, tapping her arm. "I've got all these Little Orphan Annie freckles, and—"

Had I not kissed her she would've sat there talking about nothing. The kiss was longer and deeper than the one we had earlier.

This was the woman I remembered.

The sight of her, the feel of her, the taste of her—she stirred my brain into a fiery soup of primeval emotions. God, did she smell great—and to see her in daylight only made me want her more. She was 32, maybe younger. Her hair was wavy and thick today, curled in fat loops of golden cinnabar—not the frizzy kink of frightful pumpkin she seemed to hate. Her freckles were plentiful, but they were so light in color you couldn't see them unless you were close enough to lick her face. Her skin was fair enough to require a daily shellacking of Coppertone, which is why she smelled so great.

"You're wearing my favorite scent," I told her. "It turns me on."

"The unwashed old man hands or the stale beer?"

Kissing her again, I said, "The Coppertone."

"What? You like the way this stuff smells?"

Lowering my voice, I said, "I LOVE how it smells on your skin. It's like the Chanel of the Sea."

"You just said that," Sharon said, giggling.

Her dimpled smile transformed her into a beauty. Those blue eyes twinkling above her lips transmogrified my hormones and sex chemicals into something I'd long feared to feel. I tried to tell her she was gigging my body with her sexy, Daisy Duke voodoo and Coppertone beach lotion. But I got lost in those eyes again. And then Sharon offered a coy smile before kissing me, harder.

And so, it came to pass that our kiss led to petting, which swiftly—almost instantly—grew quite heavy as it swept us down a different river altogether. Sadly, its current was taking me faster than I wanted to go. Whitewater came so quick it dumped me overboard before I could steady my boat for a longer ride.

Moments later, with Sharon's head resting on my still-heaving, heavy breathing chest, I apologized for my overzealous performance. It wasn't going to be easy slowing my roll with this catfish.

"Spill it, lady," I finally said. "Rick Shelby."

Sharon straddled my waist. "Well, Rick finally went to Sheriff Silas the day after we talked. Now he's helping the Feds with some sting to put Cash Doogan in prison."

Thinking back to the night he brought me to the bar, I remembered how torn and unraveled he seemed, how troubled and frightened he was. "What about Darl?"

"Don't know," she said, "but Rick's a free man and still an officer of the law while he puts his plan together—thank God he turned himself in,

Duddy. Okay, I need to get back," she said, buttoning her blouse. "You need to get drunk with your brother and talk to him." Closing her eyes, Sharon combed her hair with her fingers and smiled. "Help me off this thing, and then help me off this boulder," she said, laughing. "The bruises on my legs will be a topic of conversation at home for a week, I'm sure."

We began the short trek back to the bar holding hands.

"Duddy, I need to tell you something that might sound mean," Sharon said. "I'm keeping you in the dark about some things on purpose— things about me and my family, why I showed up in your life uninvited. I'm doing it for good reason. I'll tell you everything soon, I promise. I prefer telling you what I'm doing instead of saying nothing and having you wonder. Whenever possible, truth is better than a lie, yes?"

"Yes," I told her with a sigh. "I can wait."

Sharon pressed her hands together. "Really?"

"Just tell me something that makes this real," I said. "You have my heart in your hands, and you're married."

"I'm not married," she said.

"You're not?"

Sharon smiled, and I forgot what I'd just asked.

"Anyway," she continued, as if we has been discussing this wholly different topic, "Brandon would come train new deputies for the sheriff's drug task force. My stepmother was secretary. I'd go sit with her at the station and see him there. Sometimes he ate lunch with me in Silas Doogan's office. I was just a girl, but I loved him. You're not the only one Brandon Doogan hurt, you know," she said, lingering at the green baby head. "Did you know that *perdido* is Spanish for *lost*? Yeah, I was thinking about that the other day after our phone call. When they were exploring Florida, sailors had a hard time finding the mouth of the river. And then when they did, they had a hard time navigating it."

"Why?"

"The Perdido River bends and twists on itself, flips directions, gets wide and deep for no reason, narrows like a creek caked with sand dunes, and suddenly turns back into blackwater," she said. "Hence, *perdido*."

"The lost river sounds perfect to me."

"Yes, it does."

Sharon stood on tiptoe to kiss me. "I've got to go," she said. "Tomorrow morning, I'll pick you up for a nice long drive and talk."

"Talk about what?"

Her smile was my answer.

Jesus, lady, what are you doing to me?

My heart pounded as I watched her go inside. I'd been a lost bastard wandering on the banks of this lost river, where generations of lost children made terrible war and passionate love upon each other. Maybe the bastards of Uriah Shelby were doomed to wander the Perdido River until Judgment Day—maybe that was the curse.

No, it was something else. Mom had warned me about it, but I didn't believe her. Boy, did her voice ring inside my head now: "Three months, three days, three minutes, three seconds—when love flips the poles of your heart, the shift happens."

Shift happens.

Of all notions to ponder, of all possibilities to imagine, only one thing interested me now—after I met Sharon, at what moment did the shift happen?

Chapter 11

Whose Side of the River Are You On?

Monday Morning, June 6, 2005

A deep-fried nightmare woke me. I ignored the sour batter of cowchip cookie dough caked on the roof of my mouth and headed straight for the kitchen, which lured me with the promise of a juicy peach for breakfast. Yawning, I stared out the window over the sink as I bit into my softball-sized piece of fruit, its syrup streaming from the corners of my mouth.

Washing my face and hands, I toweled off and wiped the sleep from my eyes. My vision cleared of last night's fuzz, I spotted an obnoxiously big off-brand RV camper under the Graveyard Tree. My heart leapt up when I beheld the sci-fi highway relic, a bus-length Jetsons-silver cigar tube with wheels and fins and outdated fonts from the 1950s. Uncle John and Mike were here.

Two more men would counterbalance the female energy.

John Shelby was Mom's big brother, the spitting image of Grandpa with a much better temperament—well, despite the cantankerous bastard bits. Uncle John was one-fifth Navy, one-fifth genius, one-fifth father, one-fifth road warrior, and one-fifth cynical smartass. Mike was a genius not unlike his old man, but more inclined to use the right side of his brain. Although well paid as an engineer, Mike's true proclivity was music, which meant the service had a real guitar player.

After I showered and shaved, I put on my jeans and one of my brother's shirts—some god-awful torn blue thing way too tight for me. She didn't know it, but Sharon was taking me clothes shopping after our drive to the beach.

Until then, I had time to kill.

The morning sky was a sleepy golden blue. I made coffee enough to last the Exodus and sat on the porch with Eva's old guitar under my arm. Lance slept underfoot while I looked at the lyrics in my little hymnal. Committing the hymn to memory was easy-peasy. I'd all but mastered it when Amanda joined me a half hour later.

"Morning, bubby," she said. "Want company?"

"Sure, honey—sit here," I said, moving into another lawn chair. "You won't have a liver by tomorrow if you keep up with that vodka."

"It's for my bursitis," she said. "What's a liver?"

The morning was throwing its heat around the porch like a Waffle House short-order cook throwing greasy food on the grill. Comingling smells of dog food, wet concrete, damp soil, stale beer, drying vomit, and piss added a unique tang to the humid air. We didn't mind though. We sat in comfortable silence, drinking cheap beer, listening to birds and squirrels chattering. It wasn't long before Belladonna and Tyler joined our pre-breakfast party.

Mike emerged from the camper dragging a large cooler filled with ice cold bottles of his *family-famous* craft beer. Tyler dumped the last of his Natty Ice into Lance's water bowl and took a proffered IPA with a shit-eating grin. After serving the rest of us, Mike opened one and sat in a lawn chair with a tattered seat.

"Breakfast of champions," he said. "Beer before noon should be mandatory on days following family deaths. Drink up."

A horn honked—Sharon was there to collect me.

With a wink, Tyler took my guitar and started playing a song with filthy lyrics, a distraction we'd planned last night at the bar to hide my sneaking off to spend the morning with my would-be girlfriend. Her car idled at the bend in the road just beyond the house. I had no idea why, but I was anxious about seeing her. I felt like that slow kid on the short-bus unable to control his face muscles when his stop arrived.

Sharon didn't see me until I opened the door and buckled myself in. With a shy peck on the cheek, she handed me a clipping from today's newspaper, Granny and Grandpa's obituary and information about the viewing at Boudreaux Funeral Home and the burial with graveside service at Beulah Baptist Church tomorrow at noon.

Surviving family members include: daughters Brenda, Hattie, and Belladonna; son John; and grandchildren Dean Adam, Tyler, Amanda, and Mike.

Sharon seemed preoccupied, so I kept quiet as the languid curves of Scenic Highway took us around the rocky cliffs of Escambia Bay. The silence wasn't terribly uncomfortable, just odd considering our prior visits and talks. It gave me time to appreciate the damage left from Hurricane Ivan—the recovery was, in a word, underwhelming.

At the top of an exit ramp that swept us upward in a steep spiral, Sharon said, "I may pull over to vomit—be warned." She attempted a lopsided smile. "I don't know what's been wrong with me, but I've felt nauseous and seasick for a few days. I'll be fine once we get there."

We parked beneath the new beach ball spire.

Seeing Pensacola Beach so broken and wounded was a stake in my heart. Ivan had wiped out the entire beachfront after making landfall, but then he spun back into the Gulf only to return to plunder what was left before heading to Mobile. The pier and boardwalk were gone—there was only shore.

After climbing recently installed sand dunes, we took off our shoes and headed for the clear water across the sugar white sand. Under the hazy morning sun, we ambled through ankle-high waves lapping at our feet. Sharon pointed to the missing boardwalk, its bars and snack huts gone, the collapsed walls and roofs that once were restaurants, the graves of refreshment shanties and kiosks, splintered hotels and condos, crooked piles of boats masts, walls of broken things.

The ruins of Paradise Lost stretched for miles.

After we walked a handful of yards, she said, "I'm having a hard time not telling you things—and I've been thinking about this news story about this boy named Jay Greenberg who started playing cello when he was two years old. He said he just knew how to play it, like when he heard music in his head, he just started composing it—why, how? His parents weren't musicians."

"Past life," I said. "Or blood memory."

"I'm a blood memory gal," she said. "I keep thinking how we're all incestuously connected—trace our families back and they intersect more than once. These weren't soft people—they lived hard. They were survivors. I'm wondering if your blood records any of that history, good or bad. I wonder if their sins return through us." She vomited into the sand and leaned against me. "Do you have gum?"

"Always," I told her. "Here, chew that."

Sharon sat inside the hollow of my crossed legs and made a joke about me being her fun-in-the-sun beach chair with benefits. Staring at the hypnotizing ebb and flow of the Gulf, I let her sink into me and held her. I waited for her to revisit our recent chat about blood memory, which was a topic of great interest to me, of course. I thought of Pidge and smiled.

Sharon didn't want to talk.

My oxygen-deprived feet and thoroughly numbed ass cheeks did, but aside from that, our silence made this a perfect moment.

Had it not been for the appearance of a young man named Joseph Conrad, I would've sat there until sundown. But this good-looking kid with his mixed heritage dropped out of the clear blue sky and landed in front of us. It sent me ass-over-feet backward. Freed from me as her human seat cushion, Sharon screamed when this guy picked her up and spun her around like a ragdoll.

That he knew Sharon wasn't a surprise.

That she knew him wasn't a surprise either.

That I nearly went into a jealous rage because they both knew each other was a surprise—and why?

Because this tall, good-looking athletic college kid with perfect teeth and abs and glowing caramel skin was juggling MY woman, making her forget about me. To be fair, as soon as her feet touched sand, Sharon retched again—*what the hell was going on?* As soon as her legs buckled, I was there at her side until the wave passed.

I didn't give a monkey shit what this kid was to her or what she was to him—my only concern was Sharon. I needed to get her off the beach and back to the car.

A hand thrust in my face made that difficult.

"I'm Joseph Conrad," he said, waiting for me to shake. "Sharon, I'm sorry for making you dizzy." To me, he added, "I'm so sorry, man. I just wanted to surprise her—I haven't seen her in a while and—man, I didn't know she was sick."

Reluctantly, I shook his hand.

"I'm Dean Adam," I said. "I don't know if she's sick, but she was feeling better until you scared us to death and started spinning her in the air. Look, when you're young you're also oblivious—I know this better than most, Joseph Conrad, so I'll forgive you for the bad first impression, if you'll help me get her to the car."

I honestly didn't know what this kid would do, but when I let go of his hand, his face broke into a smile. "So, you're Dean Adam Doogan," he said. "I've heard a lot about you, man. Not as tall as I pictured in my head, but you look just like him."

"Like who?" I asked. "Him who? Brandon?"

Suddenly confused, Joseph Conrad laughed nervously. "Sharon didn't tell you? I mean, she wasn't supposed to tell you anything, but I know her and—what, girl? Don't 'shush' me like you're my mama. I came here to throw a football with my boys—I didn't know you were here with HIM, so don't blame me because you're sneaking around—"

With a groan, Sharon twisted herself from me and got to her feet. She wobbled, but she held steadfast to her need for balance. Then, through clenched teeth, she hissed something at Joseph Conrad before laying all kinds of holy hell into him, slapping his arms repeatedly.

"Goddammit," she spat at him. "Shut up, shut up! I couldn't help it. I had to see him. I've been waiting long enough to see him, so quit puffing up and leave me alone."

Silence.

The longer Sharon stood there saying nothing, the easier it was to let the silence unfold. I glanced at Joseph Conrad, who shrugged in confusion before he put his arm around Sharon. "I'd swear on a stack of bibles he looks like—" She elbowed him hard in the side. "All right, but you know he isn't for you. And you know why he isn't for you."

"How do you know who is or isn't for her?"

Believe me—I was just as surprised to hear me say it.

Joseph Conrad took a step toward me. "Who do YOU think you are, chump?" he said, his shoulders hunched as he bounced on his toes. "This is a family matter—back off."

Taking a foolish step toward the much taller young man, I said nothing as I stared at him.

Outside, I was calm and confident and cautious.

Inside, I was drowning in an ocean of my inner child's piss and shit and vomit. I had no chance to win a fistfight with this kid, so my only tactic was a psychological one to not back down and not make things worse by saying another something stupid. Sharon stepped into the space between us, which would've been funny had things not gotten so tense. She widened the gap with a firm push, one for each of us.

To me, she said, "Really, Duddy? Jealousy?" To Joseph Conrad, she said, "Stop being an asshole."

"I'M THE ASSHOLE? Check yourself, Sharon."

And so, it came to pass that I decided doing something stupid was better than doing nothing at all. I stepped in front of Sharon like a cave man and shoved Joseph Conrad.

Five other young men, each one an athlete from a Benetton ad, circled me. Two of them grabbed my arms, but I flailed and flung myself free. Joseph Conrad was too busy arguing with Sharon to care about me. "No, YOU provoked him, and YOU pissed me off, all because YOU didn't think about anybody else. YOU knocked him over and YOU swung me around until I puked. YOU ruined something important, Joseph Conrad! I don't care that you're going to Italy for your semester abroad in a few days. That man over there is about to bury his grandparents, but YOU wouldn't know that because YOU are a self-absorbed ASSHOLE!"

"YOU'RE SIDING WITH HIM?"

Sharon lowered her voice.

"I am this time, Joseph Conrad. YOU were in the wrong today, so do right by me. He's still in the dark, so check your ego and give him a pass.

Do it for me and for Silas—Joseph Conrad, do it for yourself. You know who he is to you."

Joseph Conrad slapped his hand as he spun into the waves. For several moments, he stood there. And after a deep breath, he returned to Sharon and took her hand. "You're right, I wasn't thinking," he said. "I was showing off because I'm leaving my friends until next year. I'll keep my mouth shut and forgive him for being AN IGNORANT FOOL," he said, glancing at me. "I WON'T DROP KICK YOUR SKINNY ASS," he said, whistling for his friends as he ran down the beach. "SEE YOU NEXT TIME, DEAN ADAM DOOGAN."

Sharon stood in the surf. She watched them toss the football. Turning on her heels, she took three great strides and pushed me hard. When I fell on my ass, she kicked sand at me and slapped my head as she shouted a barrage of epithets.

"Why did you have to be such a prick? He's my cousin, Duddy, but because YOU didn't stop and think we could be related, YOU became a jealous, prejudiced ASSHOLE."

As I waited for Sharon to finish, I wondered if she was right.

Jealousy didn't affect me—that it happened today the way it did told me it was something that went beyond insecurity or fear of losing her. My busted emotional fuse box was no excuse for what I did. Was Sharon completely wrong? If the same racist blood of Earle Adam Doogan flowed in my veins, was I also doomed to repeat his evil? Would his memories resurface?

I didn't know what to think—my heart was beating so fast I thought spontaneous combustion was as real a threat to my life as was a bullet to my head. I knew I'd fucked up. I was trying to calm down and cool my overheated jets. But then Sharon stormed off, didn't even look at me. She left me standing on the beach, got into her car, and drove away.

All I could do was stand there and watch it happen. I thought maybe she'd be gone a few minutes before she came back for me, but she didn't. I waited in the parking lot for an hour, and she didn't come back. The only open restaurant on the beach had a taxicab stand, so after three pints of beer and two bowls of peanuts, I took a cab to Cordova Mall, bought some clothes, and took a cab home.

I knew I'd have trouble doing it, but I had to forget her today—I had to forget about how I felt about her. I didn't feel a goddamn thing about Dad when he left, but I did with Sharon. Her absence was the gaping hole in my chest where a heart should've been.

•

A few minutes before noon, I came in through the living room to avoid the carousers on the back porch. Mom was in the kitchen. Her puffy face was ash and splotched with pink. When she saw me, all the color in her face returned.

I thought she was having a stroke until she grabbed me and burst into tears. "Sugar, why were you gone so long? Where were you?"

"I went to the beach and bought new clothes," I said matter-of-factly. "I shouldn't have to announce my every departure and arrival time to you when I decide to leave the house."

Silence.

Mom wiped her nose on the back of her sleeve. "You're right, sugar—I'm sorry—my mind's just all over the place with what's happened—come with me, Duddy."

I followed her into Granny's room.

Looking through the small pile of papers on the large pile of folders, Mom mumbled something about doing what she could for her children whenever they needed help.

More often than not, that meant enduring the slings and arrows of our myriad outrageous fortune changes and the ancillary maelstroms. It meant hand wringing and irrational worrying, it meant tender and hostile criticisms, or rebukes and apologies—it meant teetering on the brink inside her private holocaust.

My martyr mother—and I loved her.

Whatever this woman thought she did or didn't do to me, it would be easy to forgive her for it.

Mom handed me a fancy piece of paper with the State of Florida's seal. "Give me a dollar, sugar—it's the title for your new care," she explained, snapping her fingers until I put the bill in her hands. "Just sign the bottom line there—I hereby bequeath to you Granny's T-Bird. I know it ain't Jeepers, sugar, but it's the best I can do."

"Thanks, Mom," I said, rising.

"Happy Birthday, my barn baby," she said. "I'll spin your birth story just as soon as I can catch my breath, sugar. And by that I mean, just as soon as everybody gets here."

Kissing the top of her head, I went to sit in my new car and listen to the radio with the air conditioning set to high-def frigid mode. I returned to the family booze party on the back porch as more guests arrived. Pidge, Miss Eva, and Aunt Clara added to the stockpiles of food in the kitchen. Miss Eva's daughter Mickey was still holding the gate for her daughter Kate, who had trouble with her bags of food thanks to four-year-old Katelyn.

"Baby, get out from under my feet," Kate said, handing her heavy bags to Tyler. "You're like a psychotic kitten today—go and hug Duddy. Please go, and then keep on going. Go all the way up to the moon if you—young lady, did you just break wind?"

Katelyn's freckled face went beet red. She calmly adjusted the pink bow in her sandy blonde hair and went up the steps to the kitchen. Turning around in the doorway, she cleared her throat to speak in a thick-as-butter Southern drawl. "We came here to make y'all feel better...on this sad day. We brought ham and bacon and beef, if you want it." She excused herself for farting and slammed the door behind her.

Kate opened two beers, chugging the first one.

"Baby Hitler's gonna tell everybody how magnanimous she is," she said. "I swear, if that child ain't running her own business by the time she hits high school, she'll start her own mafia. I blame you, Mother. I wanted to drown her, but you wouldn't let me. I'd be living in Paris if it weren't for you."

Mickey thumped Kate's head. "Watch it, Missy," she said. "Open me a beer, so I may go into the cool house and partake of the ham and bacon and beef selections." She paused for effect. "On this sad day."

Food tapered our collective inebriation into a lovely buzz. It was wrong, and we all knew it was wrong, but we didn't give a shit. I know I didn't. To forget what happened earlier demanded many libations. We traipsed about like drunken monkeys. We told truly embarrassing stories about each other, which got worse the more we imbibed. Kate sent Kate-lyn away to keep her from learning our colorful language.

Uncle John emerged from the camper to join our wild rumpus. With a sweep of his arm, he opened a bottle of beer. "Dad and Mom would've wanted us to do exactly what we always do whenever we get together— God bless them," he said. "Sorry for the turd in your punchbowl, kids, but we need to move cars to the backyard and clean up this mess. Guests are coming soon, and ALL of you need to bathe, you bunch of stinkers."

A miracle happened. By four o'clock that afternoon, eight snake-drunk people sobered up, washed and dressed themselves without hospice care, and transformed a tiny house into a cozy place for a big gathering to celebrate two people. Somehow, I managed to keep thoughts of Sharon so far from my mind that I actually enjoyed the company of these crazy people. For the first time in years, I felt like I belonged.

Family wandered in and out the house.

Despite the fans circulating the poor, overworked air conditioning units, it was hot. We didn't mind—no one did, so long as the doors and windows were opened to the world outside. Folk I'd howdied but never shook with filled every room and seat. Distant and close relations laughed and mourned with us. They lifted our spirits, surrounded us with love, and kept us from sinking into despair.

After pitching a fuck-a-duck fit about being spin-doctor, Amanda set-tled into her task and played vinyl records on the Magnavox stereo. Play-ing on the muted television set were Grandpa's *Victory at Sea* tapes. Using myriad materials and methods, we somehow deconstructed and reassem-bled William Hubert and Melba Shelby into a single, Frankensteined mo-saic of life. Their 59 years of marriage had survived a World War, two Asian proxy wars, a near-miss nuclear war, gambling debts, Hattie's ad-dition, curses and feuds, deaths and births.

We broke for supper when Miss Eva whistled. "I'd eat the ass end of a dead rabbit if somebody would fix me a damn plate of it," she shouted.

Outside, Tyler had declared himself Lawn Sheriff and deputized Mike. Holding a case of Zima malt beverages between them, they drank from each one and lined the fence with half-filled bottles of the clear malt beverage. Apparently, it sucked biting insects better than anything. The bottles soon were throwing an undulating luminescence against the side of the house. Protected by rows of citronella candles, several campfires, tiki torches, bug foggers, a slobbering Boxer, and insect zappers the size of small refrigerators, the perimeter of the yard buzzed, hummed purple, and snapped like a popcorn machine.

Miss Eva and Aunt Clara were holding court in the living room. They sat like old queens, feet up on cushions, directing people or blessing them, or cursing them.

Doris regaled the room with tales of the curse.

Pidge and Mom were dancing like teenagers, as Belladonna hovered around them like a thoroughly Gothic country druid—she wore Granny's cowboy hat, of course.

There was laughter. There were tears.

There were much flatulence, name-calling, and blasphemy.

At midnight, when many of the guests had departed, Amanda softened the music selection. The women-folk filled the empty spaces of the living room, lolling on chairs, the floor, the sofa, and the unused seat cushions. The men-folk stood in smaller groups outside.

I was hanging with my uncle on the front porch. "Too much female in there," I said. "Always, too much estrogen."

Uncle John nodded. "Try growing up with it." He sipped Scotch from a tall, white ceramic mug shaped as a woman's breast—you drank from its nipple, you see. "The curse's a load of MAH-nure," he said. "I've seen strange things growing up around them, Duddy, but just because those women throw around tragedies like baseballs, you don't have to swing at them. When Mike and I lost his moth—"

Tyler suddenly popped up, his arm draping around Mike.

Uncle John shook his head. "Speak of the devil."

My brother and cousin swayed to their own music and then wandered off to the darkest part of the yard. Uncle John sucked his mug nipple. "My genius son, the lawn deputy."

"Amen," I said, raising my glass.

Inside, Mom shouted for Kate to tell the dog-napping story. Every female in the living room whooped and clapped for it until chaos reigned in joyful raucous anarchy.

The story, alas, would have to wait.

As I stood in the doorway, Miss Eva shoved two pinkies into her mouth and whistled. Aunt Clara raised her tumbler and broke wind. Miss Eva threw her hands up like a withered traffic cop until the noise subsided. "The three most important women in this family—this tri-something—shit, NEPHEW, what's that 50-cent word for 'three'? No, Brenda, not trio. Clarabelle Wilson, stop farting or I will end you with my pickle spear. NEPHEW!"

"Triage," I said from the porch. "I think."

Miss Eva blew me a kiss. "Triage! Melba, Clara, Eva—"

"The Triage of Terror," whispered Belladonna.

"Christ-in-the-Candy-Store, you crazy Gothic smartass," Miss Eva said, throwing her pickle. "Hell's bells, niece, if'n you'd listen less to Clara and more to me, you wouldn't need to cast spells or read cards. You would've been married one time 'stead of as high as I can count."

"Six fingers on her cursed arthritic hand," Mickey mumbled to Kate, who snorted.

Miss Eva continued. "You want curses? Belladonna married a man who ate his own shit and snuffled, sniffled, huffled—what's that word, Kate? Is it sniffing fumes?"

"It's 'huffed,' Boobs," Kate answered. "Huffed."

Miss Eva blew her a kiss. "Thank you, baby—do you know how gorgeous you are?" She looked at Aunt Clara and said, "She's MY granddaughter."

"Eva, shut the fuck up before I stare at you to death with my good eye," Aunt Clara replied, moving her patch to the other one. "Wait, this eye's the good one."

"Anyway, he HUFFED gas fumes and ate his own shit to hide the half gallon of whiskey he'd chugged on your honeymoon night—you had five other husbands just like him," she said, using her second pickle spear as a pointer. "I'll just say it since you won't, Belladonna—will you please, for the love of Christ, find a nice girl with lots of piercings and settle the hell down before you die? We all know you're a lesbun, baby, so get on with it and be happy."

Silence.

Sipping from his mug, Uncle John looked at me and said, "Duddy, did you know my sister was a nipple-sucking lesbian?"

Throwing up my hands, I said, "I plead the fifth."

"To lesbuns!" Pidge shouted, raising her tumbler. "HA! I've been waiting to make that toast for years, cousin! Go love on Miss Eva for outing you, scaredy bitch—damnation station! One less secret to keep in this family is cause for a pride parade in the living room."

Tears streaming down her face, Belladonna hugged her aunt. Miss Eva took her by the chin.

"You don't deserve the Big Stupid Shitbird of All Time crown," she said, gently. "Melba knew, baby—well, we all knew. Your daddy would've died from hearing his precious baby was gay—but since he's already dead, it can't hurt him or you. But you're still my Big Stupid Shitbird."

Aunt Clara laughed. "Crown looks better on you anyway," she said. "Will somebody PLEASE play somethin' by the King?"

Pidge cackled. "HA! No, another Beatles song!"

Amanda played 'In My Life' from *Rubber Soul.*

The women huddled closer. Heads leaned on shoulders. The men moved closer to the open doorway and sang with welled eyes. Uncle John kept his nipple mug at his mouth, but he never stopped singing. When the song ended, Amanda screamed.

"One side of the record's scratched to hell!"

Mom laughed. "That's because your barn-born brother used it as a surfboard on my kitchen floor when he was two years old," she said. "I should've killed him."

"Yes, she should have," said Uncle John.

Suddenly, Mike reemerged from the darkness and his secret yard doings with Tyler, his right arm smeared chocolate brown. "I just landed in shit, Dad."

Uncle John laughed. "Proud of you, son—I told you not to imbibe those malt drinks."

"I'm going to bed," Mike said as he wobbled.

"Not in mine," Uncle John retorted.

"Dammit, I want to toast our dearly departed," said Miss Eva. "Melba took care of that wicked man these last nine years with naught but a pig part-covered metal-ticking heart in her tiny chest. For loving that man, Melba deserves a spot in heaven. As for William Hubert, let's just raise a glass and say, 'There, but by the Grace of God...'"

Miss Eva poked Mom with a pickle spear. "Brat—I never liked you or your gay sister. Mickey, you're my daughter, but you can burn in hell with Buddy. John's my favorite anyway. And now Clarabelle, Our Lady of Perpetual Gas, let's to bed. Big day tomorrow."

Aunt Clara moved her eye patch. "Damnation station, will you please shut that hole in your head for one goddamn minute? We'll go after one more bedtime story."

When Miss Eva showed her gnarled middle finger, Mickey volunteered to close the evening with her dog rescue story. I always liked Miss Eva's daughter. She had a brassy voice and bright, crystal eyes that sparkled when she spoke.

"Leave it to Kate to get herself seduced by a redneck psychopath," Mickey said. "Good looking and crazy."

Kate snickered. "That doesn't run in the family at all."

Mickey kicked her. "Them three starving Rotties tied to a tree in his backyard weren't there for vacation, Kate, so when did you get a clue? Something in the boy's britches clouded your mind, cause it wasn't his Texas Chainsaw house in that cul-de-sac at the end of Burn-in-Hell Lane—nice one, honey."

"Shut the hell up, Mother, and tell the goddamn story."

"Well, you did break up with him," Mickey said. "After Kate found out he had this bitch Golden Retriever for his Rotties to screw and kill, she broke up with the bastard before I had a chance to tell her to steal that dog."

Mickey's telling of what happened would've been great had Mom, Belladonna, Pidge, and Amanda not added their own details and embellishments.

Being the butt of their jokes, Kate held Katelyn and tried not to blush when she corrected them.

Miss Eva turned to her sister. "What was your part?"

Aunt Clara grinned. "I drove the getaway car!"

The women who had participated in the First Annual Pensacola Dog

Rescue whooped as Mickey looked at Kate. The story took on a life of its own now. There was nothing more to be said. Next year, it would undoubtedly be the rescue story about a bus of orphans. Everyone had an important part and everyone else was a screw-up.

"Clara couldn't reach the pedals," Belladonna said. "I got on the floor board. She sat on the seat behind me and would step on my left shoulder to brake and my right shoulder to gas."

It was a miracle that *family-fun* didn't take a life or two.

Kate's freckled face went crimson as Pidge added details about how they almost ran over a man walking his cat. "He didn't see us because he was busy taking his cat—one of those fluffy ones that looks like it chases parked cars—HA! It had a rhinestone leash."

Miss Eva's face split. "A bedazzled cat, not a fancy dog? Christ Crunching Crackers, was the man dressed the same too? Clara, you shoulda took him out with the truck. Poor pussy's what needed saving. I'd-a taken care of that pussy. Bet the man's pussy shits in a toilet."

Kate's laughing and jerking woke up Katelyn, who'd been sleeping soundly on her mother's knee. In her thick-as-butter drawl, the four-year-old shouted at everyone for being so loud. "Y'all, hush! Mommy, stop bouncing! I'm trying to get some goddamn sleep!"

Belladonna sprayed wine as Mom keeled over into the carpet. Mickey excused herself. Stumbling away, Amanda snorted cheese and vodka. Coughing incapacitated Doris and Dorothy, both of them screaming breathless 'stop its' in mirrored hunched apoplexy. Pidge pissed herself—she literally peed on herself from laughing. There sat Miss Eva, snickering like a demented old clown next to Aunt Clara, waving her hands like a truck stop Geisha to hide her sudden, and quite loud, gaseous Morse code.

And thus ended story hour.

Someone rapped knuckles on the living room window.

Another knock followed, heralded by a catcall and drunken yodel. Poking my head outside, I hissed Tyler's name. He didn't answer. The scent of urine and BBQ smoke was heavy, and diffused moonlight shone its pale glow across the bottle-covered yard as guests departed. Miss Eva and Aunt Clara waved goodnight as the blur of a naked man bolted from the bushes.

Tyler sprinted to the backyard with a Rebel Yell. Moments later, I heard strange noises, so I went to see what he was doing and found him washing off under the garden hose. "I was naked bush diving and fell in dog crap—let's run naked in the woods and howl at the moon."

"How about we just walk and talk, instead?"

"We'll run for as long as we can through that opening," he said, ignoring me. "We can walk back, and then it'll be time for some naked fuckin' bush divin'. Compromise?"

Unbuttoning my pants, I nodded. "Compromise."

Tyler fell hard on a patch of grass at the top of a steep slope. And I fell beside him. My brother was right—running naked and howling at the moon was something to experience. From there, you could see Muscogee Road winding from the end of the Beulah Landfill, past the gates of the RC Cola plant, and to the curve at Granny and Grandpa's place. The tiny house gaped at us like a Jack-o-Lantern. Every window was an eye peering into the darkness.

"I hate it when good things are gone," Tyler said, rubbing his eyes. "Dad's gone, Granny and Grandpa are gone—sucks, boss. Nothing's good when the things you love are gone. You were gone a long fucking time—I hated it when you were gone. I hated you for wanting to be, but you got better—I can tell you don't want to be gone anymore."

We talked for a long time, both of us unwilling to move until mosquitoes forced us to go.

On the way back to the house, Tyler finally asked about Sharon. I hadn't planned to say anything more than I did at the bar last night, but I couldn't stop once I opened up to him. Maybe it was the beer-soaked naked moonlight run. Maybe it was the end to years of my self-imposed isolation. Or maybe it was because he was my brother.

I began with Memorial Day weekend.

Cotton Wilson's house. Pidge and the photos of Silas and Hank. Rick Shelby. My fight with Cash. My night with Sharon. My morning at the cemetery with Granny. Hattie's cancer. My music box quest. Auntie Claudia and the Charleston market. The secret room in Lilly's cellar and who hid there. I told him nearly everything that happened over the past two weeks and finished with the beach incident.

Tyler laughed. "Boss, you didn't ruin anything—she doesn't know how to fucking deal with being in love with you—women do that shit when they love us too hard," he said. "You survived a tornado, boss. You kept Amanda safe under a bridge on the Interstate as people got sucked into the sky—that's hardcore courage. If I knew nothing else, you'd be my fucking hero. You can handle Sharon. So, what now?"

"I might need you to cover for me tomorrow."

"Why, boss?"

Good question, but I didn't have a good answer.

Chapter 12

I'll Fly Away in a Hip Jesus Graphic Tee

Tuesday Morning, June 7, 2005

If there's one thing about living in the South, it's learning to love hot weather. I mean sweltering, no-breeze, Tennessee Williams, bayou-broiling weather. Heat that does things to fool the mind and trick the soul. Heat that makes your body weak from sweating in the heat of all seven deadly sins. Heat that knows no skin color, faith, or gender. Southern heat haunts our history, geography, and people—it's the reason for our peculiar, unavoidable collective madness.

Christ, it was hot as holy hell today.

Mom's car led the other cars to Boudreaux Funeral Home on Jack's Branch Road. We parked in a shady lot near a pair of one-story buildings and joined the other mourners gathered beneath the carport there. Inside the main building, I remained close to Mike. Neither of us knew who these people were—well, besides some serious babymakers. Their kids were running everywhere. Hordes of Jem Finch boys wearing crooked clip-on ties and hand-me-down Dickies and Scout Finch girls wearing sundresses too short to hide dirty, skinned knees.

Belladonna sidled up to us.

"Your Granny won't mind if y'all mess up her song," she said. "Miss Eva and Aunt Clara will kill you both dead if you fuck up, but your Granny won't mind. I just hope the caskets don't drop or break," she added.

"It's been a while since we had *family-fun*, and with the day being so hot, I wouldn't be surprised if they did. Nothing in the world is so set in stone that it can't be turned upside down with its ass in the air."

Mike laughed. "Who said that?"

Belladonna smiled. "Granny said that."

The lobby was cool and reeked of Pine Sol mixed with rose perfume. Beyond the closed doors was the chapel viewing room where Granny and Grandpa were on display. A felt lined, waist high board in front read, "William H and Melba W Shelby," which made it feel like we were going to the Golden Corral for the goddamn buffet.

The chapel doors opened at eleven on the nose. Ruddy-faced Buddy Lee Boudreaux, packed like a Vienna sausage in his Hugo Boss suit, stood next to Mom and Uncle John to welcome everyone. Buddy Lee's thinning salt-and-pepper hair was slicked back with Vitalis, exposing his recent Botox face-lift and a smile with too many perfect white teeth. "Open caskets the first fifteen minutes and closed caskets for the last thirty," he said, offering his arm to Miss Eva.

Tyler and Belladonna went in the chapel with the other mourners. Mike and I waited on a cushioned bench outside. We didn't want to see the bodies of our dead grandparents. Buddy Lee left the chapel and came over to talk to us. Patting my arm, he said, "Before we close the caskets, I wanted to make sure y'all don't want to go in. I've been in this business all my life, laid many folk to rest. Melba was always cute as a pair of lamb's pants, but right now, in that viewing room, she's the most beautiful woman you ever laid eyes on—she's a perfect angel at peace with Jesus. Are y'all sure?"

Mike cleared his throat. "Mr. Boudreaux, my grandmother was not a beauty—well, not in a conventional way—but she was a beautiful woman. In fact, she was the most beautiful woman in the world before you dolled-up her dead body with spray paint, hot glue and glitter. I don't mean to sound so cruel, but I don't need your grotesquery to say goodbye to my Granny. Excuse me."

Grief—it's what's for dinner.

It goes without saying that Buddy Lee avoided my cousin the rest of the day. I agreed with Mike in principle, but I also knew better than to insult the man doing our family this huge favor. Yeah, Miss Eva bought the favor with a date night, but it didn't preclude Buddy Lee having our sincere gratitude and appreciation for his services.

Mike and I went into the chapel.

The two coffins sat in a V-shape, one mirroring the other, on biers against the far wall. A blanket of white lilies covered Granny's casket— Old Glory covered Grandpa's casket.

Other vibrant wreaths, bouquets, and flowers filled the small room with sweet perfume as mourners paid their respects. Seated on a red bench near the entrance were Pidge, Mom, and Uncle John, who thanked guests before Belladonna took them to sign the guestbook.

My great aunts hid behind a large fake ficus, tittering and telling dirty jokes to break the tension, anything to relieve the heavy weight of collective melancholy. Other than the snickering, they were angels—fallen ones, of course. There was a police escort to Beulah Baptist Church. Officer Enos Percy, the one who caught me speeding Memorial Day weekend, led the procession. He deliberately winked at me before he drove away, son of a bitch.

A Naval honor guard stood at sweaty attention in the shade of the Graveyard Trees in the far back corner of the cemetery, which was an odd thing to see in and of itself, but not nearly as odd as seeing a tombstone and two open graves on the spot Granny had shown me.

Death is family.

A pair of mechanical Astroturf-lined platforms stood on shoddy scaffolds over the shallow pits. The party tent was a nice touch—it was a tent that said, *bury your grandparents while having a real fancy picnic at the same time.* Under the fringe awning were two rows of metal folding chairs covered in Cookie Monster-blue velvet.

When the family members were settled, Buddy Lee motioned pallbearers around the scaffolding to the back of the hearses. We carried Granny's casket and locked it into place without a hitch. The honor guard almost dropped Grandpa's casket when the woman in pole position buckled. We leaned forward to give psychic support until they secured the casket and straightened the flag.

An overcast sky gave way to a sunny one as Pastor Bill began his benediction. Our bald Man of God came to us by way of the Missouri Synod, but he'd have a heat stroke if he didn't lose the black robes. When he left the lectern (also decked in the same Muppet-blue fabric), he was all perspiration. The handkerchief he used to mop his face was a sopping rag, which made Mom giggle when he used it.

Uncle John nodded to my cousin and me. We thanked Miss Eva and Aunt Clara for choosing us, and after I said something about it being Granny's favorite, Mike strummed the guitar and I sang the hymn.

> *Some glad morning when this life is o'er, I'll fly away*
> *To a home on God's celestial shore, I'll fly away*
> *I'll fly away, O Glory, I'll fly away*
> *When I die, Hallelujah, by and by, I'll fly away*

When we finished, the sun ducked behind the clouds. The pastor got up to deliver a sermon that Pidge would later dub, 'Preacher Perspiration's Special Words for a *Family-Fun* Fucking Funeral.' Now, it's important to note that Missouri Synod Lutheran ministers are by-the-book folk. Pastor Bob said he could suffer some hot weather because Christ suffered crucifixion for our sins. Preacher Perspiration was about to prove Hattie's belief that God preferred to punish pride painfully and publicly.

Who would've thought that meant an afternoon apocalypse too?

•

HERE BEGINS BEULAH BAPTIST'S
BURIAL BOOK OF REVELATION

•

The FIRST SEAL broke when the sun returned.

The SECOND SEAL broke when Pastor Bob's bifocals fell.

The glasses smashed on the base of the lectern. He tried reading his note cards with the one mostly-intact lens. He said some kind words about the family, how much we loved Granny and Grandpa. He wiped his brow.

From the Gospel of John—When Mary was come... where Jesus was and saw him, she... fell at his feet, saying to...him, Lord, if thou hadst been here, my brother had not died.

To his ears, I'm sure he sounded conversational.

To ours, the slurry of sounds were like those made by a drunk Sunday schoolteacher with no teeth.

The THIRD SEAL broke when he continued anyway.

When Jesus therefore saw her sweeping Jews weeping which came with a groin spirit and said, Where have ye laid him? They said unto him, Jesus swept.

Pastor Bob asked if we'd allow him to continue without his robe, and we begged him to make himself comfortable.

The FOURTH SEAL broke upon the sound of ripping Velcro.

Pastor Bob stood before us in cargo shorts and a graphic tee with a crude drawing of Christ sitting in a dumb waiter descending from the phrase: 'Jesus Is Lowered.'

Which broke the fucking FIFTH SEAL.

Pastor Bob gripped the lectern. Trying to cover his shirt with a pasty white and splotchy arm, he apologized and soldiered on, correcting himself as best he could. He continued, bless his heart—

Then said Juice, Be-home how beloved him! Handsome of them said, Could hot men, which opened dyes the blind hovel creamed that should not have died? Jesus therefore cometh to the grave cave, said, Take yo stone, sister of him that was dead four days.

Sounds of coughing disguised rippling waves of laughter, and yet, Pastor Bob plodded through the final passages.

> *Then they turned to stone from the place laid as Jesus shifted up his eyes again, Feather, I think thee thou breast hearing arrest me always: but of the people may believe thou hazard me when he horse's spoken cried with a loud as ice, Lorenzo home front.*

Pastor Bob abruptly ended his sermon and returned to his seat. He sat so hard the right back leg of his chair sank into the soft ground, putting him on a slant.

The SIXTH SEAL broke.

The sky darkened as storm clouds covered the sun. As the Graveyard Trees swayed, their mosses, their gray shawls fringed in wisps and chiggers, lifted from gnarled fingers as the wind blew them. It took a 21-gun salute to silence the laughter and the haunting melody of Taps to ground us again. And when the American flag was solemnly passed to Uncle John's trembling hands, our grief returned.

The service ended quietly, personally, and bereft of humor.

Then I noticed the scaffolding under the caskets. Its rickety mechanical jacks were all caddywumpus on Grandpa's side. His casket wasn't secure after all. Mr. Boudreaux's assistant was re-inspecting the levers when a string of thunderclaps made him jump like a cat on crack.

The SEVENTH SEAL broke.

Lightning cracked just beyond the line of trees.

The assistant under the scaffolding bumped it, which sent shudders through the entire wobbly structure. He steadied things and quickly began tightening screws and bolts.

Then came the click-clanking, jickety-jacketing racket of William Hubert Shelby's casket suddenly dropping in his grave with a kaBOOM! The assistant under Granny's side immediately backed into the grass. Half-screaming and laughing, we wondered if we should run for cover or clap for an encore.

Pastor Bob fainted.

And then Aunt Clara, sporting a velvet eye patch covered in rhinestones, also fainted.

A cooler wind brought the first smattering of rain and the dull rumble of thunder. With a whirring clack, Granny's casket began a slow descent with delicate clicks until it rested gently at the bottom of her grave. Aunt Clara came to with a flatulent trumpet blast.

"HA!" Pidge shouted. "Now THAT was a funeral!"

And to these things I say,

'Come, my Lowered Jesus—Amen.'

•

HERE ENDS BEULAH BAPTIST'S
BURIAL BOOK OF REVELATION

•

Uncle John personally escorted the minister inside the church to cool off. Before I left for the parking lot, I helped sweat-drenched Buddy Lee check levers and pulleys. He kept reassuring everyone the caskets weren't broken. Mom and Pidge tried to convince the poor man to let his assistants finish the work before he had a cardiac arrest. He refused to leave his work until Miss Eva whistled and waved him over to escort her home.

Pidge put her arm around me. "Well, fuck-a-duck, if that don't beat all," she said, cackling. "HA! Wasn't that the best funeral ever? I hope to Jesus my casket cracks open."

A sunbeam splashed the church roof. The clouds returned. Fat drops of rain hit the hot dusty ground and quickly subsided.

Thunder followed.

Kissing Mom and Pidge, I ran to the cemetery gate and shook Mr. Boudreaux's hand. Miss Eva blushed as she took his arm and left.

Belladonna slipped a piece of paper into my hand and whispered who it was from before she ran with Amanda to Mom's car.

I read the message.

*Duddy, I'll be in the corner lot facing the church—I had to move on
something fast. I don't have time to explain, so I need you to trust
that I got your back. I'm bringing Cash Doogan to justice, and it'll
clear a path for you to find Brandon and bring him home. I'm sorry
for what I'm gonna have to do to you. Please trust me. Rick.*

Ahead were groups of mourners running to their cars before the rain
caught them. The only ones not rushing to their vehicles were Mickey,
Kate, and Katelyn, who'd managed to remove her dress as she angrily
marched with arms crossed behind her exasperated mother.

"No, Mama, I wanna go to *Family-Fun* Death Party!" Katelyn said
it with such passion (and so many extra syllables) I snorted with laughter.

Who WOULDN'T want to go to *Family-Fun* Death Party?

I read Rick's note three more times.

Move on something fast, he said.

My hands were shaking when I put the note in my pocket. I had one
more thing left to do before I left the cemetery. Taking two lilies from
Granny's casket, I placed one on the bench at her mother's grave and the
other lily at the base of Jonathan Wakefield Shelby's obelisk.

Through the gates, I crossed the near-empty lot, the gravel crunching
under my feet as I headed for the patrol car at the far side of the church.
Pulling Tyler aside, I reminded him about what he needed to do and then
extended my hand to Rick.

After we shook, I left with him.

With no mention of the note Belladonna passed to me, he asked about
the funeral, how I was doing, how the family was coping. We left the main
road for a bumpy farmer's drive and bounced along for a quarter of a mile
inside a cornfield.

A streak of lightning announced an immediate crack of thunder.

The sky opened up.

Rick stopped the car about a hundred yards short of a large farmhouse. He gripped the steering wheel, unable to hide his anxiety. His
breathing was heavy. His eyes were panicky. He kept swallowing a lump
that refused to go down.

Whether he was in trouble or I was in trouble was beside the point—

he couldn't tell me anything about the situation. Sensing he needed me to keep talking, I watched his face. His eyes widened once he caught my gaze and then shifted his chin, fixing it to his shoulder as he threw his eyes to the backseat. That's when I realized three things:

One, I was in very real danger.

Two, Rick was also in danger.

And three, someone else was in the car.

I gave a slow nod telling him I understood. The rain was loud and heavier now, and Rick relaxed as I continued to play along. I made small talk about the preacher and the weather, and the *family-fun* we had at the funeral. Rick mouthed, *'Brace yourself.'*

Silence.

"Alright, g-g-get the fuck out," Rick shouted, turning off the engine. "Open the g-g-goddamn door and stand over there." The rain was cold and the sky was thick as pitch. We were soaked in a few moments. "T-t-t-turn around, Duddy. Raise your arms. DO IT."

Closing my eyes, I did exactly as he told me to do.

Although I didn't see him, I knew that Cash Doogan had jumped out of the car. He punched me in the side of my neck. He just missed my jugular, and I went down as soon as his fist connected. I'd never felt anything like it. I almost lost consciousness. Cash would've continued punching my neck until I stroked or drowned had Rick not lifted me off the ground to put me into a choke-hold.

He let Cash get in a few punches to my face and gut.

A wave of vertigo flipped me upside down, sending its dizziness throughout my brain.

Cash Doogan suddenly lost his interest in me.

Through a curtain of queasy, fuzzy vision, I caught a glimpse of him looking off to the north. Still keeping me in a sleep hold, Rick whispered low in my ear, "We g-got him, D-D-Duddy—we fucking g-g-got him. I'm s-s-sorry for doing this to you."

Rick tightened his grip.

All I heard before blacking out were the sounds of Cash Doogan shouting and swearing, two or three gunshots, and several police sirens in the distance.

•

I woke on a sofa in a strange house.

There was an ice pack on my face over my eye, my cuts were cleaned and wrapped in gauze. It hurt to sit up, but the pain was a dull, general soreness. My ribs weren't broken.

There were voices talking in another room, the kitchen maybe, so I called out. A woman who looked like Hattie brought a fresh compress for my eye and checked my neck. Her skin was a richer brown than my godmother's, and she didn't have as many freckles under her eyes, but her smile was just as warm and bright.

After checking the bandages, she said, "It's nice to meet you, Dean Adam," she said, looking at each of my eyes with a penlight. "It's nice to put a face to the name, but you look so much like your daddy I could pick you out of a crowd—same handsome face, green eyes, same jaw."

"Yes'm," I said, wincing. "So, I've been told."

"Hmm, I'm sure you were told something," she said. "My name is Queenie. I'm a nurse—you won't need to see a doctor unless your bruises turn black," she said, leaving the living room. "Be right back, baby—just sit tight for a minute."

"Wait, who brought me here—?"

But Queenie already had gone. Leaning against the sofa, I looked around the room. Being there felt familiar, like hearing an old song from your childhood. A music box was sitting on the coffee table next to my wallet and keys. Jesus, what the hell happened to it? It was filthy, busted, cracked—its lid off the hinges, so I doubted it worked at all.

How did I get here?

What happened to Rick?

How long have I been out?

Where were my clothes?

I hated having no answers—

Just let it wash over you, Duddy-baby.

When a scratchy voice began talking behind me, I thought that maybe Queenie had brought in a music box and started the recording. I didn't turn around to see if it was there—I had no reason to think it wasn't.

I closed my eyes and listened.

"In 1918, a young woman named Echo Freedman married a handsome young man named Jasper Lincoln, a sharecropper who worked Shelby farmland in Cantonment. In September of that year, JJ Doogan violated Echo as her husband lay dying two feet away from her.

"In June 1919, Margaret Shelby and her two widow sisters hacked JJ Doogan to death with two hoes and a shovel on the spot they was fixin' to put a new barn. Next day, when Earle Adam Doogan came to the farm, there was no sign of JJ, Echo Freedman, or the baby."

There was no static when the story ended.

Silence.

When I heard the floor creak, I turned around.

Sitting in a rocking chair behind me was an old woman, a bitty thing, all wrinkles and sinews. Her wispy hair was the color of blanched bone and her skin was burnished and dark, as if she'd not known a day out of the ancient Egyptian sun. Cataracts made her eyes like ceramic orbs, with a ghostly gaze searching only ever beyond.

"Hello, young man," she said. "You feelin' better?"

"Yes'm," I replied. "Thank you. I'm Duddy Doogan."

The old woman laughed. "You know who I am even if you don't realize it," she said. "When Earle Adam Doogan murdered her son and husband, Harriet Freedman faked her death and changed her name to Confederate Jasmine," she said. "When Echo Freedman gave up one of her twins for Justice Wilson to raise as his own son, she faked her own death and raised the girl on the other side of the river. Echo Freedman died when Margaret Shelby my boy, so I called myself Lady River."

It was a mallet to my heart.

"You're Cotton Wilson's mother," I said. "You're Hattie's grandmother—you're Confederate Jasmine's daught—you're alive!"

Lady River laughed. "Lord Almighty, I never thought I'd see a white boy turn whiter than my albino son," she said, shoulders bouncing. "Yes, and here I still live and breathe too. The best way to save lives was to hide our chirren, let the river keep them apart 'til God decided it was time to reunite them. It took some years. 'Free at last, free at last—thank God Almighty, we are free at last.'"

Her light filled the space around her with *nothin' but*, and when she took my hands my skin erupted in electric tingles all over. "You better brace yourself, young man—it's time you heard the rest."

We sat at a little table in the kitchen.

I'd forgotten all about the earlier part of my day.

As Queenie filled my stomach with her food, Lady River filled my soul with her words. "We kept separate lives until Earle Adam's sons and their sons stopped hunting us. After my daughter had Queenie, a man named Alan Doogan killed her and her husband. He killed Hattie Louise's mama and uncle. He would've killed Hattie if Cotton Wilson hadn't left her with the Shelbys."

Queenie took Lady River's hand. "God's plan to reunite the Perdido River isn't easy to understand—don't forget the man I married gave you a great-grandson."

Lady River nodded. "Where are he and Miss Thing?"

Sharon walked into the kitchen. "Waiting for you to stop spinning, Grandma River," she said, handing me the broken music box, my wallet, and my keys. "Your suit was ruined, so those clothes will have to do until we get you to Cantonment. I'll explain later."

You can imagine my surprise when Joseph Conrad walked into the kitchen. "At least I know how I got here—and whose clothes I'm wearing," I said, sheepishly as I shook his hand. "I'm sorry."

Joseph Conrad smiled. "Bet you thought you were up Styx River without a coin for the Boatman," he said, looking to Sharon. "Let's go, girly—Darl and I got work to do."

Queenie hugged me warmly before Lady River squeezed my face between her hands. "Your grandfather saved Hattie's life just as Margaret Shelby saved my son's life—I can hear Dr. King's words clearly now. God speed, young man."

Sharon and Joseph Conrad ushered me quickly from the house and into the front seat of the car in the driveway. I had no idea where I was, other than a strange subdivision with friendly houses and manicured lawns. There was a golf course and lots of trees. It wasn't quite twilight, which meant I hadn't been gone long enough to be missed.

"Should I ask questions now or later?" I asked.

"Later would be best," Sharon replied.

Joseph Conrad laughed. "You might as well pretend like you have all the answers until things blow over."

Sharon laughed.

"All we can do is tell you what we know," she said. "It's not much, but it'll be enough until you're back on the Florida side of the river."

THE TOWER

Chapter 13

The Truth Will Set You Back a Day

Cantonment, Florida—Tuesday Night

We stopped on the shoulder of Muscogee Road. Around the bend ahead was my grandparents' house, which bustled with twice as many people as last night. As to what happened earlier today, there was good news and bad news.

The good news: Rick Shelby had cobbled together a last minute plan to use me as bait to get Cash Doogan to that middle-of-nowhere farm, a front for his Perdido River meth hub. Darl overheard his brother talking about killing me after the funeral and told Rick. Darl and Joseph Conrad carried me to safety as soon as Rick's sleep hold knocked me out. When the raid was finally done, Cash Doogan would rot in a prison cell until Kingdom Come—I prayed Rick wouldn't do the same.

When I got out of the car, Sharon handed me an envelope. "I'll be back in two hours, so bring a change of clothes—or two, considering what you'll be doing. You won't be back until late tomorrow night. Go show your brother what Darl found."

And that was the bad news. Darl had found the broken music box in his father's (my uncle's) mobile home back in an Alabama swamp off the Styx River. He'd found the diving watch with a sun charm clipped to the band, caked with mud but still ticking, and the music box, also caked with mud but very broken. Dad's remains were in the mobile home too, but

Darl thought I should be the one to retrieve them. I didn't agree with him, but when he told me what his father was capable of doing to himself, to his things, and to others, I changed my mind. Darl was now taking me to his father so that I had a chance to bring what was left of mine home to Mom.

See? Death IS family.

"Why do you need me tonight?" I asked Sharon.

Joseph Conrad snorted. "Your boy's thick, girly."

"Ignore him," Sharon said to me. "Go read that letter."

When the car's red taillights disappeared, I headed to the house, wending around dozens of cars crammed along the road. Avoiding the rush of people gathered in the front, I went around back, each step its own thought and heavier than the step before it.

My neck hurt like hell, and my gut throbbed from the ache of a thousand sit-ups. I felt powerful magic at work—in the back of my mind, I heard Hattie telling me about fools who put on shoes before pants.

Heading across the yard, I ducked under the clothesline and went around the corner of the house. I sat on the concrete slab next to the garden hose. The window there had a soft, brilliant reading light far from prying eyes.

> *Duddy, I'm sorry I left you stranded. I was sick. I was angry at myself for getting lost in you, for letting you into my heart, body, and soul. JC did ruin a lovely moment, but who knew YOU were such a jealous monster face? It's partly my fault, and I might've been flattered had I not been barfing all morning. Even so, I never should've said those horrid things. I have no excuse. I was sick and I let my temper get the best of me. You deserve better. Let me make it up to you tonight. Let me give you what you've given me. Let me show you I haven't done anything to your heart but keep it safe. Sharon*

At the end of the note was a lengthy, very detailed, and alarmingly graphic postscript that filled the rest of the page. Darl and Joseph Conrad had a plan tomorrow, and Sharon had a plan tonight, one so vividly crafted and plotted I had to take a cold shower. Fucky-lucky me—the garden hose was right there.

After a wash and scrub, I tiptoed naked through the yard and enlisted Tyler's help to fetch my things and a towel. Dressed and ready for my night with Sharon, I joined Mike on the porch when he started an Eagles set. Tyler gave me the stink-eye all the way through 'Hotel California.' Finally, I said, "Stop it—I'm not that late."

Tyler's eye continued. "I was this close—thank God Mom's been too high to pay attention to anything."

Uncle John raised his mug, a lit blunt in the nipple. "Mike, don't look at me like I just kicked your Legos, son—it's not my first rodeo. I'd offer you a suck on my tit, but—"

Mike grimaced. "No, Dad—no, no, no, no, no, no."

Poking her head outside, Aunt Clara whistled.

"Duddy-darlin'—a word."

My great aunts were sitting on the bed waiting for me in Grandpa's old room. I sat on the floor and waited for one of them to say something. They both looked nervous. Finally, Miss Eva said, "We're ready to go, Nephew, but my ugly sister and I wanted to see you before Mr. Boudreaux took us home."

Aunt Clara nodded. "You and Mike better sing that same goddamn song for me when my table's ready—vicer-verser for Eva too. Duddy, you know I'm about as psychic as Goddamn Tater most days, but I saw something in your cup the night of that storm."

Taking her hand, I said, "Before you say anything, I love that you women have the Gift, but I don't give a flying crocodile shit about what you saw. Over the past two weeks, I've been hit daily with something I didn't know was coming, and I wouldn't want it any different."

Aunt Clara smiled. "Pidge said you'd surprise me," she said. "I told the little twat she was a hubby-killing ignoramus, but I was wrong. Eva, you talk—I got emotional."

"Death is family, you old bat."

"Damnation station," Aunt Clara said. "You buck-toothed pig fucker, making me cry—this is worse than the funeral."

Putting on my best *devil-thinking* face, I said, "Hey, I've been having carnal knowledge of a Perdido River woman since Memorial Day." It was the first thing that popped in my head, but it got Aunt Clara laughing.

"Just when I thought my admiration couldn't go higher."

"Sluts, sluts, everywhere sluts," Miss Eva said.

Aunt Clara flipped up her patch. "Hello, Pot—I'm Kettle."

"Ignore her, Nephew—I've known for years this old cow's heart was gold beneath the tar, bourbon, and skidmarks. Did you put the music box in a safe place? Good. Cotton Wilson and his secret drawers and puzzle shelves—when I sit on a chair, I don't want my fat ass falling into Narnia."

Aunt Clara pulled the patch down. "All right, Duddy-darlin', I'll see you when I see you." Without lingering, Pirate Clarabelle Wilson left the room. Miss Eva got to her feet and punched my arm.

"Proud of you," she said, rubbing my back in a quick circle. "You better sing that hymn for me when I'm dead, or I'll haunt you."

She left before I could tell her she already did.

Saying goodbye made my knees buckle.

I fell to the carpeted floor with a thunk.

I sat there staring at the bottom drawer of Grandpa's dresser. Opening it, I found stacks of old photos, and albums of old photos, and sleeves of old photos. I popped the cracked rubber band on one of the stacks and shuffled through images of Dad arrested in time, each one a singular moment of joy lost forever to the ether. The last picture in the stack was his smiling face staring at me.

"I'm coming, Dad," I whispered.

Closing the drawer, I put the picture in my pocket and headed to Belladonna's old room. I opened the door to see Tyler on the floor with a Ouija board on his legs.

"Where'd you get that?" I asked.

"Closet," he said, tossing his head. "Amanda and I tried using it, but we kept getting some weirdo who loved the Bee Gees. Anyway, Mom wants to see you about something. Oh, and you left that on the porch." He pointed to the broken music box at his knee.

"Take that and wait by the T-Bird. Amanda too."

Tyler stretched the muscles on his arms. "God, I am ready for a workout—this sitting around drinking all day isn't good for me. Why's this box so dirty, boss?"

"I'll explain when I get out there," I told him.

I went to the noisy bedroom next door. The family witches were sitting on the floor (sans the two great aunts). Clothes were everywhere—robes, pants, slippers, shoes, blouses, skirts, hats, muumuus, and shawls. Belladonna wore a nightgown around her neck like a boa. Mickey wore a pair of Granny's underwear on her head. Pidge had the cowboy hat.

The others also wore something, but the bright pair of pajamas Mom wore took the prize. Packed in the seat was a fake butt my grandmother bought herself at Frederick's of Hollywood. "Sugar, I wanna tell your birth story," she said, taking my hand. "Let me do this. Here, sit next to Cowboy Piglet." When Mom finished, she said, "Shit, I forgot to say Madame Fynoe licked your body clean and ate the placenta. Don't you make that face—I swear to you that cud-chewing dairy cow was my second midwife. It's a true made-up part to the story."

"HA! Happy Birthday, Duddy-doodle-doo!"

"Y'all are high as kites," I said.

"I know, sugar—where're you going?"

"I met a woman and I'm going to spend the night with her." When the applause died, I looked at Pidge. "You and I are gonna have some words, capish?"

Pidge tipped her hat. "Lookin' forward to it."

"Madame Fynoe licking the baby clean," I said, leaving the room with a grin. Miss Eva didn't name her beloved bovine before entering her in the county fair. Uncle John was double-checking the entry form and spotted a blank for the animal's name. When he asked for the cow's name, Miss Eva replied, "Hmm, damn 'f I know."

Another *family-famous* legend was born.

Tyler was smoking next to the T-Bird. Its lid torn from one of its hinges, the music box sat silently on the trunk. Dad's diving watch lay just as silently beside it. I lit a cigarette and sat on the bumper.

"Uncle John and Mike turn in?" I asked.

Tyler nodded. "They're leaving early," he said. "And you don't have to explain anything."

Amanda was sitting on a root beneath the Graveyard Tree nearby. Getting to her feet, she tossed her cigarette and wiped her eyes—she'd been crying. "So, you know where Dad's body is," she said, wiping her wet face. "Is that what you're doing tomorrow? It'll be good to know for certain. I won't tell Mom—be careful, Duddy."

She kissed me on my cheek and headed to the house. Stopping at the gate, she grabbed the cord to the 'Beware of Dog' bell and started pulling the thing like it was supper time on the prairie. The cord tore away, tattering to frayed string pieces in her hand. The echo of the last ring faded into silence. When Amanda looked at us, the old nails holding the post broke and sent the bell, stake, and sign backward with a loud clanking crash. "Fuck-a-duck," she said, laughing as she went inside the house.

Two years had passed since we left the grounds of Magnolia and said goodbye to Brandon Doogan. *Here we go again.*

"Tyler, can you stay until I get back?" I asked.

He looked hard at me. "Duddy, why are you doing this?"

"Because I volunteered."

"Bullshit, boss—I call fucking bullshit," he spat. "Can you promise me you'll be safe?"

"No."

"Can you promise me you won't get hurt?"

"No."

"Can you at least promise to come back alive? I don't care if you lie— promise me."

"I promise," I told him. "Tyler, it's a short walk in the swamp and a quick boat ride back."

"I bet that's what Dad thought—don't die, boss"

After Tyler went back to the house, I took another drag of my cigarette and looked at the broken box. Rusty cogs, a filthy note comb, busted springs, mirror shards, bent rods, ruined wires, cracked casings—if there was a recording, it was gone. I was curious about that one more than the others I had yet to hear. But then, even if it were intact, how was I supposed to play it? I still hadn't a clue as to how the thing worked.

Maybe I could try tinkering with it tomorrow.

I slipped Dad's mud caked silver diving watch in my pocket and tucked the box in the trunk beside the one Miss Eva gave me. I doubt Hattie knew Dad had one, or if she did that it'd ever be found. Hell, there could've been a secret collection of boxes she didn't know existed—it's not like Cotton Wilson was the forthcoming type.

I had to assume there were two music boxes to get, and Pidge had one at her place in Flomaton. So, who had the other one? Staring into space at the ass-end of my T-Bird wasn't going to reveal that mystery, so I grabbed my overnight bag and headed to the curve of Muscogee Road.

•

Sharon banked the car hard right down a dirt road. Where we were going exactly was a surprise, but she promised I would love it because the river was nearby. "Almost there," she said, squeezing my fingers. "It's hard to see it at night. It's shaped like a tombstone."

"Death is family," I said.

Sharon seemed more at ease tonight. She looked as if she'd suddenly reached the end of fulfilling a long and grueling obligation. She kept smiling, which made her so achingly beautiful I couldn't keep my eyes off her. I was ready for my head and heart to take a rest from tragedy and secrets. Tonight, I didn't want to shoulder any burdens.

The car stopped abruptly. "The river's a few yards away. If I'd kept driving, we'd be wet. I put two cars in that river last year," she said. "Come, on—I need your help."

"This is heavy," I said, huffing and wincing in pain a few minutes later. "What are you trying to keep out, bears?"

"Lift and swing your end, and pull the metal fence back to the tree trunk," she said, climbing back in the car. "Don't let go 'til you see my tail lights. It'll pop back on its own."

Pop back, she'd said.

The spring-loaded fence suddenly screeching from my hands was one thing—the sonic boom it made upon slamming into its metal pocket was altogether different from a pop.

Sharon laughed as we headed down a root-strewn road lined with thick brush. Bats chased flying beetles and horseflies, their mad flight patterns crisscrossing the car's high beams. The road sloped down into the south end of a large clearing about three acres across. Sitting on a small hill at its center was a large Florida cracker house with a wraparound front porch. Sharon turned off the engine and pressed the button of a remote control clipped to her visor.

Suddenly, the house was bathing in lights.

"We're here."

"Where's here?" I asked. "I know this place. I've never seen it. Why do I know it?"

Sharon took my hand and led me up the steps. "You know it because you know who lived here: Justice Wilson, his wife Ruth, his albino son Ewell Curtis. I'd be happy to show you where Confederate Jasmine kept her herbal remedies, where Margaret Shelby hid her pipe and flask, the small schoolhouse in the backyard—what is it? Besides the obvious shit."

It felt like standing on holy ground. The shock of recognition hit me like a blast of icy air in the face. I couldn't stop the tears welling in my eyes or the corners of my mouth from trembling. Sharon leaned her head against my arm and rubbed my lower back.

My composure regained, I wiped my eyes and said, "If it's all the same to you, I don't want another history lesson or secret revelation tonight. My brain's done. My heart's done."

"I'm more interested in your body naked in my bed."

"What do you mean *your* bed?"

Shaking her keys, Sharon said, "It's my house, and so everything in it, including the bed, is also mine," she said, unlocking the door. "That goes double for the man who—"

I picked her up in my arms and carried her over the threshold. Tonight, there was nothing I needed her to tell me and there was nothing I needed to hear. All I wanted was directions to the room with this bed she'd mentioned. When I asked for them, Sharon closed the front door with her foot, dropping her keys as she kissed me.

With eyes closed and lips pressed firmly to hers, I bumped into every stick of furniture as she guided me there without saying a word.

Chapter 14

A Light in the Heart of Darkness

Cantonment, Florida—Wednesday, June 8, 2005

As exhausted and sore as I was the day before, I was a new man to-day. Although we hardly slept, I felt rested, relieved, and holistically satisfied, balls to brain. The first thing I saw when I opened my eyes was Sharon's face.

"Morning, sleepyhead," she said, kissing my neck. "Here, drink this. It's good and cold, and you're sweating like a pig."

"This better not be moonshine—ooh, river water."

Sharon laughed. "I've been up since noon watching you sleep. You were cute as a bug's ear 'til you started dreaming—Jesus H. Cricket, your eyeballs were going back and forth like demon windshield wipers. What were you were dreaming?"

"Can't remember—something about ghosts," I said, wincing as I sat upright. "I'm gonna be sore for days. How'd you get this house?"

Sharon smoothed my arm. "Cotton Wilson owned it and renovated it when my sister Alice fell in love with him and got pregnant," she said, matter-of-factly. "She wanted to leave Flomaton to have her baby closer to home. Lady River wanted them both closer to home. But then he died in the fire, and then Alice had the baby and hanged herself. House went to me. I'm rarely here. I never had a man stay over before either—well, besides Joseph Conrad and his friends."

Taking her hand, I said. "It occurred to me that I hardly know anything about you. It doesn't seem real, being with you here and feeling like
this. I couldn't care less about swamp walkin' with Darl when I haven't
discovered you yet."

"You discovered me plenty, Midnight Cowboy," Sharon teased.
"You'll have to wait, Mr. Doogan. I love waiting. It shows me the differ-
ence between what I want and what I'd sell my soul to have. How long I
wait measures the distance from my heart to my soul, like an astrolabe
does the stars." She took off her T-shirt, and after wiping my chest with it,
she tossed it to the floor. "I say we swim naked in the river until it's time
to go. C'mon, let's get dirty while we're getting clean."

Oh, this woman—Heaven, help me.

You'd better believe I chased her from the house.

Later, as I sat naked on the riverbank, I gazed at a melting green
willow nearby. Leafy stems dipped in and out the water with the breeze
and seemed to be dancing with Sharon, who stood inside the green dome
washing her body. As I watched her bathe, I listened to the river swirling
eddies and little currents that babbled and splashed around her. These
were the sounds of blood, the words of hate and love mingled into the liq-
uid symphony of life here.

My thirst was deep, and the names and sins of this river were water.
I drank them all.

    Baby.

        Sugar.

            Slut.

                Witch.

                    Mother.

                        Nigger.

                          Bastard.

An enormous Graveyard Tree stood above me. Its branches and spin-
dly drapes of gray, like the weaves in a latticework, seemed to press the sun
against the sky, holding its light there like a dream catcher. With the tastes
of earth and water on my tongue, I felt young and alive. I loved afternoons, when the summer part of the day teeters on the brink of autumn.

My favorite thing in the world was watching the sinking sun turn my blue sky blood orange.

"Duddy—look what I found!" And there was Sharon, naked as a baby and screaming in delight as she swung on an old rope over the river. Dropping feet first into the deep rushing water, she let the current carry her to the shallows where I was sunning myself. She spat a mouthful of water and demanded that I get off my boulder.

"You're sunburned," I told her. "You're pink as a labia."

"Nice image," she said, pulling me into the icy eddies.

In and out of each other, we rolled and swam between Florida and Alabama, measuring the distances from our heads and hearts to the destiny pulling us toward the Styx River.

•

The Baldwin County Sheriff's Department had a small satellite office nearby. Darl and Joseph Conrad were waiting for us in the parking lot. It wasn't a surprise to see him there after what happened yesterday, but he seemed anxious—brave as hell, but anxious. Shaking his hand, I told him he wasn't the only one. "If you hadn't held back your brother's arm at the bar, I'd be less pretty, so thanks for that too."

Darl frowned, not knowing how to take the compliment. "Well, I ain't my brother." To Joseph Conrad, he said, "I don't hate black folk. Don't hate nobody really. A sumbitch can be any color—most the ones I know are white as feather down and dumber than a Catholic priest lookin' for love in a beauty parlor. I better load this gear."

Joseph Conrad looked to Sharon and me. "Cash Doogan took Rick Shelby hostage, and there was a standoff until about an hour ago," he said. "Cash put bullets into more than a few men, including Rick, before he put the gun into his mouth. Rick's at Sacred Heart in the ICU—they don't know if he'll make it. DEA and Customs are combing the watershed for storage, product, labs, and people now that they cut off the snake's head."

Sharon touched Darl's shoulder. "Sorry about Cash."

Darl closed the trunk.

"I guess somebody has to be," he said. "All I ever done is try to keep my daddy safe after Cash put him back to work making that shit. Daddy was just like Uncle Hank, batshit from the get-go. Crank and Cash made him worse, but I didn't care. He got nobody but me to look after him. I always tried to hide Daddy in one of his swamp trailers. Cash hated when I did it. He'd beat me into blood sleep unless Rick was there to stop him. I'm glad it's over. Death is family, I guess. Isn't that what them Shelby women say all the time?"

I grinned. "Yeah, they do."

"'Cause it's truth," Darl said with a grin. "Cash swore he'd kill me in my sleep. He did and said worse things to Daddy. It's how he kept you in line. I'm glad he's gone." Darl's voice broke. "I feel like I ha'n't slept in years. Poor Rick knew it was gonna be a bad scene once Cash figured out who turned on him. Rick was brave and wanted to fix what he'd done. He wanted redemption, I reckon."

"Maybe his blood told him he could have it," I said, smiling at Sharon. "Maybe his blood told him he had to go through with what needed to be done. Maybe he made a promise."

"We ought to head to the dock," Darl said.

Joseph Conrad sat in the backseat with me. It was it easy to like the man beside me. I could tell he was someone to have at your side when furtive, secret dangerous things needed doing. The plan was simple—we go to Dale Doogan's trailer and keep him busy until a crew of Baldwin County's finest arrived with paramedics.

"Remind me why I agreed to this," I whispered.

He chuckled. "You're showing off for the female behind that wheel up there—oh, don't even glare at me, Miss Daisy. Eyes on the road while you're driving me. Anyway, I'm leaving for Italy tonight. Sharon doesn't need to be in that swamp. Darl needs you, and you need him. Quit being so damn thick."

We turned down a road that bounced us under two flanking maples and a dead peach tree. Grasshoppers jumped and danced amidst choruses of toads, crickets, and tree frogs. Dust coated the tall grasses of the narrow drive that dipped beneath a mossy elm into a clearing of hair green willows. The boathouse sat on the river beyond a row of sassafras shrubs and jasmine.

We parked and followed the sloping path to a rickety dock. Hanging from a rusty lamp was a crippled wind chime and a broken wooden sign that read, *Styx River Ferryboat Landing.* Darl and Joseph Conrad brought the bags of swamp gear to the crumbling pier. Sharon asked what the metal sticks were for.

"Depth checks, mostly," Darl said, spraying us with insect repellent. "Keeps you steady as you walk the spoils, pods, and mud flats. Good for whacking snakes and gators, if you need to protect yourself. I've used 'em as stilts in deep sudden quicksand a time or two."

Sharon shook her head.

"Quicksand, gators, Dale Doogan—which one is worse?"

Darl snorted. "Depends if Daddy's tweaked," he said, putting on his gear. He helped me with mine, inspecting my chest waders and boots, checking for holes around my feet and waist. "It's thigh-deep in a few places, but you won't drown or get leeches," he said, tying a bandanna around his head. "It's hot as hog balls once we're in—least we get a river ride first. Near-to-sunset is my favorite time to be on the Styx."

"All we do is stay put?" Sharon asked. "Doesn't seem fair."

"Life isn't fair," Joseph Conrad mumbled. "We can fish."

"How far's the walk?" I asked.

"Half-hour or so," Darl replied, inspecting me again. "There's one way into the swamp and a hun'erd different small trails that go deeper into Alabama than most folk'll ever know. We ain't taking a safe way either—those trails take hours, but I do stop an' look at orchids and birds."

Joseph Conrad grinned. "You know an orchid trail?"

Darl blushed. "It's a hard hike—lots of roots and bog holes and gators. I'd be happy to take you along next time I go, if you want."

Sharon shot a look at Joseph Conrad. "Just because you're going to Italy doesn't mean you're the swamp master," she said, turning to Darl. "Do they all go to Dale's?"

Darl shook his head. "No, but it's real easy to find the ones that do," he said. "That's what I think happened to poor Brandon. Daddy always shoots first an' asks questions later if I ain't there. Alrighty, we got drinking water, repellent, walkin' sticks, breadcrumb flares, and these old baby walkies I hope don't die in the next two hours."

Sharon took my hand. "What if this doesn't work?"

Darl looked as if he'd never thought it wouldn't. With a crooked smile, he said, "Swamp walkin' switches on survivor instincts so, we'll think of something. Nothing bad'll happen, Sharon—a half-hour or so there, a half-hour or so waiting there. The sheriff's fan boats only got a ten-minute trip over the flares. Now, where's our ferry to hell?"

Joseph Conrad pointed to the boat tied to the rotten pier. Sharon and I laughed. Darl did too, but more for politeness' sake (I doubted he understood how funny it was that our boat was called *Heart of Darkness*). A breeze blew off the dark water.

And then Darl quietly said: "Going up that river was like traveling back to the beginnings of the world, when vegetation rioted on the earth and the big trees were kings. The long stretches of the waterway ran on into the gloom. You lost your way 'til you thought yourself bewitched, cut off from everything. And there were moments when the past came back, and you remembered with wonder amongst this strange world of plants, and water, and silence. And this stillness of life did not in the least resemble a peace." He turned red. "I butchered it," he said. "I get real nervous public speaking."

And so, it came to pass that my journey on the River of Hate into the Alabama underworld began, as did my vow never to judge another man by his Southern accent again.

•

We'd left the cool breezes and currents of the Styx River for the viscous soups of its secret marshes. The air was warm, heavy, and sluggish. I'd never been so thirsty in my life—I wanted to suckle my canteen like a bottle. The lush growth of vines and reeds, and fat mosses dripping low from the tops of cypress trees, was a canopy of weaves that blocked sunlight and stifled breath.

I somehow managed to keep up with Darl's pace.

"Duddy," he said, as he lead me onward, "there's a patch of old roots in the mud 'bout six yards ahead that'll snap your foot if you don't tread lightly. We'll be at the far end of the yard after that. And ignore that moccasin swimming behind you—go slow an' he'll pass on by."

"Jesus Christ, that's a big one," I said.

Darl chuckled. "Nah, he's just a baby snake."

When we reached the other side of the hidden root trap, it was easier going with better footing. We went up a steep incline to a clearing with gaps in the trees directly above it. I was about to ask where the trailer was when Darl pressed a finger to his lips and guided me behind a fallen tree, its trunk hollowed from years of rot, and families of lichens and big red mushrooms.

"Keep low and quiet—on your belly," he whispered, craning his neck and grabbing a stone. He threw and ducked when it left his hand. And then a barrage of gunfire split the air into pieces and sent thousands of hidden crawling things into fits of escape. "Wait—he'll shoot if we don't wait," Darl said.

When the insects and frogs started to chirp and croak again, Darl got to his feet and cupped his mouth. He then made a bird call, a loud cawing-clicking sound from the back of his throat that was as eerie as it was incredible. He repeated the call and crouched beside me.

Moments later, the same call came back to us. Darl breathed easier now. Helping me to my feet, he motioned me to follow but to keep quiet. "Daddy, it's Darl," he shouted, using that same bird-calling to make the words. Turning, he explained, "Cash never learned Daddy's calls. That's how Daddy knows it's me, you see. Lemme go an' talk to him—wait 'til I call you."

"Darl, I can't even see the fucking trailer."

"That's 'cause I did a good job hidin' it, Duddy—stay put," he said. "That wasn't no BB gun he was shooting, and he's got a homemade rocket launcher he's been itchin' to use too."

"Why does he even have guns?"

"I keep taking 'em away, but he's got stashes throughout the swamp," Darl said. "He's never pulled anything on me, but that don't mean a thing. It be like keepin' a lion for a pet—all it takes is the one time he suddenly scratches your brain outta your skull."

"Darl, you can't guarantee I'll be safe?"

"Only guarantee in life is death takin' you at the end."

My hands shook so much from unsteady nerves that I spent most of that time kneading them and making fists. I followed a strange bird call to a dwelling that was little more than a shell of rusted walls and molded tin roof. Darl waited for me at the top of the rotted stairs.

"He's been up for at least three days—that's good," he told me, pulling a deck of Bicycle poker cards from a leather strip around his neck. "Here, he's been into betting games lately and might not give you the remains without playing for 'em. Make the stakes high when you bet something—you'll win no matter what."

"What the hell do I have that's worth anything?"

Darl smiled sadly.

"He's crazy, Duddy—remember what we talked 'bout on the way here? Remember what I told you about how he gets?" He patted my shoulder. "Sheriff'll be here in thirty-forty minutes—ignore the evil and just be with him. It'll take a while, but he'll settle. Here."

Darl took out another bandanna and a small pouch of dried flowers and herbs. He wrapped it inside the bandanna and tied it to my wrist. "Keep breathing that in, Duddy. You're walkin' into squalor you ain't never seen. Them herbs will keep you relaxed and your sinuses as cleared up as can be. It's noxious as a Farm Hill hooker's yeast infection in there."

With a deep breath, I opened the door and went inside the trailer. It was worse than any landfill. My breathing bag immediately went to my face. I fought the urge to vomit as I took deep breaths, deep-deep breaths. I looked around.

There was not a stick of intact furniture, just old ripped sleeping bags, broken bookshelves, shredded carpet covered in dirt and shit and undiscovered molds, bits of bedding with urine-soaked feathers from ripped pillows. Parts of the roof had fallen into what had been the living room. Empty cans littered the floor—there was a blanket of oozing metal tins six inches thick.

Rats were everywhere. And cockroaches the size of dump trucks scurried over the unwashed dishes and garbage bags piled on the counters and sink with no bottom or plumbing.

The rest of the trailer was a large makeshift laboratory filled with vials, tubes and beakers, and unlit or used up burners. Bags of chemicals lay in stacks beside the broken cabinets. Dale Doogan sat hunched over what was left of a table in his utterly unlivable mobile home. He was naked and filthy, oblivious as he cut chunks of white crystal chalk with a long razor blade comb. He argued with himself as he sliced, like an insane chef mincing ingredients for crazy stew.

He's not all there, Duddy.

Just use his broken mind against him.

"Uncle Dale—I'm Brandon Doogan's son."

Dale ignored me and kept cutting, saying nothing as he worked. His leg began to bounce. The up and down motion became a jerking series of twitches. He started giggling for no reason and continued cutting. His skin was pale, the color of grub worm, and his eyes were set back in his skull. He wore a listless, toothless smile.

"Pretty, pretty boy," he said. "So pretty-pretty, this boy of Brandon's. Such a dreamy doll. What's his name?"

"My name's Dean Adam Doogan, and—"

"I HEARD YOU—I'M TALKING TO HIM," Dale shouted, leaping from his chair. He grabbed my throat and shoved me against the wall. He looked at my neck for a long moment and pressed his lips there, breathing in the scent my skin.

Dale reeked of rotted meat and soured shit.

Then he began to grind against my leg.

"Pretty-pretty doll doesn't speak 'til Dale marks him, makes him worthy," he whispered, his fetid breath quickening. "Not much longer for the mark to come. Yes, pretty boy doll—come for you, pretty-pretty. Big Dale's juicy juices—just—like—there, now. Much better for pretty-pretty doll and Uncle Dale 'til the next marking time. What do you say, pretty-pretty?"

Darl had warned me about this. He'd warned me about many things. One of the reasons I wore rubber waders and a heavy long sleeved shirt had as much to do with being inside this space with this man as it did with the muddy trail here. There was nothing to do but pretend it didn't happen and continue with the visit until it was over.

"Uncle Dale, thanks for marking me."

Dale grinned in surprise.

"Gratitude makes pretty-pretty a bee-YOU-tee-full boy," he said. "Where are my manners? Come sit at my table-table, so we can visit. Had

I known company was coming I would've straightened the house. Dear Dean Adam, sad would-be son of Beautiful Brandon, our tragic Doogan since Hank Doogan. Yes, murder, murder most foul is what happened to Hank."

Uncle Dale burst into tears. "I'll sit on the floor—you sit in my chair," he said, weeping uncontrollably as he plopped down. Abruptly stopping, he played with his penis, pointing it at one of the cabinets, and pissed. "Dale doesn't like it when pretty-pretty boys say words that are lies. I know what you did, pretty-pretty. Tell me what you did, the truth. I heard it in a music box. I had to take it apart to make it play the words. Someone stole it from me. But I remember Beautiful Brandon said the words—he told me what you did-did, Duddy-Duddy. Would you like the head that came with the box?"

"Yes, Uncle Dale."

"I had to hide it after the thief took my music box," he said, still holding his penis. "No such thing as free-free, my pretty-pretty, so we'll play a game. If you win you get the prize—I know it's why you're here, Dear Dean Adam."

"Uncle Dale, do you play poker?" I asked.

His eyes widened. "Ooh, high-stakes poker sounds fun, pretty-pretty," he said. "But Dale needs to test you. First, a test of truth. Second, a test of strength. And third, a test of trust."

"Of course, Uncle Dale," I said, drawing air through my wrist bag. "Test one."

Dale blushed as he ran a finger down my leg. "Did you kill my brother? It's okay if you did because he would've killed you good and dead. Just tell Dale the truth."

Swallowing, I said, "I honestly don't know."

Silence.

Dale nodded. "Good answer," he said, reaching for a cardboard box beside him. "Test two, pretty-pretty—here, open this tiny baggie and snort the dream powder. Go on, it's this week's batch, one of my better ones. It won't burn or bleed you. It'll take you on a zippy trippy trip—time can't find you. I like to put mine in my nose and eyes, and the back of my throat when I don't use my other openings. Go, on—test of strength."

"The whole bag?"

Dale blinked innocently. "What do you think?"

I opened the packet and poured the white dust into my palm. My experience with this and other similar substances told me I was holding three doses, maybe four. When I asked him what failing the test meant, he pointed a pistol at my face.

"Don't fail the test, Dale says—test of strength requires an A+ to pass, Dear Dean Adam. Up your nose with a rubber hose."

My bowels seemed suddenly quite watery.

With a curt nod, I snorted the white powder in my palm.

"It doesn't burn," I said.

Dale clapped free hand to pistol grip. "And now, the test of trust," he said, flipping open the cylinder to empty all but one of its bullets. "There, and now we spin and spin—no whammies, no whammies—STOP!" He handed me the gun. "Into your mouth the barrel goes—here, let me pull the trigger. It's like a jack-in-the-box. Ready? One-two-three...BANG!"

Click.

"BANG! BANG!" Dale shouted.

My heart pounding and my skull swimming in terror, I watched as he did the same thing to himself. Cylinder spin, barrel in the mouth, pull of the trigger.

Click.

Silence.

"Congratulations," Dale said with a satisfied sigh. "We passed the tests, so let's play a hand of poker. Stakes are high, pretty-pretty. You call the high stakes we play."

"The remains of Brandon Doogan," I said, shuffling the deck.

"That's a fine win for pretty-pretty," Dale said, clapping. "Yes, we should give the Brandon trophy. He's in a secret place. Stakes, pretty-pretty—you lose, then Dale gets to mark you on the inside. Yes, Dale marks Dean Adam, named after Grand Wizard Earle Adam Doogan, who begat JJ Doogan, who begat Alan Arthur Doogan, unholy father of Dale, Hank, Silas, and secret Brandon, bless his severed head. Yes, mark you on the inside 'til it hurts inside."

Dale snorted another packet of powder and wiped his nose.

My heart began to race now—the inevitable high was about to envelop me. As I shuffled the cards, my mind began to clear and sharpen. The fog of fear and racing disorganized thoughts were ending. Replacing them were razor sharp order, clarity, and focus. Powerful and sexual and infinite—I was becoming a demigod now.

I know what to call this lightning dust.

"Kingmaker, Uncle Dale," I said, offering the deck.

Dale knocked it twice. "What's Kingmaker?"

"The name of your product—that's how great it is," I said, dealing cards. "Game is Perdido River stud—deuces wild. One hand, winner takes all."

Betting against a man not playing with a full deck was like shooting crippled babies in a dumpster. My aces and deuces handily beat his pair of fives, but Uncle Dale was so happy he got up and danced a jig. "You won, pretty-pretty," he said, "and now, your winnings, my boy. Sorry Dale doesn't have a bag for you to carry my Brandon doll head home. But first, a drink!"

Dale plucked two coffee mugs from the debris at his feet and filled them from a half-full bottle of moonshine, warm and neat. He wiped his nose. "Make a toast to your Uncle Dale—yes, cheers to Dale and cheers to you. Amen, amen, amen."

"Death is family," I said taking a gulp.

Yes, I know what you're thinking, and yes, you may fall prostrate at my feet and bow to my Kung fu—that was the most incredible toast ever made.

But then I had another one—it just came to me, as if my mind were a sacred vessel of awe-inspiring toasts.

"To 'Kingmaker'," I said, raising my mug again. "And to Uncle Dale." Again, I was simply the vessel.

"To us, yes, and to death," Dale said, suddenly lucid. "Daddy Alan, Hank, Brandon—how did you know death was family? Who taught you this wisdom?" And again, he burst into tears, collapsing in a heap of uncontrollable sobbing. Then, after a sudden fit of clapping, he crawled to a spot near the back wall and pulled the carpet. "Take your prize and go, pretty doll," Uncle Dale whispered, eyes streaming with tears. "Forgive me, but Dale is just another Perdido River bastard. Tell me true, Dean Adam, are you an angel or a bastard?"

It seemed like an odd question only if you didn't know the answer. "Yes, Uncle Dale. I'm both."

"So you are," he said. "Careful with Brandon now."

Of all the things I'd done in my life, the greatest labor thus far began and ended with my time in the trailer with Dale Doogan, who killed his half brother Brandon and kept his dead body close to him for comfort and company. Dale wept when I retrieved those remains.

Amidst the sounds of grief, the monster at my feet became almost human. But what kept me sane as I went about my grisly business was the packet of 'Kingmaker' I snorted.

The drug stopped my mind from crumbling to dust. There was only a piece of Brandon Doogan left. You'd think that after two years of sitting around a damp swamp the decay would've been dramatic, that the features would've looked far worse than they did, that he would've been erased and replaced with ooze. You'd be wrong. And I would've sold my soul for something I couldn't recognize. Oh, but I did recognize him—it was a night terror made real.

To this day, I still have dreams.

And so, it came to pass that I pulled the severed head of Brandon Doogan from the floor and staggered outside holding it under my arm like a fucking football.

I found myself standing in a lawn filled with decayed cypress leaves and grassy reeds. The twilight sky was clear, orange and purple hued, and the air was rich with moist trees and damp earth. I didn't know what I'd find when I stepped outside—a shot in the back maybe, or an ambush. There were flashing lights and boat engines.

There were several uniformed men and women shouting in garbled voices, milling about the property with flashlights and walkie-talkies. A flare gun fired a sparkling shot of red flames that arched into some cesspool a hundred yards away.

From inside the trailer, a single gunshot.

BANG!

I don't know how long I stood there after I heard the crack of that bullet tearing through the rotted brain of Dale Doogan. I vaguely recall coming to when someone touched my shoulder and gently took my arm at the elbow.

Night replaced twilight—*when did that happen?*

Around me were flares marking the perimeter of the swampy island. By now, the *Heart of Darkness* was back to the Sundays' boat dock. Sharon would be waiting at the station. And Joseph Conrad would be home packing for his flight to Italy. Or was that flight yesterday? A deputy led me to the place where Darl and I made our landing earlier. He passed me to another officer, a tall man, and broad in the shoulders, with piercing green eyes and a shock of gray hair.

"You'll be going back now, son," he told me. "Here, let us carry that. It's okay, son—just let it go, Duddy. Be right back."

It was surreal, all of it.

And after I let go of my father, I sat beside Darl in one of the flashing fan boats as he also struggled to let go of his father. I couldn't do much to comfort him. He couldn't do much to comfort me. Darl handed me a canteen of warm water to help me swallow the pills he gave me after the paramedics were done checking my vitals.

Time skipped backward and forward.

I couldn't focus on any particular memory or incident, so I put all my efforts into breathing. *Just breathe and keep breathing,* I told myself. My heart was pounding. My brain was buzzing.

And I was certain both would burst soon.

Why the fuck would you do this on purpose, Duddy?

Why, why, why, why, why?

"What did you give me, Darl? The pills, what were they?"

"Some tranquilizers Silas told me to give you," he replied. "Silas said they'd calm you down."

"Silas," I said, lost in thought. "Sheriff Silas, that Silas?"

Darl patted my arm. "We're back at the station."

"What? When did that happen?"

"An hour ago," Darl replied, snickering. "You talked more'n that time then I've heard anybody talk. Don't you remember?"

I told him I didn't remember, but I didn't remember a number of things that happened after I left Dale's trailer.

I've since had to rely on others to fill in the blanks.

My vertigo was set to lather, rinse, and repeat, so I don't know how I got to the station. I don't remember shaking Joseph Conrad's hand. I don't remember Darl helping me out of my waders and boots. Or Sharon getting me clean and dressed. Or me talking about what happened in the trailer and not stopping once I started. Or me blacking out and coming to. *Why the fuck did I do that to myself?*

I was surprised to find myself sitting in an office chair when I came to. The lights were particularly bright. By then, Darl and Joseph Conrad had gone. Sheriff Silas was speaking to Sharon, who was sitting in the chair next to me holding my hand. Her eyes were red from crying. I had no idea what the discussion was about, but it made me angry. They were talking about me, and it made me angry. I shouldn't have felt a thing, but I was paranoid and angry.

"Enough secrets—I want the truth," I shouted. "BANG!"

Silence.

Sharon pulled me gently back to my chair.

Sheriff Silas put his hands behind his neck. "I was beginning to wonder if I needed to dunk your head in cold water," he said. "I'll take you back to Cantonment in a few minutes," he added, calmly. "The meth is short-circuiting your brain, so you're off kilter."

"Maybe we should take him to Queenie," Sharon said.

"I'm feeling better," I said, adding, "I just need sleep."

"The paramedic said the same thing," Silas said. "This blacking out and coming to is from something else—you've had that since you were eight or nine."

"It's why I stopped doing drugs," I said. "How did you know I had blackouts?"

"Brandon told me," Silas replied. "Why the hell did he go looking for Dale? He knew not to do it alone—you saw the circus act it took just to get close to his trailer. Brandon had a nasty habit of keeping things to himself. I knew he wasn't alive, but I never imagined it was because of this. Darl discovered the remains two, three weeks ago. He told Rick Shelby and gave him that busted music box and diving watch. Rick waited too damn long."

"How's Rick doing?" I asked.

"The same—he was shot up pretty bad," he said. "Christ, if he'd come to me, we could've prevented all of this, including your jaunt through the swamp—I wasn't told that part either. Darl would've had a deputy, not you, son. We could've put crazy old Dale Doogan in a facility before he killed himself, and—"

"Dale didn't kill himself on purpose," I said. "It was redneck pistol roulette."

Silas swore. "Brandon and Rick should've come to me. Goddammit, if those two idiots had told me the truth we wouldn't be here. Christ, I know I bend truth to keep me in office—I'm a nickel short of a Huey Long dollar bill when it comes to politics—but I draw the line at putting family in harm's way. I'm ending this lie tonight. Duddy, you never would've had that accident if your mama and Brandon had told you the truth."

And suddenly it dawned on me.

"Brandon wasn't my real father," I said, matter-of-factly.

Silence.

"No, Duddy, he was my mine," Sharon said. "I'm sorry I didn't tell you. I made a promise not to say anything until it was time," she said, wiping her eyes. "Silas raised my sister Alice and me when the woman who gave birth to us left. Brandon didn't want us either, but he was always around like he wanted to be. I didn't know the truth until he went missing. When Alice killed herself, I struggled too, Duddy."

Sheriff Silas patted the top of his desk. "I think we should head to Cantonment now. I'll tell Brenda the news—she should know what you did today anyway, and I—"

"You're my father," I said. "Sorry for interrupting."

Silas Doogan. There it was, the truth hiding in plain sight, right here before my eyes. I saw my face clearly in the face of the man before me—there was no doubt in my mind.

"Pidge told me I should come see you," I said. "Hattie and Pidge both decided to do the right thing when Mom couldn't."

"Wouldn't and couldn't," Silas said, "are separate things. Brenda wouldn't. Brandon wouldn't."

Silence.

I felt like I'd been dropped buck-naked in the ice cold, inky black Styx River headfirst and left to swim back to the Perdido in the middle of a hurricane.

Soon we were on our way to Muscogee Road.

Sharon sat with me in the backseat of the squad car. Silas talked about how he and Mom had been a couple. How she was pregnant and planned to marry Silas until Brandon showed up. How she ran off and refused to let Silas be a part of my life. And now I knew why Grandpa was furious.

It wasn't hatred for all Doogans.

His knocked up daughter eloped with the wrong Doogan.

No wonder he wouldn't speak to Mom until I was born—she forsook the father of his first grandchild.

FUCKING HELL.

As Silas busied himself with radio chat to the dispatch center, Sharon nodded toward him.

"You're a lot like him, you know, so he wasn't surprised at what you did today. He said your blood was calling you home."

If that were true, then my blood had a better memory than my brain. I didn't want my brain to remember anything. I didn't want it to think, to solve puzzles, to figure things out, to make sense of my recently flipped-upside-down world. I was too fucking tired, too angry, too confused, and too sad. A residual surge from my earlier high smacked me. Suddenly, my thoughts were zipping and bouncing inside my skull like ping pong balls.

Mom was pregnant with me, but she wasn't in love with Silas. She eloped with Brandon after falling in love with him, and the families on both sides of the river kept the secret. But Brandon couldn't keep away from his Alabama kin. He lived with Silas after Mom kicked him out of the house and didn't come back for three months. Brandon met a woman at some bar. Silas later raised the girls his brother had abandoned, and the same brother kept coming back to see his secret daughters like some sleaze ball from a movie on Lifetime.

I didn't want to put these connections together.

I didn't want to make sense of these secrets and lies.

Sharon squeezed my hand. "We're here."

Silas turned into the drive and parked along the fence. I wanted nothing more than to jump out of the car, take off all my clothes and run like hell through the backyard and into the woods howling at the moon. There were other more important things, I told myself. I was near the end of my journey, and I didn't have much of me left.

I don't remember going into the house.

I don't remember the wailing keen of my mother when she saw Silas. I don't remember Sharon sitting between Tyler and me at the dining room table. Or how long we sat there before Belladonna came through the kitchen with Aunt Clara and Goddamn Tater. Or Buddy Lee Boudreaux with Miss Eva. I don't remember my voice breaking every time I tried to speak. Or my mother glaring at Sharon and refusing to make eye contact with Silas. I don't remember saying goodnight or going to bed.

I only remembered the nightmare and waking up alone.

Chapter 15

The Gospel of Duddy Doogan

Cantonment, Florida—Thursday Morning, June 9, 2005

Two years had passed since we first said goodbye to Brandon Doogan. Mom was ready to tuck him into the earth with her own two hands, but there wasn't going to be another service until it was time to put her into the ground.

Only Buddy Lee Boudreaux knew about those arrangements.

I mean, I only went down the Styx River, walked through a gator swamp, wrestled a demon out of the Old Testament, braved a drug overdose, played Redneck Roulette, and got whacked in the face with a burning two-by-four of truth for my trouble.

It was just as well.

I had nothing to say to or about Brandon Doogan that wasn't spiteful, and I needed to get to Flomaton. I gave Mom the sun charm from the diving watch, but she didn't say anything, not a word of thanks or gratitude when I put the piece of pewter into her hand. Although she had a look of calm on her face, behind those hazel eyes of hers brewed a tropical storm, and my family had a saying about those things.

When Mom hugged me goodbye, she marched back to the house stubborn as a toddler and fit to be tied. She didn't know what to say or do about what she must've felt.

I'd endured Hurricane Brenda's gale forces for two weeks, so I suspected years of pent-up guilt and shame were collapsing around her feet. I wasn't going to make her talk to me—she was a grown-ass woman and needed to stand in the ruins of her fucked-up decisions for a few days.

Tyler didn't see it the same way. He had more than a few choice words for our mother, which I won't repeat. After his tirade ended, he hugged me and said, "I'd take you as my half brother over the whole brother I thought you were any day, boss. I'll give you a call when Laine and I work through things."

"Will y'all be okay?"

Tyler grinned at me in silence.

Amanda held to me until I groaned in pain—I was still quite sore and bruised. She kissed my cheek and walked into the house with Tyler. Belladonna left earlier to go visit Rick in the hospital, so Pidge and I were alone in the yard. Surprisingly, she didn't knock me down when she hugged me.

"I put the last music box down in Cotton Wilson's cellar for you," she said, quietly. "I figured the only way to get you to go down there and face your past was to put it—"

"I need two more boxes—the broken one doesn't count."

"Not true," Pidge said. "It's real simple, Duddy-darlin'. Rick called Hattie and me two-three weeks ago to tell us what Darl found in the swamp. He wanted to call Brenda, but you know how she feels about that poor fallen Shelby angel. We hated lying to her, but we didn't have a choice. We saw this as the right time to bring you home and put you back on track."

"Mom will blame Rick for what happened to her husband until she's dead and gone," I said, kicking a root. "Mom got me to keep my promise to her and Hattie though. She brought me back home, Pidge."

"But we knew your mama wasn't gonna tell you the truth you needed to know. We knew she'd keep that a secret 'til she died too. We had to move quickly."

"Did you know my quest would take me to Dale Doogan's Alabama swamp? As soon as I saw that broken music box, something in my blood told me I'd be the one to get those remains."

Pidge burst into tears. "Oh, Duddy-darlin', we never expected there'd be any remains. Rick told us about the broken box Darl brung him. It gave us the idea about getting you to the other half of your family tree. You deserved to know all the missing pieces of your life, not just the forgotten bits of a really bad summer day. Even a country road to hell is paved with good intentions. Duddy-darlin', I'm sorry. I mean, I'm not sorry at all, but I am. Don't give me that look—makes me feel like I just gave you two black eyes again."

I laughed. "Because you know I can take the hits."

Pidge smiled. "It's why I don't feel sorry."

Silence.

"I don't know how to play the recordings," I finally said. "I couldn't figure out that whole 'hiding in plain sight' business, so I've not listened to any of them besides Lilly's, and—"

"Damnation station, darlin', press the damn keyhole like a button," Pidge said with a chuckle. "You've earned the right to know the answer to any question, so the next time you're stumped, ask me. I'll open a can of farmhouse whoop-ass on anybody who disagrees. HA! But the answer was right in front of your dumb blind ass." She tossed the keys to her Jeep in the air and caught them. "All right, I'm off to Sacred Heart."

"Who put Sharon in my life, you or Hattie?"

Pidge smiled as she climbed into the Wrangler. "We both helped a bit, but y'all did the rest of it. Y'all did it lots and lots of times, from what I've heard. HA!"

•

I left the tiny house my grandparents bought for $10,000 back in 1968 and made my way from Cantonment to Flomaton in Granny's T-Bird. Having a car with real air conditioning was like a Country Cornfield of Goddamn Dreams. Alone with my thoughts, my brain wandered backward. Two weeks ago to the day, Mom called to remind me about a promise. A fortnight later, I was a numbed head filled with too many memories haunting me, teasing me, and punishing me.

Too many demons and angels warring over my soul.

Too much history. Too much truth uncovered. Too many stories and secrets. And too much Southern heat.

I know I needed the transfusion, but JESUS! Was playing life and death games in Uncle Dale's swamp requisite?

Death is family, Duddy-doodle-doo.

"No," I said out loud, "Death is *family-fun*."

HA!

Aunt Clara would've been so proud.

The blue sky was bright as God's cotton when I turned down the dusty road. Its shoulders were tangled in bushes of blackberry briars, a mile-long weave of red braids and Sleeping Beauty brambles on either side. In another week, the bursting pods of pink fruit would deepen to purple sun-swollen blackberries.

My mouth watered from thinking about the taste.

Instead of keeping to the road that ended at Pidge's place, I turned left into the cotton field where a steeper drive took me up to Cotton Wilson's house on the hill. I parked under the Graveyard Tree and sat in the car wondering whether I should get the damn box or get my ass up to Montgomery.

To everything, there is a season, Duddy-baby.

I knew the season, time, and purpose. Still, how would I find my way back to the light once I'd descended into the goddamn shadows? How would I find my way back to the people I'd begun to love so hard?

I went around the back of the house. The workshop with the cellar was an empty garage now. The shelves had no tools, no bins, no benches—there was nothing inside but dust floating in the pencil-thin beams of light kissing the floor. It felt like a dark place, even in the sunlight. The shadows were unnatural, pointed like shards of mirror glass toward the cellar door.

Under the window to my left was a copper sink with an old-fashioned water pump bolted to a raised plate with a brass handle. I washed my face and then rinsed the sour acid taste from my mouth after I vomited on the floor. From the window, you could see the tree-lined pond and the willow jutting from its left bank. It draped over the water where I'd sat throwing rocks on the day of my accident.

Hank Doogan must've been at the sink where I was standing.

He must've been here when he spotted a boy skipping stones a hundred feet away from him. He must've looked over to the cellar door and smiled. Thinking about the what-ifs of Hank Doogan suddenly led me to how I felt when Lilly took me into a world I never knew existed until she showed me a hidden room behind the bookcase down in her cellar.

It was there that she told me one truth I won't forget—*not all secrets are shameful, young man.*

But if that were the case, then why could I not remember what happened to me? Or what happened to Hank Doogan? My brain was keeping that secret—whether it was from me or for me was the mystery. After the gaps of time I experienced the night before thanks to Uncle Dale's magic Kingmaker, I understood that better than ever now.

"It's time to dig up buried things," I whispered. "Time to shine a light on the monster in my fucking closest."

I went to the cellar and opened the door. Standing at the top of a staircase, I flipped the light switch, took a breath, and descended into the stale, musty belly of the workshop. I always had a hazy recollection of the day, as if I'd dreamed it in a dream. The smells of a morning rain and green grass and dirt. The feel of running barefoot through pastures of grazing dairy cows. The warmth of the sun and the tit-tit-tit splash of a perfectly skipped stone. The recent addition of sour sweat and moonshine triggered nothing more than a vague sense of terror and fear and unbounded rage.

The music box was waiting for me on the bottom step. And as instructed, I pressed the keyhole—brilliant, that. A crackle of static was prologue to a voice that only could've belonged to Brandon Doogan.

Ewell, I need to get my ass down to Baldwin County before I head back to Charleston—that's a long drive at night. All right, I'll do this now—no, you're right. It's important. If I knew I was going to die tonight, what would I tell Dean Adam? I always wanted to tell you face-to-face over a pitcher of beer, but a message in a box will have to do. I never told you about your accident because it was important you remember on your own. Was your injury more than physical trauma? Did your memory break from the fall or from what happened before it? Here's what we think happened: my half-brother Hank dragged you in the cellar to violate you. Something in your blood must've snapped, Duddy, because you got hold of a shovel and hit him in the head, repeatedly. Wasn't much of Hank left by the time we got to you. You must've climbed the cellar steps, got vertigo at the top, and then fell backward. You were gashed to hell and lying in chopped up pools of Hanks bits. We only told Sheriff Doogan of Baldwin County, and Silas told us to cover it up. He said justice had been done and you didn't need to know a thing. You ought to go see him if you get a chance. Duddy, I gotta go up the Styx for an errand, so... Silas Doogan—look him up. And keep listening to your blood. I always admired that about you.

The recording ended in static and silence.

And I started laughing. As I was laughing, I pressed the keyhole to listen again. After a second time, I still hadn't remembering anything new about my accident (let alone turning into a cold-blooded killer).

So, I continued laughing until I cried.

Silence.

"You know, they poured a foot and a half of concrete over Hank's bloody hacked-up body after you went to the hospital—no wonder they didn't want you to know."

When I turned, Sharon was sitting on the top step. "Pidge told me when you left so I got here as fast as I could," she said. "I've been here since you played it the first time. I didn't want to disturb you. I just wanted to be here when you finished. So, is your memory hole all filled up with concrete truth?"

Shaking my head, I said, "You heard me laughing."

"I bet it hurts too much to weep, Duddy."

"Chopping my lecherous, pedophile uncle to death when I was eight years old shouldn't hurt that much."

"Yes it should," Sharon said gently.

I knew Hank Doogan was still under my feet.

I knew Cotton Wilson took a page from history after I did exactly what Margaret Shelby and her sisters did to JJ Doogan back in 1919.

It was in his blood as surely as it was in mine.

It was disappointing to reach the bottom of my rabbit hole though. The music box didn't make me bigger or smaller, but it made me realize how much Brandon loved Mom. It would take me some time before I'd forgive him, but I couldn't hate the man who loved my mother—I couldn't hate the man who sacrificed himself to hold her.

Now I understood how he felt.

The woman on the stairs had me under a crazy spell. Seeing her made it easy to let the poison go. It was time to leave these ugly things where they belonged—in the cellar. I'd fiddled enough with my smiling soul. Picking up the music box, I stood in the center of the floor and said, "Uncle Hank, I forgive you, but I'm not sorry for making sure you didn't lay a finger on another child again."

Silence.

"I'm sorry I lied to you, Duddy."

"You didn't lie to me, Sharon."

Silence.

"But I kept things from you."

"And I hope you always will."

Silence.

"After Alice hanged herself in the tree outside," Sharon said, "Pidge and I spent a lot of time together. I saw your picture on the wall in her den. I knew I'd give you my heart if you'd have it. For the longest time, Pidge said it wasn't meant to be because it would take a miracle to bring you home. A miracle is worth waiting for, so I prayed for one and made a promise to wait for you. Two weeks ago, I went a bit crazy because the miracle was unfolding right in front of me and I was too excited to wait. I didn't think I'd ever get up the nerve to drive up to you."

"I'm glad you did."

Silence.

"What do we do now?" Sharon asked.

"About the fact that you're Brandon Doogan's daughter or that I'm Silas Doogan's son? We could spend a week living in bed and swimming in the river. I'd also be open to figuring out how to forgive the man I knew as my father for not even trying to be a real father."

"Would you be open to YOU being a real father?"

Silence.

Somehow, I found myself two steps below her seat on the top step. "You can't be pregnant."

"Yes, I can be pregnant."

"But you can't be, unless you've been with—I had a vasect—"

Thoughts of Auntie Claudia shut me up.

"You're the only man I've been with in two and a half years, Dean Adam Doogan," Sharon said. "I'm hoping you'll be open to that talk because I want the father of my baby to be a *real* father to my baby." Her gaze never wavered from mine, not even when her tears began to flow.

Or mine.

I moved up a step to be closer.

There was nothing more to discuss. The story about why I bothered to get a vasectomy didn't matter, not even with an added bit about my apparent Immaculate Reversal as a Madam Fynoe type of button to end the story. I'd made up my mind about what I needed to do anyway. And since I was more or less already on one knee...

•

It was an easy pleasing drive beneath puffy cloudscapes over green hills with motley wild flowers. The Georgiana exit ramp was still under reconstruction. I told Sharon about the tornado that night, the images like fuse-lit firecrackers going off in my head. The drive took longer than usual, as I kept my speed just under the limit.

We reached Old Alabama Town without another weather incident, or a nuclear holocaust, or a super volcano erupting. A stretch and walk around the yard un-knotted the muscles in my back and legs. The speckled shade of the trees played in the grass near the carriage house. Sharon ran for the hammock and refused to let me on—we wrestled and tickled for the chance to be its only occupant.

With a foot, she shoved me toward the house. "Go see Hattie," she said with a look of *devil-thinking*. "I know my way around."

Of course, you do, I thought.

Grabbing the music boxes, I let myself in the house. The kitchen counters were bare. Nothing simmered on the stove or sat cooling on the rack in the window. The house was quiet as a mummy's nursery. I crept upstairs. "Hattie?"

Her bedroom was the closest to the stairs and the only one without a sitting area. I opened the door and went inside. Her floor-to-ceiling window curtains were half-open, letting in the sun. The lamp on her nightstand glowed with soft light for reading. Hattie's enormous four-poster bed was empty save for the closed bible on the pillow.

"She must be in the carriage house," I said to myself.

Of course, she's in the carriage house.

I sensed more revealed secrets in my future.

I tiptoed down the hall to Sara Nell's room two doors down. I didn't know what to expect—I took a deep breath, opened the door. Brandon Doogan's mother was as mighty and capricious as a Roman emperor, a proud woman who either loved or hated you. Time had laid waste to her body and mind—all the glorious pomp, her righteousness, the sheen of her Aqua Net beehive coif—all had crumbled.

"Sara Nell, want some company?"

She sat in her rocking chair and stared at me with a look that went from confusion to joy, her eyes brimming with fat tears when I knelt on the floor beside her. She trembled as she gingerly took my hand and pressed it to her bosom.

"Brandon, I was wondering when you'd stop by," she said. "Weren't you in a boat accident, son?"

"I'm not Brandon—I'm your grandson, Dean Adam."

Sara Nell's face sank. No, I wasn't her boy, and now she knew. She did seem to want my company, so I kept to the sunny side of her good graces and talked about church and bible stories, which lifted her mood. She looked out her window with a lazy smile as she held my hand and listened.

It was my fault, you know—our silent war.

After the memorial at Magnolia Cemetery two years ago, Sara Nell gave everyone a piece of her Methodist mind—she laid into all of us and told us she never wanted to see us again. I mean, the woman lost her only son, for chrissakes. I was a prick not to let the outburst go. I know my resentment toward her had more to do with what I felt toward her son. It was easier to keep my distance than it was to make amends. The woman who once told me to burn in hell and never come back was letting me hold her hand now.

"Up close, you don't look like Brandon, Dean Adam," Sara Nell said, turning my chin toward her. "Tyler's the spittin' image of him. Not you. Seems like I was far away for a while, and when I came back, you were here with me. I'm glad you came to visit—I want us to part as friends."

"I brought something for you."

As soon as I put the diving watch into her hand, her eyes welled. "Where did you find this?" she asked. "Brandon loved this watch."

"A swamp off the Styx River some miles north of Mobile," I said. "Mom wanted you to have it, Sara Nell."

Her lip quivered. "They find his remains?"

"Not much, but some—Mom's made special arrangements for their burial, but you should have something of him."

"We had a fight," she said, picking mud from the band. "It was about you, Dean Adam. I recall telling Brandon he'd done you wrong. It was a lie he told you—I said he was like half of his daddy. Not the cruel half of Alan Doogan, but the selfish, cowardly, lying half. I never would've married that man had I known he had three boys in Cantonment. He abandoned them and lied to me. I'm glad I left him. Did you know Brenda's father killed Alan Doogan?"

"Grandpa? No, I didn't," I said, and meant it.

"It was after he took in Hattie," she said. "I was remarried when I heard Alan was shot."

"Do you remember why?"

Sara Nell thought for a moment. "Hattie answered our ad—we needed a housekeeper for our house in Wetumpka. When my second husband died, I had no money, so Hattie offered to buy this house and promised to let me stay if I sold it to her. That's when she told me she knew Alan Doogan was my first husband—not at first, but when she figured it out, she said it was God's will that led her here and it was God's will she stayed after. I still grieve knowing the truth."

Sara Nell's voice trailed off as her eyes glazed over. Clutching the diving watch, she said, "I don't want to bury this, Dean Adam. I don't want to bury Brandon's watch."

Unbuckling the band, I said, "Wear it to remember him—we'll have it resized." After we said a prayer for Dad's soul, Sara Nell looked cockeyed at me for a moment when I got up and kissed her cheek. She didn't know me anymore, but I thanked her for the visit just the same and left to find Hattie.

Her bedroom was still empty, so I took the music boxes downstairs and headed to the carriage house. As I marched across the grass, I watched a sweet gum sway in the breeze against the brick fence jutting from the back of the building. I walked into the parlor.

"Hattie? Sharon? Y'all in here?"

"Hoo—we're in here, Duddy-baby."

Hattie always did this funny hoot with her voice that tickled me to death. It came from the living room, and there I found her on the sofa sitting next to Sharon, Queenie, and Silas. On the floor was a chubby mocha-skinned one-year-old girl with sable black, curly hair and the brightest green eyes you ever saw. Confused, but decidedly rolling with it, I put the music boxes in Hattie's lap and sat on the floor.

"Who's this tiny pudding head?" I asked.

"Shelby Louise," Sharon said. "Willow's my niece."

"And my half sister," Hattie added, cooing at the baby, all dimples and drool and apoplectic giggles thanks to Sharon's monkey toes. "Not quite the scene you were expecting?"

"No, it wasn't," I admitted. "I expected to see you weak, nothing but bones and ashy skin, with an oxygen tank squatting like a robot toad beside you. Thanks for the worst quest ever, godmother. You didn't lie about the cancer, did you?"

Hattie laughed.

"Fool, don't make me whack you with my spoon in front of company," she said. "I know you've been through the ringer, but you better check yourself and visit properly before my sedative kicks in and I go take my nap," she added, tsk-tsk-tsking.

Looking at Queenie and Silas, who were both quite relaxed as they watched me play with Willow, I said, "Should I ask the obvious or hold off until Hattie takes her nap?"

Silas laughed. "We're here for the meeting in AJ Cobb's office tomorrow morning." Queenie laughed. "But tonight, my husband and I are staying at a bed and breakfast," she said, kissing his hand. "We need a break from cranky grandmothers, excitable sons bound for Italy, drug lords, the redneck mafia, and cute, demanding babies."

The look on my face must've spoke volumes.

Sharon and Hattie burst out laughing.

"I'm still jittery from yesterday—don't make fun," I said, trying not to smile. "If I have to learn one more secret, I'll eat my own head."

So, Silas was my biological father. Queenie was my stepmother. Joseph Conrad was my younger half-brother. Sharon had been Willow's nanny for the past six months, dividing her time between the carriage house here, Justice Wilson's old house on the Perdido, and the house where Lady River lived with Queenie and Silas.

"Joseph Conrad," I muttered, shaking my head.

Sharon kissed my cheek. "Now you know why you kinda pissed me off at the beach."

Thump-thump-thump!

On the kitchen counter was a baby monitor—the pounding sound came from there.

Thump-thump-thump!

"The soothing sounds of Sara Nell," Queenie said, patting Hattie's hand. "I'm on it, girl—let a nurse handle the monster."

Hattie hooted with relief. "Sara Nell's been the biggest pain in my ass," she said. "I'm gonna poison her, and I won't shed a tear because my Jesus wants her home. What's with your neck, Duddy-baby?"

"Granny's casket fell on it," I said.

Like a kitchen ninja, Hattie produced her wooden spoon and hit me three times on my shoulder. "What happened to your neck, boy?"

I looked at Silas, who grinned. "You're no help," I told him. "Rick Shelby's choke hold did this to my neck, Hattie. Cash Doogan punched me there first."

Silence.

There was no need to repeat what happened.

The moment she took my hand told me she knew. She knew I'd lived more these past two weeks than the whole of my life before. I refused to give in to my grief just yet—I hadn't begun to deal with any of this. Hattie let go my hand and played one of the boxes for Willow, who gurgled at the tinkling sound.

"You better give that heartache up to God while it's still fresh," she said. "I know what it's like to swallow pain for too long, what it can do to your soul—best to give it up sooner rather than later."

I changed the subject. "How many more chemo hits?"

"Three," she replied. "Maybe less if Sara Nell falls off the roof accidentally. See? I can change the subject too."

"I stopped by her room," I said. "I made peace with her."

Hattie smiled. "Glory to God," she said. "Duddy-baby, I didn't know how to tell you the truth about everything 'til Rick Shelby called about the broken music box. Piglet and I decided to put you two lost birds together and go about it through the family history—there was deceit to get past, secrets to keep or tell. I was 'bout to lose my mind up here waiting for things to happen. Silas know you're knocked up?"

"Hattie!"

Silas turned bright purple as Sharon said, "Queenie promised to keep it a secret until I knew for certain—it's too early."

Hattie guffawed. "Soon's I heard, I had a vision of Doris and Dorothy. Then I had a vision of my daddy and his sister."

My heart skipped. "Twins? Dear God, please don't tell me you had a vision of Hank and Dale Doogan."

Sharon's face was in her hands. "A vision of Alice and me?"

"Yes and yes," Hattie replied, clapping. "Twins."

There was a long stretch of time when nobody spoke—the only thing you could hear was the baby babbling and gurgling and giggling on the floor. When the color of his face returned to a ruddy pale peach, Silas looked directly at me. "Duddy, the man you'll be for the rest of your life is the one you're becoming now. If ever I see you revert to a *primitive* state, I shall personally escort your ass back to your current state. Understand me, son?"

"Yes, sir—I understand."

Sharon pressed his arm. "You're not angry?"

Silas rolled his eyes. "Sharon, you're a grown woman—I'm just shocked is all, baby, and I'm trying to do the math in my head," he said. "Half-half first cousins ain't as bad as it sounds. It's more distant than most married cousins."

Hattie sighed with joy. "God put these two together."

"No, YOU put 'em together," Silas replied. "You wanted a permanent bridge for the Perdido River bastards to cross. You wanted old wounds to heal and you wanted to rewrite the legacies of Uriah Shelby and Earle Adam Doogan with love instead of hate. I may be an old redneck sheriff, but I'm no dummy."

"Never thought you were," Hattie said. "Too many souls have been lost for too damn long. It's time Uriah's children were washed clean. It's time to see the Perdido River as the Promised Land."

Sharon beamed at me. I always knew Hattie's weapons were love and forgiveness. Her calling, her mission in life, was sharing that love. She played the music box lullaby and sang to Willow.

> *I know dark clouds will gather 'round me*
> *I know my way is rough and steep*
> *But golden fields lay just before me*
> *Where God's redeemed no more shall weep*

"Silas Doogan, if ever there were two souls who belonged together, it's these fools here," Hattie said. "That she got herself with child in record time is a sign from God—woo-hoo!"

When Queenie returned, we sat at the kitchen table and talked about the appointment with Judge Avery Jebson Cobb in his Old Alabama Town office tomorrow. Hattie didn't reveal any details, only that the family would benefit from the meeting and that she was missing her Ladies' Friday Breakfast and Prayer Group at the Village Inn just to see my face when I heard the news.

When Silas and Queenie left for their romantic evening, Hattie helped us clear and clean, and to our surprise, she picked up Willow, kissed us goodnight, and went out the door with a wave.

•

Later that evening, I shuffled into the kitchen of the carriage house and poured a glass of wine. Sharon was barefoot on the porch in one of my shirts looking at the moon. Her face was bright and alive, and I didn't recall her eyes ever being so blue. I chalked it up to the whirligig of our recent bedroom romp, but I sensed deeper things stirring in her. I felt them too. We were wading in different waters, the new shores of an uncharted sea. I sat on the bench as Sharon stood behind me rubbing my shoulders. I decided to ease back on the booze and stop the smoking altogether.

"Duddy, are you ready for this?"

"Ready for what?"

"This new life," she said. "Are you ready for it?"

Was I ready for a new life?

Two years and two weeks ago, Hattie told me we had a responsibility to do something meaningful with our life that pleases both God and Man. For my godmother, she lived only to Love a continual action that had nothing (or little) to do with her feelings. The act of loving unconditionally was to lift up others, especially your enemies, above yourself. Hattie told me the meaning of life, and I was plotting to kill myself.

Was I ready for a new life?

Two weeks ago, I took my first step down a different road simply because I wanted to keep a promise. I dreaded every step afterward, but looking back at those 14 days—my *Family-Fun* Deep South Fortnight—I became the man I'd always wanted Brandon Doogan to be.

Sharon squeezed my shoulders.

"You didn't answer my question, Duddy."

"I don't know if it's the right question," I answered truthfully. "It's the same life on a better heading now that I'm with you."

"Good answer," she said. "More wine?"

I shook my head no.

As I looked up at the moon, I thought of Hattie's genius. She changed the legacy of an evil man from a cursed one to a blessed and beloved one. I wondered about the legacy I'd leave behind. I wondered if I was worthy of this grace given to me, this gift bought with the blood and tears of generations of my family.

All those lives, like so many stars in the night sky, were mere specs of light until you gazed at them from Time's window. Constellations become clearer. The pictures of those stars are the stories we tell, the maps we use to navigate the uncharted oceans of life until we reach our final destination. And I didn't see them as the branches and roots of a large, sprawling tree anymore. I pictured a vineyard of crisscrossing vines of muscadine grapes growing in the rich soil along the Perdido River.

Sharon led me back to the bedroom.

I still felt as if I were dog paddling in the deep end of intimacy, which was a stranger until recently. This went beyond me, beyond her. Two lost and broken people had found each other and made each other whole through love—it was hard to imagine not feeling so complete.

"What are you thinking about?" Sharon asked.

I mumbled something about being a homunculus of emotion. Simple thoughts were all caddywumpus in my head, and the words twisted in my mouth when I tried to explain. I wanted to say how excited (and terrified) I felt, how blessed and humbled. I wanted to tell her I was ready to let go and love her hard for the rest of my life.

I was trying to keep it together.

Sensing my distress, Sharon tried a different tactic. "You know, the world will be fine without you thinking for a while," she said. "Here, let me hold you for a bit. You can't carry all that weight by yourself, not while I'm breathing."

I put my head in her lap and closed my eyes. Sharon said nothing. She touched my face, smoothed my brow. She hummed a sweet melody I'd never heard before. I knew she could carry a tune, but then she started singing, and I marveled her voice.

I have loved you for such a long time,
But here in my solitude, I had time,
So much time.
I wanted to tell you for such a long time,
But speechless ineptitude took all my time.
Every time.
I watched the sun in your hair,
Those traces of June will always be there.
I wanted to kiss you for such a long time—
Courage I never knew,
But I knew time could give me time,
And all that time, I wasted time.
When I saw the love in your eyes,
I shattered that moment when
You recognized me.

So, will you meet me in Heaven?
I promise, I'll wait for you there.
I won't be a no one in Heaven.
Please say you'll meet me in Heaven—
I'll save a seat for you there.
I won't be a no one in Heaven.
I could be a someone in Heaven,
Without you, there's no one,
Or Heaven.

I opened my eyes. "Lady, you can sing," I said. "I didn't know you could sing like that."

Sharon blushed and kissed my nose. "There's a lot of things you still don't know about me—but there's time."

"So much time," I said.

Sharon told me to be quiet and then sang another song, and then another song. One after another, she sang, and all original compositions, all beautiful and unique as she was. I couldn't understand why this woman wanted anything to do with me. What did I do to deserve this gift?

Then I realized the truth.

It had been hiding in plain sight ever since the weekend Hattie and Pidge put me to task, ever since the night I first met the woman now singing me another lullaby. Sharon was the music box. Cheesy as that sounds, it was the truth—she was the miracle I needed, the quest I sought to claim, not for Hattie but for myself.

And that's when grief finally found me.

The one truth I couldn't take broke me into splinters. I collapsed into weeping, and I let the torrent I'd held back take me to wherever it wanted to go. Never in my life, before or since, have I wept so hard for so long.

When the tears finally stopped, the drive for a different kind of release consumed me, and then consumed Sharon. Like a sudden hurricane of body and soul, we both let go and let God, spinning out of control and loving each other hard enough to break the fucking world.

THE WORLD 11

Epilogue

Southern Covens

Flomaton, Alabama—Afternoon, July 4, 2014

On the day of our sixth official Perdido River Family Reunion, the summer sky was all raspberry-Slurpee blue with not a cloud in it. Considering the date and geography, it was a most pleasant and unexpected surprise. Pidge said this year's reunion was set to have twice as many people than the previous reunion, which had over 90 Shelbys, Doogans, Percys, Wilsons, Lincolns, Freedmans, and a handful of Ravenhairs. The last one sounding like a name from the Harry Potter books, I often used it to poke the ribs of my girls, who never failed to correct me.

Their passion always amused the hell out of me, which is why I continued to do it. And today, as we were crossing into Flomaton, the volley of outrage from the backseat was very passionate. A dissonant chorus erupted behind me with particular fury.

"It's Raven-CLAW, Daddy!"

That was Angelica, arguably the loudest of the girls bouncing behind me. The other two were also quite loud, but Angelica, or Little Miss Bossypants, was easily the most demonstrative, as she was usually the first and last to express her opinion. "Row-ENA Raven-CLAW!"

"And then comes Helga Huffle-PUFF!"

That was Zoe, Angelica's non-identical twin sister (our Little Miss Saucypants), who interrupted with her own contribution.

"And then there's Salizar Slythering—"

"No, Zoe, it's Sli-ther-IN, like a snake slithers IN the yard."

And that was Hattie's baby sister (and Sharon's niece) Willow. Little Miss Smartypants wasn't technically ours, but she might as well have been. Sharon homeschooled all three girls at our place on the Perdido River, in the same schoolhouse where Lilly once taught the Hell's Belles and Cotton Wilson.

Willow spent more time with us than she did with Pidge and Hattie, who shared the farmhouse with Kate and Katelyn.

"And THEN Godric Griff-in-dor!"

See? Angelica, my bossy bookending daughter, had to have the last word. Oh, did I pity her future husband. The girls burst into cheering and clapping.

"*Expecto patronum!*"

"*Expecto pimento!*"

Although the drive was short, the trip brought out Grandma Brenda's saucy temperament in the girls.

"*Expecto banana!*"

We'd had Willow on loan since Memorial Day weekend, an unusually long extended stay thanks to Darl and Joseph Conrad's five-week project to makeover Cotton Wilson's hilltop.

I wasn't allowed near Flomaton until today.

"*Expecto BAMBINO!*"

Again, the laughter behind me.

Sharon squeezed my hand. My beautiful wife was a shade of tequila sunrise and beside herself from chortling. She believed the girls shared a psychic link that was destined to get stronger and more annoying as time went on. Having been baptized in *family-famous* waters, the girls were by-products of generations of strong Southern women.

"Queenie swears they have the Gift and will be finishing each other's sentences soon," Sharon whispered. "Ooh, big kick—Duddy, feel this. Hattie says I have the Gift."

The Gift. The Sight. The Big Pain in My Ass. Putting a hand on my wife's swollen belly, I said, "THIS is the only gift, honey."

Sharon laughed. "No, THIS is the accident—we have yet to see if he's a gift. I'm so ready to meet this boy today. I'm psychic. I will."

"Careful what you wish for," I sang.

"We'd like to meet our brother today, Daddy," Zoe said, apparently speaking for the trio. "I'd like his name to be Sirius Cedric Black Doogan. Angelica would like Draco Ronald Doogan. And Willow likes—what did I do now? Daddy, they're giving me the stink eye, all two of them!"

"Please, no stink eye," I said. "Willow, what's the name you like?"

"It isn't my place to say," she said matter-of-factly while crossing her arms. "Besides, it's better to pick family names. Even Hattie says so."

"Even Hattie says so," Angelica teased.

"Even Hattie says so," Zoe added.

Then came fresh peels of laughter from all three girls.

"I'll have this baby today," Sharon said, rubbing her belly with a strange smile. "Might be good for the girls to help Queenie and Pidge with the delivery. I hear Kate and Katelyn have prepared a space big enough to fit me and several horses."

"What about the midwife from the Atmore reservation, Queenie's cousin? I thought she was the baby puller, your New Age weirdo with her placenta cookies."

"She's not coming—you know how hard it's been convincing our Ravenhair kin to be a part of these reunions. My womb isn't shackled to a hospital or doctor anyway. Today, I'll deliver how nature intended. And you WILL eat one of my cookies."

"You naked and moaning knee-deep in a kiddie pool in the back of an old barn makes me nervous," I said, adding, "and no cookies."

Sharon grinned. "Face it, Duddy. I have the Gift. My dream is coming true today. I can't wait to see the look on your face and you will LOVE my cookies. Excuse me. I need to distract these screaming girls before my water breaks in our new car."

Sharon kept them from arguing by making them apply sunscreen to each other—twice. Despite the light milk chocolate tone of her skin, Willow burned easily, thank you very much, and needed as much as Zoe and Angelica did. My daughters had skin like mine—light and semi-freckled at the start of May to a ruddy brown freckled glow by October.

Sharon already slathered herself with Coppertone Anti-Nuclear SPF

9000, and I know this because of the erection knocking on my zipper. As soon as we reached Pidge's place, I'd have to untuck my shirt before getting out of the goddamn car. And my wife knew what was going on—she was laughing herself into another shade of tequila sunrise as surely as my man bubbles were turning blue.

"You okay?" she giggled. "Careful with that thing."

"You're to blame for my swollen condition."

"Well, you and your fetish are to blame for MINE."

"Who's sick?" Willow asked.

"What's a fetish?" Angelica asked.

In a panic, Zoe said, "Mommy, did a bee sting Daddy? I'm 'lergic to bees, and I can't find my"

Angelica patted her shoulder. "I got your Epi-Pen, Zoe."

Looking out her window, Willow said, "The road to my house has LOTS of cars. I thought the reunion wasn't supposed to start 'til later."

"Well, this year is special," Sharon explained. "The museum is finally finished, and the memorial gardens have new additions—Uncle JC and Uncle Darl have been working hard to finish the new landscape for the hillside."

Zoe frowned—I saw her sudden pout in the rearview mirror. "I'm not going up that dumb hill," she grumbled. "It's full of dead people and not fun anymore."

Willow and Angelica vehemently disagreed. They'd had this discussion a number of times, so I ignored the argument erupting behind me and made an announcement. "Girls, look up there—it's Uncle Tyler and Grandpa Silas," I said, pointing to the top of Cotton Wilson's hill. "Look, they're waving. Girls, wave back."

Dad and my brother were securing the bandstand for the concert later tonight. Now that he'd seen his granddaughters, he was leaving Tyler to his own devices and making his way down the hill.

Where was he going?

"Look at all the picnic tables," I said. "I think they're underestimating the number of people coming."

"Well, we do have fireworks this year," Sharon said, the corners of her mouth trembling before she burst into tears. "My hormones are making me a wreck. Damnation station, I want this baby OUT today! He's coming out today, Dean Adam Doogan, or YOU'RE sticking your hand up in me and pulling him out when we get home."

A chorus of disgust from the backseat: "Ew, gross."

A chorus of joy: "Damnation station!"

All three in precise unison both times too.

To be fair, they were allowed use of a few PRE-APPROVED swears to honor Great-Great Aunts Clara and Eva. Had they been alive, they would've made certain the swear words were more colorful and decidedly NOT approved. Deep down, the hand-me-down vulgarity would've been like church bells to my ears. I missed those two biddies. It broke my heart knowing my girls wouldn't have two of the three original *family-famous* Hell's Belles to nudge them toward a wrong-but-so-right direction.

I think even Granny would've approved.

My favorite dirt road, now paved with asphalt, took us past the sea of cars parked on either shoulder. At the house, we had a space reserved next to the old Wrangler, rusted out and sans back tires now. It was no surprise to see Pidge waiting for us, with half an ass cheek on the porch railing and both feet dangling, a jug of sweet tea bouncing on her left bionic knee. I barely had time to turn off the engine before the car doors flew open and shot-put the girls onto the porch with her.

"AUNT PIGLET," they screamed.

"Our new car has an eject button," I said to Sharon. She slipped a hand to my crotch and whispered something naughty in my ear, to which I replied, "Honey, that's a stick, not a button."

As if she could see through our tinted windows, Pidge cupped her mouth with a free hand and called from the porch. "Dean Adam Doogan, tell your fat horny wife to get off your swizzle and go help Hattie and Queenie in the goddamn kitchen," she shouted.

When we got out of the car, she added in a softer voice, "Belladonna's burned the biscuits twice, Amanda's ruined Queenie's banana pudding three times 'cause she keeps sneakin' out to the vineyard to shimmy up Jacob Ravenhair's totem pole."

"Jacob Ravenhair? Really? How did that happen?"

"Amanda met him at the casino in Atmore," Pidge said, rolling her eyes. "Anyway, we're expectin' over two hundred today. HA! Oh, Sharon-darlin', we're all ready just in case your baby cork pops."

"It will," Sharon said, waddling into the house with the three screaming girls in tow.

"Lord A'mighty, Duddy-doodle-doo," Pidge said when we were alone. "You look like hammered shit, boy. I done told you them girls would age you. Help me off this railing. We should take them to see Brenda."

"So, the museum's ready?" I asked. "Finally?"

"Laine just did the last of the wall this mornin', but the rest of the Perdido River Family Museum was finished last week," she replied. "And wait 'til you see the Italian landscaping Joseph Conrad and Darl did. Makes sittin' with my dead mother and sisters almost a vacation. Hell's bells, I hate bein' so fucking old. All right, let's corral the girls."

•

The girls decided to race to the top of the hill from the gazebo—well, once we wrestled them from Queenie and Hattie, who wanted everyone out of their kitchen.

I briefly waved to Belladonna and Amanda (sans her new boy-toy) as they went to help select wine barrels for tonight's music and fireworks show. *The Vineyards of Southern Covens* was the official company name and label for Pidge's *family-famous* wines and brandies. After Aunt Clara's passing seven years ago, Pidge poured the money left to her into the business. When a drunk driver killed her mother and Miss Eva in downtown Pensacola six months later, Kate had Miss Eva's barn transplanted up here from Cantonment and sold the land to purchase equipment for the business. She also poured in more than her fair share of money.

As did Sharon and I.

Hattie called to me through the kitchen window. "Duddy-baby, tell them heathen girls to go pick daisies for Brenda before they head up there," she shouted. "I'll smack 'em with my spoon if they don't."

With a wave, I passed my godmother's missive to the girls playing chase around the gazebo. Only when Pidge repeated my words to them did they start picking flowers.

We started up the hill, a pleasant climb, what with the weather being so perfect for our reunion. "We're so blessed, Duddy-darlin'," Pidge said. "We've buried so many of our brave vanguard up there."

"Death is family."

"Indeed it is, Duddems."

I laughed. "Angelica and Willow keep teasing Zoe about the ghosts haunting the Perdido River family graveyard," I said. "I wish I could explain to her there was nothing to fear."

"Is Darl here yet?" I asked.

"He'll be here after while— I think ol' Darl might've found himself a girl who won't chew him up and spit him out for once," Pidge said. "He said he'd bring her, but anything can happen between now and then. That poor boy, bless his broken heart. And here we are."

There was the history museum (Cotton Wilson's old house). The workshop was gone. In its place were the reflection pool and a near-perfect replica of Lilly Middleton's Charleston cellar. The spot of my *family-famous* accident was a secret hiding in plain sight, a shadow at the entrance to our renovated cemetery. The weeks of transformation really brought home the oft-quoted notion about the Grim Reaper being close kin.

"The watershed's healing, Duddy-darlin', but it'll always need three Hell's Belles to keep people on their toes," Pidge said. "One day, your girls will be large and in charge, just like Hattie, Brenda, and me."

"Just like Granny, Miss Eva, and Aunt Clara."

Pidge took me to one of the refreshment stands for a refill of her fantastic new batch of summer blush, perfect for a warm sunny day.

"This wine's so good ice cold," I said.

"It's our biggest seller thanks to Katelyn," Pidge replied.

Kate's daughter joined the family business only last year. She took to running it like a duck to water. Her innate bossiness, incredible palate, her savant way with numbers and logisitcs—*Southern Covens* was officially in the black because of a brilliant high school teenager.

Pidge put her hand into the crook of my arm. "HA! I remember when I could climb up here and not break a sweat or a hip! Lord, I'm takin' one of those trucks back down—this walkin' uphill shit ain't for me."

Tyler greeted us at the museum house. "What's up, boss-daddy?"

"Hey, little brother—where's Dad?"

"Silas went to help the girls pick flowers," he said. "Laine won't be back from the hotel for another hour, so I'll pick flowers too. Mike's not coming, did you hear? He's taking Uncle John to the Mayo Clinic again. He asked if we could fly up in August."

Pidge took me into the house. I'd already seen the second floor, which were rooms filled with donated old family furniture, clothing, and folkart. The first floor was new to me. In one room were floor-to-ceiling family pictures and shelves of history books and bibles. In another room, painted as a mural across each of the walls by Tyler's insanely talented wife Laine, was the Perdido River Family Tree accented with grape vines.

"She did a fantastic job," I said.

Pidge sighed. "Your contribution ain't too shitty either, Duddy-dip-stick," she said. "And I shall now read it aloud for you, in order to make you feel REAL fuckin' awkward. HA! *Family-fun,* right now."

> *Ours is a family laced with trace elements of Puritan and Celt-ic. Creole and Gullah. Native American and Scottish Highland-er. Buccaneer and Carpetbagger. Southern Gentleman and Afri-can slave. Our progenitors drank elixirs of strange, genetic alloys, marrying into stronger families and absorbing other lesser ones. They fought and died. Lived and mourned. Murdered and betrayed. Sacrificed and worshiped. And they loved. All that fire and pas-sion accumulated like magma pools within the collective soul of our hard-loving men and women. Now, as we traverse the edge of a new day, we know peace and the sweet ache of passing time, and we are renewed. Our family has many names, but we share one home. Lost no more, we are now reborn in this holy Perdido River—may it car-ry our blood on the back of its sacred water 'til Kingdom Come.*

"Amen," Pidge said, smiling hard.

"It's heavy-handed," I said, rolling my eyes.

"Yeah, well, so's this fucking family." She took me to the collection of music boxes, which fit together like puzzle pieces on a large table in the middle of the Family Tree room. Each box was part of a tapestry of stories that told fragments of our family's long, complicated, and intricate histo-ry. The display Joseph Conrad and Darl made looked great—only three of the boxes worked now.

From one of the surviving audiotapes Hattie discovered in her basement came the last recording, and a short one at that. Ewell Curtis "Cotton" Wilson began to tell us why he'd spent the last years of his life recording stories, but his voice abruptly cut out. All that work, forever lost to Time, made this endeavor a *family-famous* legend now. I thought it fitting, that the boxes didn't work the way he'd planned.

As I understood it, oral history isn't meant to be summoned by the press of a button. It isn't meant to be heard by a disembodied voice from the dead. Only the living can share the past to us. And we must one day pass our recollections down to the next generation, a communion through the ages to bind past to present to future for all time.

"How's the near-photo perfect brain, Duddy-doodle-doo?"

"Still don't remember killing Uncle Hank," I said, pointing to a large bible-thick book beside the music boxes. "What's this?"

"Darl had our completed Perdido River history book bound on homemade paper," Pidge said. "It's gorgeous, ain't it? Look at the prints of his wood block Tarot deck he made for Belladonna."

It was so much more than a book. The carved wooden cover depicted a flaming house and the figure of a man rising from the fire and lifting his tools toward the heavens. The clouds spilled onto the back cover and swirled as a hurricane above a woman carrying a baby through a storm. There was Pidge's history book, with my latest additions, and handwritten transcripts of each music box recording on motley-speckled leafs, each page as distinct as a fingerprint. In the margins were sketches of herbs, plants, maps, flowers—each page was tended to, as a garden of memory, moments of time preserved like so many pressed butterflies.

"I get teary-eyed when I see this beautiful thing, Duddy-darlin'."

"I had no idea Darl had this talent."

"Bullshit," Pidge cackled. "You saw something in that young man. Why else would you go into a fuckin' swamp? You wanted to help him save his father because you couldn't save yours. Fuckin' deep, right? Truth comes out when it's time. Must be something in the blood."

Without warning, Pidge hugged me. "What you did for this family, Duddy—I didn't imagine this was gonna happen in my lifetime."

"That's enough love," I said. "Let's go see Mom."

We left the museum and made our way to the memorial grounds. We took pit stops along the way to greet kin I knew and kin I'd never shaken hands with yet. When the Italian hillside came into view—Jesus Christ, what a view—I couldn't move. Pidge took my hand as we both stood there, our feet firmly planted at the ridge of the overlook. In less than five weeks, Joseph Conrad and Darl created an unbelievable wonder.

For a town like Flomaton, it was akin to having Stonehenge or the Giza Pyramids suddenly appear in your backyard.

The Perdido River Family Cemetery began at the reflection pool and continued down the western face of the hill. The side with the steepest slope had ten beveled terraces carved into it like the tiered mounds of an Italian village, each one a step that crept to the vineyards below.

The vines on the memorial tiers bore the same varietals of muscadine and scuppernong grapes that served the *Southern Covens* label. Also growing among them were flowering trees and shrubs ensconced by serpentine walls of fieldstone and benches of marble to mark burial plots and memory fountains.

The Perdido River Family Trust, which Hattie and Lilly had established the day after my engagement to Sharon, owned this place. Queenie operated the trust, which essentially bought and sold land for the descendants of Uriah Ephraim Wilson Shelby, including all of his bastards.

The trust nearly bought enough land to OWN the city of Flomaton for generations to come. Vineyards were the primary development. Housing for the elderly and the disabled were the secondary development. The burial grounds made up a tiny portion, but in many ways, it was the most important part.

Here, no one was lost or forgotten. Here, no one was evil, even those whose deeds were decidedly so. But had the children of Uriah Shelby never been born, then we wouldn't be here now, not even my girls.

For that, I've often caught myself thanking the evil bastard.

Like now.

I watched them put their armfuls of handpicked flowers over their Grandma Brenda and Grandpa Brandon's grave. Buried in a single casket with the remains of her beloved husband, Mom rested here in a place made with *nothin' but* love and forgiveness.

Across the pond and under the Graveyard Tree were the graves of Ewell Curtis and Alice. Lady River was nearby, as were some of Lilly Middleton's ashes, which Helga and Auntie Claudia had delivered when the hill was first dedicated. Aunt Clara and Miss Eva were laid to rest in the top tier, which was nothing more than a chiseled edge when Darl had the small mausoleum built. The ashes of Kate's mother Mickey were there, as were the ashes of Rick Shelby, who did die at Sacred Heart.

Sara Nell was in a grave near her son and daughter-in-law.

Dale Doogan and Cash were laid to rest in one of the new tiers toward the bottom of the hill, which Darl had built for them personally. Other Doogans were there, but only because Darl demanded that they lie with his brother and father in the Bottom Ring of Doogan Crazy.

Watching my girls honor the woman who gave me life caught my breath. I hoped they'd understand how powerful and magical she was to me, as they understood the same thing about their own mother. I prayed they'd have courage to love as hard as Brenda Shelby Doogan loved her husband and her children.

I kissed my fingers and touched the headstone. Mom and I didn't speak much after the summer Granny died. She was there to welcome her granddaughters, but she never took a liking to their mother, for obvious reasons. Having to face the truth was too much for her. It was hard watching her rip her bond to Pidge and Hattie. It was harder still watching her do it to Tyler and Amanda, and then me. Mom couldn't forgive herself for keeping that secret and refused to let anyone else forgive her. As the self-appointed martyr for her children, she took it upon herself to die under the weight of her and her husband's sins.

Still, I deeply missed my troubled, passionate mother.

"I kept my promise," I whispered. "Love you, Mom."

"C'mon, Duddy-doodle-doo," Pidge said, taking my hand.

In my family, love was no more a curse than walking down a country road, even if it went to hell and back. My girls would have plenty of chances to carry pieces of Doogan and Wilson, Freedman and Percy, Ravenhair and Lincoln, and other names we'd discover in time.

They'd scatter their beauty and voices and fears and passions like seeds, and those seeds would grow along paths and rivers as wild and un-tamed as blackberry briars and scuppernong vines.

They were the fruits of a place filled to bursting with too many secrets and too much love. A new triage of feminine power ready to wreak havoc on the Perdido River watershed, and woe to any man that dared come between them.

My girls ran down the hill, all three of them suddenly screaming and mad as balloons. I laughed and choked back tears wishing Mom could've lived to see this—*Hush, sugar, I see fine right where I am.*

Uncle Tyler and Grandpa Silas were chasing the girls down the hill toward the farmhouse—probably to play with Pidge's lumbering new bas-set hound puppy, Holy Goddamn Clara.

Apparently, they were running for another reason.

"Goddammit, Dean Adam Doogan," Pidge said, shaking me. "I told you Queenie shouted for you to run to the fuckin' barn. You better run. I ain't walkin' down—TYLER! Come bring that truck 'round."

Tyler jogged past me as I started down the hill.

"Which barn?" I shouted.

Pidge cackled. "HA! Miss Eva's barn, Duddy-doodle-doo!"

The new expansion for *Southern Covens* wasn't some pristine, gorgeous thing—it was old as Cotton Wilson's hill, and I knew it quite well. Kate-lyn had started to fill it with equipment and casks, metallic vats and wood-en barrels, and a costly refrigeration unit too. Passing the farmhouse, I sprinted around Pidge's old barn and headed for the other one.

Queenie was at the corner when she shouted, "Dean Adam Doogan, move your ass! Sharon told you it would be fast and easy!"

It was that moment when I actually spun in a circle like a frightened dog, not knowing which way to go.

"What are—dear God, where? Which door?"

"There's only one door, you crazy fool!"

Queenie was right—there was only one door, and I had to run around to the other side of the building because I was a mindless idiot.

Amanda was there to meet me. She and her new boyfriend Jacob Ravenhair were holding the door for me. Kate guided me inside to the area they'd prepared, which so happened to be the remains of one particular horse stall, an area she swore was cleaner than any hospital delivery room. Turing the corner, I found myself staring at Belladonna and Katelyn behind my wife, holding her as she floated in the knee-high wading pool, which Darl had built for the occasion.

Joseph Conrad embraced me and took me to over to Sharon, who was half-naked in the pool of water with a newborn whining and squirming on her chest. "Come meet your son," she said, taking my hand and placing it on his skin. "You should hold him while they get me clean and into my soft chair. I'm SO ready to get out of this nasty pool to feed him."

Hattie rubbed my back.

"Congratulations, Duddy-baby," she said, her eyes filling with tears. "You should tell him his birth story while we clean things up. Oh, and he looks just like you did."

Silence.

And so, it came to pass that I lifted my screaming boy into my arms to spin his story.

"You were born in Miss Eva's barn on July 4, 2014," I began, voice breaking. "Pidge kept your daddy and grandfather and sisters busy outside while your psychic mama squatted buck naked in a temperature-controlled tub of water beneath two scuppernong wine barrels.

"You were surrounded by so much love when you came into the world. There was Queenie and Belladonna, Hattie and Kate, who caught you as you spilled out into the pool Uncle Darl built. There was Aunt Amanda and Uncle JC, and the guardian ghosts and angels of the river. Your mama dreamed this day would happen, but your daddy didn't believe her until he held you for the first time.

"And when he finally did hold you, he christened you Curtis Brandon Silas Doogan."

Oh, how my boy cried.

He quieted down the longer I held him close and kept him warm and rocked and whispered to him. Nothing in my life prepared me for the surge of emotion that came at me. It split my heart so wide and open that I could've worn it as a fancy hat for the reunion.

Oh, how I laughed.

I grew up surrounded by the love of too many women, a family with too many secrets, and a curse as real as a portrait of Elvis made with too much velvet. And I couldn't wait to share all that insane, sublime, beautiful nonsense with my boy.

Don't get me wrong—my girls were the stars in my firmament, as surely as my wife was the moon floating in it. But here in my arms, born in a barn like his father before him, here was my son, my sun.

The End

ABOUT THE AUTHOR

D. Byron Patterson writes fiction for adults, teens and kids. His short works have been published in *Elephants & Other Gods, Ramble Underground, Shalla Magazine, Larks Fiction Magazine,* and *Cerulean Rain.* Books for young readers include *The Christmas Witchling* and *Little Tiger and the Dragon King of Beijing.* Books for early readers include four illustrated Lamby Lambpants storybook adventures and a Lamby coloring book.

Byron is a songwriter, vocal and artistic mechanic, classically-trained actor (Shakespeare's Globe Theater, for starters), sometime-puppeteer, graphic designer, illustrator, co-founder of a toy company, and a 1st Runner-up National Karaoke Champion (don't tell anyone). He is married and lives in Tarpon Springs, Florida, with his wife Tina.

Want to see the entire Perdido River Family Tree?

Sign up for my mailing list @ Facebook.com/dbpatterson.author and I'll email it directly to you.

First Printing: 2014 | ISBN: 978-0-692-24629-0

DBP Press | Post Office Box 399
Tarpon Springs, FL 34688

facebook.com/dbpatterson.author

Made in the USA
Charleston, SC
07 October 2014